CW01630654

SECRETS OF THE DEADLY NIGHTSHADES

HEATHER G. HARRIS & ELLA STONE

PUBLISHED BY HELLHOUND PRESS LIMITED

HELLHOUND PRESS

Published by Hellhound Press Limited.

Cover Design by Christian Bentulan.

AI: No AI was used in the writing of this book, or the production of the cover art. The authors expressly forbid their book to be utilised in training AI.

Heather's Dedication

To Ella, for making this so much fun!

Ella's Dedication

To Zoey, for her amazing strength.

Contents

Chapter One

'I'm your grandfather.'

Old Jacobson's lips were moving up and down but I couldn't hear his words. There was a bizarre ringing in my ears, like I'd suddenly got tinnitus, and my chest felt absurdly tight.

I kept looking around the room – anywhere but at him – it was as if my eyes couldn't stop roving. When I started swaying, I realised I was in shock; I'd felt this horrible sensation once before.

I took several shaky breaths and finally looked at the man who had just upended my world. My grandfather. My only surviving blood relative – well, I *assumed* he was my only surviving blood relative, unless my grandmother was still alive. That thought threw a switch in my brain and I almost moved from shock to panic.

'Were you married to *her?*' I asked in a wobbly, raspy voice that I barely recognised.

'No!' he said quickly. 'She used me for my sperm and moved on. I was in love, she wasn't. Years later I found out that she'd had a child, and I just knew it was mine. I spent years tracking him down.' The old man's face crumpled. 'But when I finally found him, it was at the graveyard.'

The grief in his voice was real and I almost reached out a hand to comfort him, but I wrapped it around my stomach instead. I didn't know this man who claimed to be my family, and he hadn't known my dad, not like I had.

I'd loved Dad with all that I was. I'd known the foods he liked, the books he loved and the music he had adored, and my heart stung as I realised that Jacobson hadn't had the chance to know any of those things about his own child. He was grieving for someone he'd never met, an ideal child; he hadn't known any of Dad's flaws either, like his irritating humming or his irrational hatred of irises.

Jacobson could never – would never – know Dad like I did, but I could give him *something*. He deserved the little I could give because I could feel his grief, and it was still raw even after a decade.

'He hummed a lot,' I blurted inanely. 'Dad,' I tacked on. 'And he hated irises.'

Old Jacobson was looking at me like I was a ticking time bomb. 'I didn't know that,' he said carefully.

'It was you who left the irises on his grave?'

'Yes. I thought that since his wife was named Iris … and they were Dahlia's favourite flower.'

Dahlia Bleakman was Grandmother Dearest's name. Now that I'd found out she'd loved irises, it made perfect sense that Dad had hated them with such passion because there had been no love lost between them. And yet, here we were. A family built on murder, floristry and unfortunate name choices.

I pressed a hand to my temple. Yes, I could feel Jacobson's grief but also a desperate thread of hope, hope that he and I could be family for each other. It cut me to my core; I had accepted long ago that I had no family and that knowledge formed part of my identity. Now he was forcing me to change my very perception of who I was.

Everything was suddenly far too much.

Only a few hours ago, I'd seen flames billowing from my ancestral home – and not eternal ones. My best friend, Maddie, had been inside, unconscious and succumbing to the dark magic she had unknowingly been wielding.

The cherry on the shitty cake had been chasing down a murderous eel shifter who had shot me. I knew that he'd shot me because my top was covered in blood, but thankfully I was all healed up. Yanni or Fraser must have fed me a potion whilst I was unconscious because I'd come around in Fraser's arms, wrapped in his jacket and feeling decidedly less dead than I'd expected.

And now Old Ernie Jacobson, the curmudgeonly hermit of a witch who'd saved Maddie, had just declared that he was my paternal grandfather. Obviously I knew I must have had a grandfather at some point – I do know how babies are made – but I'd thought he must have died. Instead he'd been living here in Witchlight Cove. Why hadn't he bothered to find me sooner? I'd been so damned *alone.*

He reached a hand towards me. 'Beatrix, I understand—'

'No,' I said sharply, cutting him off. 'Whatever you're about to say, I guarantee you *don't* understand.'

I felt a sudden heat behind my eyes but I didn't want to cry in front of him; he didn't know me and he'd think his granddaughter was some sort of snivelling weakling, the type who'd lose the Eternal Flame... Oh wait. I'd already done that.

It had been a long, emotional night; I was so exhausted that my bones felt heavy and my eyelids could barely stay open. My mind didn't have the capacity to deal with this right now. It was time for a classic Bea move: when the going gets emotionally tough, run the fuck away.

I needed to escape. *Now.*

Maddie was in the next room with her grandmother, Yanni. They were my family, DNA or not, and they were who I needed right now. All I wanted was for Yanni to wrap me in her strong arms while my retriever Eva nuzzled into me. I didn't want to deal with Jacobson's bombshell, not now and preferably not ever.

'Is everything alright in here?' Yanni asked as she opened the door. If I hadn't known her better, from the way she appeared just as I was thinking about her I'd have thought she had psychic powers, but Yanni was a hundred-percent bear shifter.

Eva slipped around the side of her and raced across to me. She sat at my feet and stared up at me, eyes wide with concern. She was another part of my family, and I owed way more to my four-legged friend than my so-called grandfather. She laid her heavy head on my lap and looked at me dolefully.

'Thank you for what you've done for Maddie,' I said to Ernie Jacobson. I blinked back the tears and straightened my back. 'But I should be getting back now.' I turned to leave, but there was one last question I couldn't swallow. 'Why didn't you look for me?' I whispered. 'You must have known I was alive. You knew I'd lost my parents and you didn't bother trying to find me?'

Yanni frowned, stepped closer to me and held out her arms. As I stepped into them, the tension inside me eased. I knew she was being gentle because my ribs didn't creak even a little bit. 'Bea,' she said softly. 'Is everything okay?'

'Apparently Ernie Jacobson is my grandfather.' Despite me trying to hold it back, a tear ran down my cheek.

She looked astonished. 'What do you mean?' she asked, aghast. I was glad it was news to her, too, because it would have destroyed me if she'd been hiding something like this from me.

'He's my father's father. And he didn't even bother looking for me.'

The old man's voice wobbled. 'I did look. I could sense that you were alive, but that was all. I repeatedly tried to use magic to find you but you were being hidden by something – a ward. I couldn't find you, no matter what I did. I assumed your parents had taken steps to keep your grandmother from finding you.'

They might have taken steps but she had found me all the same.

Jacobson licked his parched lips. 'In the end I resigned myself to waiting for you to come home, but the years rolled on and you didn't.' He winced. 'When you finally did, you looked so much like Dahlia that I panicked and reacted very badly. I was mortified. I knew I had to keep away from you until my emotions and magic were stable again. As you noticed, when I'm anxious or upset my magic can get out of control – that's another reason I keep myself to myself. When I saw you at the coffee shop, my emotions were all over the place. I promise I didn't consciously throw Fraser around. I'm very sorry.'

I felt almost pleased that he looked so utterly miserable because he'd abandoned me in my hour – my *decade* – of need. A voice in my head pointed out that he hadn't done it on purpose, but I shushed it because I wasn't ready for logic. I was in the chokehold of my own emotions, and if anyone understands the impact emotions can have on a person, it's me.

'I know I should have done more. I'm sorry, Beatrix.'

When Ernie's emotions struck me, they were pure and laser-focused: all he was feeling was pure, unadulterated regret.

I was stuck between the desperate urge to run away or to stay and learn about the man in front me. If I stayed, even for a few moments, maybe I could get some answers about my past. There was so much to absorb – and there was still the matter of the missing Eternal Flame. Mentioning that now felt like a mistake; there was already more than enough shit to shovel without adding more.

‘Where do we go from here?’ I asked, my voice muffled by Yanni’s shoulder.

‘Maddie needs to stay with me for at least another hour so I can monitor her,’ Ernie replied quietly. ‘Perhaps we could use that time to talk.’

I looked down at Eva. She had way better sense than the average canine – and better sense than most humans and non-humans, too. I realised I must be in a poor state if my emotional compass was a retriever with a questionable love of stealing my keys.

She dropped onto her belly, as if to say we should stay and listen to whatever Ernie had to say.

Yanni weighed in. ‘Perhaps you should hear him out. But only if you want to.’

Two votes in favour of listening. That was it, then; decision made. I swallowed the lump that was thick in my throat. ‘Fine,’ I said, turning to my grandfather. ‘You have one hour. But after that, I’m out of here.’

Chapter Two

The five of us, including Eva, were sitting in Ernie's living room. Maddie had been dozing when we came back in; she was obviously having difficulty staying awake but that wasn't surprising after what she'd been through.

When I sat beside her, she opened her eyes. 'Sorry, I must have dozed off,' she said sheepishly. 'Is everything all right? What's going on?'

'Ernie here is my grandfather,' I announced.

'What!' Maddie's eyes flew wide open then her expression switched instantaneously from shock to outrage, just the way a best friend's should have done. She glared at the old man. 'You'd better have a bloody good reason for abandoning her!' She jabbed the air with an accusing finger. 'Do you have any idea what Bea's been through? Do you have any idea how much she's suffered alone – and all this time she actually had family?'

Her anger on my behalf was so potent, it warmed me. She was the best. I touched her shoulder lightly. 'I've always had family.'

Her eyes softened. 'Damned right you have.' She pulled me into a hug. 'I'm so sorry that fucker let you down.' Her voice was loud enough for Ernie's ears.

He didn't reply; he seemed to be shrinking into himself like a balloon losing air. I did my best to ignore the less than subtle twinge of my conscience; he *had* tried to find me, after all.

As we sat down, he remained standing with his hands deep in his pockets, rocking back and forth, his eyes downcast. It was hard to believe this was the same powerful witch that had thrown Fraser across Sonny's coffee shop. Albeit reluctantly, I was starting to feel sorry for him.

'I guess the best place to start would be with Beatrix's grandmother? How you met her?' Yanni's tone was businesslike; she was using her police interrogation techniques to get the most out of him. He wasn't a felon, but he was definitely a person of interest who'd been sparing with information.

Ernie took a deep breath and his regret was replaced by anxiety; it came off him in such great wafts that I almost drowned in it. Despite myself, I didn't want him to feel that way in his own home; no one deserved that. 'It's okay,' I found myself saying. 'I know this must be hard for you. Just ... tell us the truth.'

He nodded and some of his anxiety receded. 'You've seen that I have a lot of power,' he started. 'My ward around this house and the spell I used to disappear at the coffee shop are just a fraction of what I can do.' He wasn't boasting or threatening us; his tone was matter of fact.

'My powers were already formidable when I was young. As you can probably tell from my accent, I grew up in Spain. News of my power spread. It might surprise you, but I was quite a looker back in the day and a lot of young ladies tried to court me, but I wasn't interested in any of them. I was only interested in my magic and using it to serve the good of the world. That's all I wanted – but then *she* came into my life.'

'She?' Maddie whispered but Ernie didn't even glance at her. The way his eyes glazed over made it feel as if he wasn't just telling us about his past, he was reliving it.

'Dahlia.' As he breathed her name, a soft smile touched his lips. 'She was magnificent. Beautiful, powerful. I could sense her urge to do more, to be bigger, but I thought she was like me and she wanted to use her power for good.'

The mist dropped from his eyes and his jaw tightened. 'But she didn't. Not at all.'

'My grandmother,' I said, my tone resigned. 'She romanced you?'

His emotions were rolling over one another and there were too many for me to make sense of them.

'I – I don't know if she seduced me. I didn't *think* she had – I thought her feelings were real, like mine were real. I thought I knew her, but I was wrong. She was only after one thing – to have my magically powerful child.'

'Well, isn't that just lovely?' I muttered. 'A magical gold digger, except instead of mining for money she was after genetic quality. What a keeper.'

I was living proof that a magical pedigree was no guarantee of magical strength and, for all my grandmother's plotting, my dad hadn't been *that* powerful – had he? I frowned. Dad had always avoided magic, preferring to use his wits and his hands to accomplish what magic could have done more easily. I'd thought that he wasn't very strong magically, but there again he'd always been able to use magic when he really needed to. And when *she'd* come, he'd stood toe to toe with her. I hadn't thought logically about that night before, but actually Dad had been a force to be reckoned with – so why had he avoided magic for so much of my life?

Ernie paused and I could hear my heart drumming in my chest. This was the start of the story of how my father came to exist, and I already knew its tragic ending. But what was in between?

'I didn't know Dahlia was pregnant when she left,' Ernie said, answering a question I hadn't asked. 'She said we wanted different things, that we'd become too dependent on each other. It broke my heart.'

He shook his head. 'Once she'd gone, I did everything I could to forget her. I was heartbroken and my confidence in myself was shaken, so I threw myself even more into my magic. A friend came back from travelling and told me that he'd run into Dahlia in a small magical community in the south of Italy and she'd been with a small boy of about six or seven.

'In that moment I knew in my heart that there was a child of my blood out there in the world, and a simple scrying spell confirmed it. I spent three decades looking for him.'

'If you're so powerful and you could scry, why couldn't you find his whereabouts just like that?' Maddie clicked her fingers.

'I tried, but when I did that first scrying spell Dahlia sensed it. I'd inadvertently alerted her that I was looking for my son, so she cast spells to throw me off. Whenever

I looked for him, I got a different location to where they actually were. Oh, she was clever! I didn't know that she'd been practicing sorcery, so I had no idea that she could do that. It took me an embarrassingly long time to work out what she was doing – she sent me on a wild goose-chase for a whole decade! Then, a few months after I realised what she was doing, all signs of your father vanished.'

'Do you mean he died?' I asked, only to dismiss that idea because the dates didn't line up.

'No. I always assumed that he'd taken measures to hide himself from her. Did your father often do big, flamboyant magic?'

I shook my head. Dad had made himself less so that Dahlia wouldn't find him. 'No,' I admitted. 'He was always very reserved about his powers. It was only when she came that I saw how strong his magic was…' I slumped. 'But it wasn't enough to save him.'

'Sorcery is hard to beat,' Ernie said grimly. 'It is the ace of hearts of the magic world – it trumps all.'

'Then how are we supposed to defeat it?' Maddie huffed.

'As we did that night when your grandmother came here,' Yanni said. 'Strength in numbers.'

That night it had taken the deaths of eight good people before Dahlia Bleakman had been vanquished. Although she'd been beaten, her body had never been found and that had left a big question mark as to whether dear old Granny was still prowling the world, pretending to the big bad wolves that she was an innocent old lady when she was actually the baddest of them all.

Ernie nodded. 'Exactly so. I think Greg tried to avoid attracting her attention. News of what had happened here – a sorceress trying to steal a child, and the many lives that had been lost to defeat her – reached me in Austria where I was living at the time. I knew it was her. I prayed that I was wrong but when I saw the grave, I knew ... I knew my son no longer walked the living plane.'

'And you gave up on finding me.' My statement was more hurt than accusatory.

'I did.' He held his hands up in surrender. 'I searched for you, Beatrix, I promise you that – but no matter what I did I couldn't scry you. And I had just lost my son.' He looked at me, begging me to understand. 'I was a broken man, and I have been broken ever since.

'Finding your father had become my life's work so I knew about you and how you had left Witchlight Cove. But I also knew you were guardian of the Eternal Flame and I believed in my heart that you would come back.' His breathing hitched. 'I should have done *more,* but I couldn't bring myself to leave your father to search the world again. I finally had a chance to be by his side – even if it was only at the side of his grave.'

The desperate rawness of his grief resonated with me; at least I could understand that. Grief was something I knew well. 'But if you expected me to come back, why did you react so badly when you finally saw me?'

He gave a sad chuckle. 'Let's just say I hadn't anticipated you'd look quite so much like *her*.'

I didn't like that remark at all and the temptation to change my appearance was immediate.

My brain was thrumming and suddenly it was all *too much*. 'I can't do this right now.' Finally giving into the overwhelming urge to flee, I stood up. 'I need to go.'

Maddie and Yanni immediately got to their feet. 'We'll come with you,' they said simultaneously.

I shook my head. 'No, I'm fine. I just need— I just need space.' I patted my hip as I marched towards the door. 'Come on, Eva.'

'Beatrix?' Ernie called but I shook my head.

'Another time,' I said, before looking back at him and holding his gaze so that he could see straight into my eyes. 'Thank you. Thank you for telling me all of that and thank you for what you did with Maddie.'

'You'll come back, though?' he said desperately. 'You'll come back so that we can talk more?'

I bit down on the inside of my cheek. 'Possibly,' I said. 'Probably,' I amended as I saw how stricken he looked. 'I just need some time to process it all.'

I pulled my jacket closer around me as I walked down the shingle path towards the beach with Eva at my heels. Stopping for a moment, I reached down and ran my fingers through her fur. Back in the house I'd said I'd had to get out because I needed space but I didn't; what I needed was to be comforted. Luckily, my own therapy dog was right there with me.

I sighed. 'What do you reckon, Eva? On a scale from one to ten of catastrophic family reunions, how bad was that?'

Eva gave a short huff that sounded like a world-weary sigh.

'Yeah, I thought so too.'

Chapter Three

I stared at my phone, willing it to ring or at least beep with a message. I desperately needed a distraction, and my hormones were willing to supply me with one in the shape of Fraser Banks. Wickedly, I let my thoughts circle back to him and the way he'd looked walking out of the sea.

Every step I took towards home, I considered changing direction and going to his house instead, which was ridiculous because I hardly knew him. Sure, we'd shared a couple of heartfelt conversations and I'd liked him – even before he'd saved my life – but it wasn't as if he knew about my family the way Maddie and Yanni did. But maybe that was the whole point: he wouldn't be there with incisive questions and inquisitive eyes.

I was halfway home when Yanni's old police car drew up beside me with Maddie in the front passenger seat. She wound down the window. 'Do you want a lift or do you want to walk?' she asked, and I felt a pang of gratitude. It was cold and dark and yet she knew better than to order me to get in. If I said I wanted to walk by myself, she'd accept it. Instead, I opened the back door and got into the car with Eva.

'Good choice,' Yanni said. 'This thing might not have heating but at least it has working doors. Mostly.' She was taking a humorous jab at my own rust bucket, Rosie, whose driver's door didn't open. I appreciated her trying to lighten the mood and offered a weak smile.

Silence swelled around us as we all tried to adjust to what happened both to me and to Maddie. Ernie's announcement had affected them too; it might not be at the same level, but Yanni would have been perfectly within her rights to be pissed at him. After all, she was the one who'd had to look after a seventeen-year-old because we'd thought I had no relatives who could do the job.

'How are you feeling, Beatrix?' she asked. 'After being shot and ... everything,' she clarified.

'I'm fine,' I said airily.

I saw her grimace in the rearview mirror but she didn't say more. My PI instincts were tingling but I was too tired to dig into whatever she wasn't saying. When she dropped us home, I didn't miss the way her sharp eyes lingered on me. Yanni was worrying about me. I sent her a too-bright smile that she didn't buy as I waved her off.

'You don't mind if I head straight to bed, do you?' Maddie said as we flipped on the lights. 'I know you've had a bit of a crazy one, but I'm feeling pretty wiped out.' She flopped onto the sofa.

The house still smelt of the mess Maddie had made in the kitchen. We'd only had time to open the windows to let out the smoke, not to clean up, and the pink cauldron was still stinking the place out. I'd deal with it when Maddie was in bed. She looked shattered.

'Of course I don't mind,' I said instantly. It was ridiculous that she even needed to ask. Okay, I'd been shot, but it hadn't been that serious. I was totally fine. Well not *fine* fine, but I was alright. Besides, my head was swirling and the last thing I needed was another person's input. 'Plus, if we keep talking, there's a strong chance we'll start making terrible life decisions, and I've met my quota for the week.'

'Bea, I'm really sorry about the whole dark magic thing.' Maddie looked down at her feet.

I sat on the sofa next to her. All the emotions she'd been keeping hidden since I'd first arrived – the fear, the hurt, the loneliness she'd felt since I'd left – couldn't be hidden now. It was as if any barriers that had stopped me from knowing every inch of her emotions had been removed and I could feel them all, just the way she did.

I edged away from her, taken aback by the deluge of sensations. I'd never felt multiple emotions so clearly before, but she was my best friend and I had almost lost her. Maybe that was why my magic was so raw. I struggled to push it back behind my barriers.

'I promise I didn't realise what I was doing was dark magic,' Maddie continued. 'I was trying to keep on top of everything – the tattooing work and the Flame disappearing—'

'You don't have to apologise to me.' I reached over and took her hands. 'I should never have left you to do everything by yourself. That was unfair of me. Whatever has happened to the Flame is not your fault.'

'But maybe... I don't know. Maybe it went and didn't come back because it knew I was doing something dark in here.'

I offered her my most withering look. 'You only started using darker methods when the Flame had already gone, Mads. Don't lose focus on that. And besides, it's a *Flame* – it doesn't make decisions. We'll work it out. Now Yanni knows the truth, I'm sure we'll figure it out in short order,' I said with a confidence I didn't possess.

'And Fraser,' she pointed out.

'Sorry?' Hearing his name come from her lips caught me by surprise.

'He came into the house, right? He found me. That's what Yanni said when you were talking to Ernie. If he came in, then he knows about the Flame too.' Her bottom lip wobbled. 'And I guess he'll use it to kick us out of the house.'

I shook my head. 'Fraser's not like that,' I said firmly. 'I've spoken to him about the Flame and other things. He's ... he's a good guy.'

She gave me a look usually reserved for people who claimed to enjoy kale. As her face screwed up in disbelief, I decided it was probably best not to go into him saving my life; that felt like more than she could take in one night. As someone on my own knife edge, I recognised the wildness in her eyes.

I squeezed her hands. 'Look, worst-case scenario we have to live in a cave and become mysterious witches of the woods. Best case, we don't.'

She snorted gratifyingly at my attempt at humour.

'Either way, I promise we'll work it out.' I squeezed her shoulder again. 'Don't worry about Fraser. He won't be a problem. Now, get some sleep – you need it, and so do I. I've got the early shift on the phones tomorrow.'

Yanni had officially fired me from my job on the phones, but we hadn't discussed a notice period and it seemed churlish to leave her in the lurch. I still had the shift noted in my diary so I intended to honour it. I realised that I hadn't had the chance to tell Maddie I'd been sacked but now didn't seem the right time to mention it.

'I love you, Bea. You know that, right?' Her eyes were earnest.

I smiled. 'I love you, too. To the ends of the universe and back.'

As she pulled me into a hug, I felt the weight of her head drop onto my shoulder and again I was hit by her emotions, clearer and crisper than I'd ever known them before.

'Come on. Sleep time.' I coaxed her off to bed. When I was sure she was in her room, I went and tackled the devastation of the kitchen.

The walls were a little stained from the magical smoke but that was nothing a lick of paint wouldn't fix. It took a good half hour of scrubbing, but finally I had the cauldron gleaming the way Mum had always liked it. I set it neatly in Mum's larder where it normally lived. Making me clean her cauldron had been her favourite punishment, but now it just made me smile wistfully.

I spent another half hour setting the kitchen to rights, then went into the lounge to collapse on the sofa and stare at the woefully empty grate that somehow still seemed to call to me. What I wouldn't give for the magical flames to leap up, a veritable rainbow of fire that had always warmed me in more ways than one. Without strong magic of my own, knowing that I lived with the power of the Eternal Flame had always comforted me. The walls of my cottage felt cold and lonely without them.

Thoughts of solitude brought to mind how I could end that situation: Fraser Banks. I'd reassured Maddie that she didn't have to worry about Fraser, but the same couldn't be said for me. 'Worry' wasn't really the right word, but I couldn't stop thinking about him and that was *not* good. I needed to be happy with myself before I could add a man to the mix; I wasn't in a relationship-y place.

As I stared at my phone I could almost feel him doing the same, sitting in a deep green-leather armchair, staring at his screen, wondering if he should be the one to message first or whether it should be me.

It was all in my imagination: I had no idea what the inside of his house looked like. For all I knew, he didn't even have a green armchair. But my vision felt vividly real: I could almost smell the aroma rising from his whisky as he swirled the amber liquid in a cut-glass tumbler.

As I found myself once again unable to think about anything other than Fraser, I considered how Yanni had spoken to him when he'd pulled me out of the water. My mind had been fuzzy, but I was sure she'd been angry at him. Why? Why hadn't she thanked him for saving me? Had he used some dark magic to do so – though from the little I'd learned about him that didn't seem likely. If he'd been a dark magic user, I was certain the situation between his mother and father would have ended very differently.

I'd promised to message him when I was home safe, so I did even though it was late. It was hard to put down the phone when I wanted to stare at it until he replied. Thankfully, he messaged almost immediately.

I'm glad. I hope Maddie is well too. Sleep well, Beatrix.

She's doing okay, thanks. Sleep well, Fraser, I replied then I put down the phone so I could focus on anything but Mr Tall, Dark and Becoming-Less-Mysterious.

When I wandered up to my room and prepared for bed, I *definitely* didn't imagine Fraser doing the same.

I finally fell asleep with Eva's soft snores reverberating in my ear. I was so tired, mentally and physically, that I could have slept for days; I would have done were it not for the veritable raft of issues I had to face like dealing with my grandfather, finding the Eternal Flame – and ignoring the delicious Fraser.

Chapter Four

I stumbled downstairs, only to stop at the sight of Yanni in the kitchen. 'Yanni?' I yawned. 'What are you doing here?' I checked the time. 'I'm not late for my shift.'

Her eyes softened. 'I told you I'd pay you one month's severance. After all you've been through, I didn't expect you to turn up today.' She paused. 'Or ever.'

'Ever?' Maddie repeated, appearing in the doorway with the keen look of someone who knew drama when she heard it. 'What's going on?'

Oops. 'Yanni fired me,' I said lightly.

Yanni snorted. 'I *freed* you.' She looked at Maddie. 'Bea can do her PI job just as well down here as she can in London. I'm giving her one month's pay and the freedom to lie in.'

Maddie blinked. 'Yet she's still up at the crack of dawn.'

I glared. 'I wasn't planning on leaving Yanni in the lurch, I was going to serve my notice period.'

‘I appreciate the thought,’ Yanni said, ‘but we’ve got Sam to divert the phone to my mobile or Dove’s. It’s a pain, but it’ll do for now.’

I winced on her behalf. ‘I’m sure you’ll both love being woken up at ungodly hours to listen to people report missing garden gnomes and seagull-related crimes.’

A grimace crossed her face before she could squelch it.

Maddie was looking far brighter than I’d seen her in days and her cheeks were flushed with a healthy rose glow. She was wearing gym clothes and trainers and had clearly been up and out early. ‘You went for a walk?’ I asked, gesturing to her clothes. I am queen of the logical deduction.

Maddie filled a large glass with water and took a long gulp before she spoke. ‘I woke up a couple of hours ago. I don’t know what Ernie did to me, but I feel the best I’ve been in weeks and I wanted to go for a run.’ She polished off the water and made a face. ‘I guess I’m going to have plenty of time to get fit now that I can’t do my tattooing.’

She made the comment flippantly, but I heard the sadness in her voice. With a quick mental push, I ensured all my barriers were up. I suspected a barrage of emotions were about to fill her and the last thing I wanted was to be struck by them and start my day with a banging headache. My powers had been a bit wonky for the last day or so, and I didn’t know why.

'Shit. This is crap.' Maddie's hands were trembling. 'I was going to open a shop. Tattoos are my business – my life. I don't even have a way to earn money without them.' Her panic was rising; any minute now, she would explode.

I placed a hand on her shoulder. 'It's fine. Ernie will work with you. A witch as powerful as him – I bet he'll know how to make your ink without the Flame. And if he doesn't, we'll simply have to downgrade him from "powerful witch" to "regretful pincushion" until he figures it out.'

She gave me a wan smile for my efforts.

And if he doesn't, I'll make him find out how to do it, I thought. It was the least he could do after giving up on finding me. I'd call in my first 'biological granddaughter' favour if that was what I needed to do.

Maddie's panic was fading slightly, though it hadn't disappeared entirely. 'That doesn't change the fact that I still have to earn some money.' She bit her lip. 'I've got a bit set aside but it won't last long.'

I shared her pain. Since moving back to Witchlight Cove, I'd lost my income from my self-defence students who came to pay-as-you-go classes, and I hadn't picked up any PI work other than Maddie's task of digging up dirt on Fraser Banks. That hadn't been paid, nor had it gone quite as planned. I'd had a guaranteed income from working the phones at the police station but now I'd lost that too. All in all, it was a crappy situation. Unless...

'Maddie, you're still good with early mornings, aren't you? When you're not doing dark magic, that is?'

She offered me a glower for my sass. 'Better than you. Why?'

'Why don't *you* take over the job answering the phones at the police station? I'm sure Yanni would be flexible and you could still do your sessions with Ernie – and you'd have an income. In the meantime, I'll look at setting up some self-defence classes and hopefully pick up a couple of PI cases. We'll be fine.'

I watched her ponder the suggestion, then realised that I probably should have checked with Yanni first. The two were as close as any mother and daughter, but for all I knew working with Maddie could be Yanni's idea of a nightmare. However, from the smile blooming on Yanni's face I suspected that wouldn't be the case.

'Would you be okay with that?' Maddie asked, looking at her nana.

'What? Having my favourite grandchild working with me?' Yanni grinned. 'I guess it's something I could cope with.' She winked.

The two of them beamed at each other, and in that moment I had a clear memory of us here together. It had been one of my few happy moments in the Cove after my parents had died. Yanni had just been promoted, and we'd been so proud of her that it had been enough to cancel out everything else. It had felt like there was something to look forward to, a future for us.

That's what it felt like now. There was a future – it was just difficult to understand what it would be like.

Yanni broke into my thoughts. 'I asked Dove to come in for an early shift so I could check on you two. But could you start this afternoon?'

'This afternoon?' Maddie blinked.

'I know it's a bit quick, and given everything you've been through, I'd want to give you longer, but...' Yanni paused for dramatic effect. 'The Order of the Nightshades arrive in town tonight and Dove and I really need to bring our A-game. I don't want to risk being distracted at the wrong moment. This would be the perfect solution for me.'

It said a little about my poor phone-answering skills that she'd been willing to flounder on without me. I tried hard not to be too insulted and focused instead on the intriguing part of her sentence.

'The Order of the Nightshades?' I queried. Technically I wasn't working for Yanni any more, and I probably didn't have a right to know what was going on, but I couldn't help myself. Prying is in my nature. Besides,

Maddie needed to know, didn't she? I was helping *her* with my questioning.

'Who are they?' I probed. I'd never heard of them, which meant that they hadn't been in Witchlight Cove when I was last around.

I lowered my shields because I was nosey and was surprised to feel the level of Yanni's nervousness. Huh. I couldn't remember ever feeling that Yanni was nervous before, and it was as unnerving as fuck. Who were the Order of the Nightshades to affect her that way?

'It's not a straightforward answer,' she said grimly.

'Are they a knitting circle with a dark side? A terrifying cult of coffee-addicted baristas? A group of tax-loving accountants who've finally snapped?'

Yanni's lips twitched but her expression remained serious. 'Worse.'

Chapter Five

She paused dramatically – too much Am-Dram in her past. 'They're a guild of deadly vampire assassins, and – here's the part that gets me – they operate outside the boundaries of the law. Centuries ago, the order got special dispensation from all of the sects. They're like diplomats, untouchable under law.'

I gaped. No wonder Yanni wasn't thrilled about their arrival: they had carte blanche to do whatever they pleased with no consequences. It was a pretty terrifying prospect. 'That's insane.'

Yanni grimaced. 'I know. But because of that, their leader keeps a tight rein on them, and they're only supposed to perform authorised kills. If they went around creating mayhem, the sects would revoke their status, so they're careful to toe the line. They're also pretty philanthropic,' she added. 'They do a lot of charity work to minimise their bad reputation as hired killers. The fact that they're hired guns is one of those secrets that everyone knows but no one is rude enough to point out to them, if they're unlucky enough to meet one of them.'

'You're telling me there's a group of vampires who claim to be philanthropists but are, in fact, a not-so-secret guild of assassins who are above the law?' I said slowly.

'That's it,' Yanni agreed. 'They have existed for a very long time – centuries – and they're very secretive. Think of the Masons, but with murder and death.'

'Do they have their own secret handshake?' I asked, intrigued.

'I imagine so, but I'm not going to ask. Asking questions of the Nightshades doesn't end well for anyone.'

'Vampire assassins.' I shook my head in wonder. 'That sounds like the kind of thing you'd find in a particularly intense PowerPoint presentation at a supernatural careers fair.'

'Everybody loves a PowerPoint.' Yanni nodded approvingly.

Maddie snorted. '*No one* likes a PowerPoint. If the Nightshades are coming to Witchlight Cove, does that mean there's someone here they want to kill?' Her eyes were wide as she asked the question that had been on the tip of my tongue.

We had only just dealt with Witchlight Cove's most recent – and first – serial killer, a man who had murdered his own father, stepmother and his sister's boyfriend to secure his inheritance. He'd caused a crazy amount of destruction – and he was just an eel shifter. That still baffled me: of all the terrifying predator forms, he'd been a sea noodle. I guessed it was a lesson in not underestimating people; despite his less than terrifying form, he'd still managed to be as deadly as a man-of-war.

I couldn't imagine what destruction an entire guild of vampire assassins could do. Or rather, I didn't want to imagine it.

'No, I don't think they have a target.' Yanni's tone wasn't as certain as she might have wished. She clearly felt the same because she cleared her throat and tried again. 'Apparently they are coming to Witchlight for their Annual General Meeting.'

'Assassin's guilds have AGMs?' I said incredulously. 'I wonder what their keynote speech is—"Maximising Efficiency in Murder: A Ten-Step Guide to Strategic Stabbing"?' I imagined what the minutes would look like: 1.1 Death. 2.1 More Death. 3.1 Extra Death.

'This one does,' Yanni replied. 'At least, that's what we've been told. I guess they knew they couldn't hide the influx of vampires coming in through the barrier, and telling us why they're here is an attempt to ensure they're given all due courtesy. They don't want anyone to jump to the wrong conclusion if anything nefarious happens while they're in town. Even so, I'd rather have extra help at the station to handle the phones so I can focus my attention on them.'

I felt guilty; I should have hidden my dislike of early mornings better then maybe Yanni wouldn't have fired me and ended up short staffed. Still, I'd been shot less than twenty-four hours earlier, so maybe I should cut myself a little slack.

'How long is the Order staying in town for?' Maddie asked. 'Lorenz is opening a new bar over by the harbour tomorrow night and everyone is planning to be there. Murderous vampires might put a dampener on things.'

'I thought you were going to Shady's tomorrow with Ezra?' Yanni shot me a glance as she said Ezra's name and a grin flickered on her lips. The werewolf had been one of my best friends growing up and yes, it was true that he'd grown into one beast of a man – literally. But I just didn't see him the way everyone else seemed to want me to see him.

'I forgot to say – we got a message that Shady's is closed tomorrow for a private function,' Maddie said. 'Which works perfectly for Lorenz – he'll have no competition for his big opening night.'

‘I bet Shady’s private party is the Order of the Nightshades,’ I mused. ‘If it is, then at least we don’t have to worry about murderous assassins gatecrashing Lorenz’s big night.’

I looked at Yanni to judge her reaction but she was giving nothing away.

‘I don’t think you’ll need to work tomorrow night,’ Yanni told Maddie. ‘Like I said, I’m not expecting anything out of the ordinary. If anything, I hope having the Order in town will mean people are on their best behaviour.’

‘Will the residents know who they are?’ I asked.

‘They gave the hotel their name clearly enough so, as with most secrets in Witchlight Cove, everyone will know soon enough. I give it three hours before it’s on the specials board at Sonny’s coffee shop.’ She looked at Maddie. ‘So can you start work at two this afternoon? It would be a great help.’

Maddie nodded enthusiastically. ‘Sounds good. I said I’d go to Ernie’s around lunchtime for some more treatment, so I’ll come straight from there. This is going to be perfect.’

‘I’m glad that you think so,’ Yanni replied. ‘And I’m sorry it didn’t work out, Bea. For what it’s worth, I loved working with you ... even if you never did manage to actually get the coffee.' She paused. 'Or answer the phones.'

I winced. No, I hadn't done either of those things.

She chuckled and turned as if she were going to leave, only to stop and look back at me. A thin line appeared between her brows. 'Have you heard from Fraser today?' she asked.

'Fraser?' I tried to say his name casually as if I hadn't been thinking about him almost every second. 'No. Why? Should I have?'

'Oh, I thought he might have contacted you, that's all.' Her jaw tightened, but she made an effort to relax it and smiled instead.

I called bullshit. 'What potion did he give me?' I asked gesturing to my stomach.

Yanni blanched. 'You'll need to ask him. All right girls, I'd better get back to work. Have a good day.' She bent down and gave Eva a rub on the head. 'Look after them, won't you? I'm pretty sure you're the most sensible one in this house.' Eva barked as if she agreed.

'Hey,' I laughed. 'Smart or not, remember who opens your dog food! You need opposable thumbs for that shit.'

Yanni snickered before leaving me and Maddie alone with Eva.

'Why exactly does my grandmother think Fraser is going to ring you?' my friend demanded immediately after Yanni had closed the door. 'And what potion were you talking about? Is there more going on between you two than you're letting on?'

The image of Fraser and me standing on the beach immediately came to mind, then I thought of him stepping out of the water, droplets trailing down his tight abs. I'd seen less-sculpted statues in museums. If I hadn't turned around and shown a hint of self-restraint, who knows what I might have seen? That thought alone was enough to make my cheeks colour – at which point I remembered Maddie was still standing there looking at me, and I blushed like a schoolgirl.

I cleared my throat awkwardly. 'No, of course not! He was there last night and Yanni probably thought he'd want to check on how you're doing, that's all,' I hastily cast around for a way to change the subject. 'And while we're in interrogation mode, we need to set up some ground rules for when you speak to Ernie. I don't trust him yet – not entirely – and I don't want you to, either. We need to learn more about him before we roll out the red carpet. And I'd appreciate it if you don't talk about me too much.'

'About what?' She arched an eyebrow.

It was a good question. What didn't I want my grandfather to know about me that he hadn't already figured out? That I was a dud witch? That my friends were my family, and I'd do anything to protect them? He already knew that. 'Just don't trust him, okay?' I repeated. 'And I want a debrief of everything he tells you. And I mean *everything*.'

A smile lifted the corners of Maddie's lips. 'Look at you, all caring and stuff.' She winked. 'Fine – as long as you tell me everything that goes on with you and Fraser.'

I opened my mouth to respond. There was so much I needed to tell her, from the conversation at the beach to Fraser's exchange with Yanni and the fact that he'd saved my life. I didn't even know if Maddie was aware I'd been shot, and that was definitely something I needed to tell her.

'About that,' I started, but before I could continue, there was a knock at the door.

'Jeez, it's like Grand Central Station here today,' Maddie huffed.

When I turned towards the door to see who had interrupted my confession, part of me was secretly pleased. Some things between Fraser and I felt intensely personal and I wanted to keep them to myself for a little while longer. But I'd have to admit to the events on the boat sooner rather than later.

Chapter Six

Maddie opened the door to six-foot-six of pure muscle attached to a sweet face that was grinning down at us. Even the ominous scar running through Ezra's right eyebrow didn't decrease his charm; if anything, it added to it. There was clearly something wrong with me that I didn't find him attractive.

'Maddie, Trixie.' He greeted us as he rocked back on his heels. He sent me an amused look. 'I hear the job didn't go too well.'

I stepped aside and let him into the hallway. 'Bad news travels fast.'

'News of *any* kind travels fast in Witchlight,' he said lightly. 'Except, apparently, the fact that I am the most handsome man in town. That seems to be taking its time.'

I rolled my eyes at him. Good-natured amusement was radiating off of Ezra, a subtle, sweet emotion, and for the second time that morning I was surprised by how clearly I could pick up on another person's emotions. Had meeting my paternal grandfather unlocked something within me? Maybe witches needed to be in covens because without family their magic didn't manifest properly?

I pondered the idea for a moment before dismissing it. If that were the case, my powers would have formed while my parents were still alive, the way most young witches' powers do. I was grasping at straws – but it didn't change the fact that something within me had definitely shifted and I was damned if I knew what or why.

'Trixie, you okay?'

I blinked. Ezra was staring at me as if he was waiting for me to respond to something. I had no idea what the hell he'd asked me. 'Sorry,' I offered lamely. 'I drifted away for a bit.'

'Yeah, we noticed,' he said.

'Ezra was saying about last night,' Maddie clarified.

Last night? 'Yeah,' Ezra added. 'It's crazy – I can't believe Gilbert would kill his own dad! That's so cold. I heard you handled the situation like a pro, though.'

Oh: *that* last night.

I wasn't sure getting shot was something a pro would do but I wasn't about to say so. 'I'm glad we caught the real killer,' I said diplomatically. 'Actually, while you're here, I might as well tell you both at once.' I took a deep breath and relayed the previous night's events as dispassionately as possible.

'You got shot?' Maddie squawked. 'And this is the first I'm hearing of it?'

I shrugged. 'Fraser gave me a potion or something and I'm totally fine.' I lifted my shirt to show them my unblemished skin.

'That's one helluva potion,' Ezra said slowly.

'Fraser saved you?' Maddie asked. I nodded. She sighed dramatically. 'Fine. My grudge against him is officially null and void.'

Ezra and I exchanged amused glances. 'Is that why you came over?' I asked Ezra. 'To talk about Gilbert?'

It was surprisingly nice having the three of us together. From when we were little kids up to when I'd left, we'd spent almost every day together and I hadn't realised how much I'd missed it. Maddie was right about us needing some proper time together again, even if she was wrong about Ezra and I making a decent couple.

'Actually, I came to ask if you'd be interested in some work,' Ezra said hopefully. 'Also, any chance of a cup of tea before I waste away? I feel my life force draining away by the second.'

Not that he was being overdramatic or anything; it was good to see some things never changed. 'Of course!

Wouldn't want you to waste away – any scrawnier and the wolf pack would kick you out,' I joked because he was solid muscle and the furthest from scrawny he'd ever been. 'And yes, I'm definitely interested in work.' I wondered what he might be about to suggest. Was it too much to hope for a lost family heirloom that he desperately needed me to recover for a huge payout? Probably.

Ezra followed me into the house the same way he'd done hundreds of times and for a second it was like no time had passed. It was only when he got into the living room and froze rather than going through into the kitchen that I realised my catastrophic mistake.

'Er, Trixie, Mads?' he said slowly. 'Is it just me, or is there something really big missing from that fireplace?'

Oh fuck. I'd let him in without thinking that he didn't know the Eternal Flame was gone! I'd lost count of who knew and who didn't. There was a *reason* Maddie and I had been talking about serious stuff in the freaking porch, but in the moment I'd just clean forgotten. I winced. This was a mess.

'You can't tell anyone,' Maddie jumped in. 'It's not Bea's fault.'

'It's not anyone's fault,' I corrected. 'It's complicated.'

'And it's very much a secret,' she added.

'Is that why you came back?' Ezra asked softly.

'Pretty much,' I admitted.

He nodded, his eyes lingering on the empty fireplace for a moment before he turned to face me. 'Well, it's a pity that it's gone – but honestly? If that's what it took to get you back here, I'm kind of grateful to whoever took it.'

Maddie hit him. 'It is not a *good* thing! And we don't think someone stole it, because all the wards are still working. It's just ... gone.'

'It's a mess,' I sighed. 'Come on through to the kitchen, let's make you that brew.' I spoiled the effect of my offer by yawning wildly; early mornings and I do not get on well.

Ezra laughed. 'Don't worry, I'll get it myself. I know where everything is.' He reached for the cupboard where the mugs were stored then retrieved the tea bags. I wondered if he still popped around regularly for tea with Maddie, or if his knowledge of the house came from all the time he'd spent there with me.

'I'll leave you two to it,' Maddie said airily. 'I need to grab a shower.'

I shot her a glare. She was about as subtle as an exploding cauldron.

She paused by the door. 'You're still up for Lorenz's tomorrow night, Ez?'

'You know it,' he promised. His gaze swept over her and some of the tension in his shoulders eased. 'And Mads? You look good today. Really good.'

She beamed. Obviously, Ezra hadn't known about her dabbling with dark magic any more than I had, but it was good that he could see a difference in her now that it was gone. Hopefully now she knew how much it had affected her, she'd never be tempted to go back to less than savoury practices.

As Maddie drifted upstairs, Ezra and I went back into the depressingly flameless living room. 'So, what is it?' I asked eagerly. 'What job have you got for me?'

I was sensing a deep sadness radiating from him, blended with a fear-based tension and tinged with an underlying anger – not to mention guilt. Four emotions at one time: my powers really *were* improving, but instead of feeling happy I felt concerned because I didn't know *why* my magic was changing.

Eva jumped up next to me on the sofa and Ezra sat on the other side of her. After ruffling her fur, he sighed. 'It's my nieces,' he said. 'I don't know if you ever met Hallie and Roz. They've only just turned ten.'

Ezra had a lot of family, including a multitude of nieces, nephews and cousins. Since coming back to Witchlight I'd only seen his dad and his cousin, Pepper. I frowned as I cast my mind back. 'I think I remember your sister being pregnant. They're twins, right?'

'Yeah,' he said with an affectionate smile. 'They're chaos. Super smart, super sassy – and obviously, I'm their favourite relative.'

'Of course.' I pressed a hand to my chest. 'Poor you. The burden of being adored must be exhausting.' His smile was sweet. Ezra would do anything for the people he loved, and I assumed that was why he was here. 'So what's going on with them?' I asked.

He sipped his tea, but I got the feeling it was to steady himself rather than because he was thirsty. 'Bullying,' he replied finally. He gritted his teeth and a wave of anger rolled off him. 'At school – and outside of it too, apparently.'

'That's so crap,' I said instantly. 'I'm sorry. It must be shit for them.'

'It is. Bullies are vermin. When we were kids, my mother always tried to convince me it wasn't their fault, that they had things going on at home that made them act badly, But you don't have to be very old to know the difference between right and wrong. And it's not like all bullies see the error of their ways and stop when they grow up. Plenty of adults still think it's acceptable behaviour to make you feel bad about yourself.' His dark glare told me he was thinking about someone in particular.

'Who's doing it?' I asked. 'Surely you've spoken to them?'

'Oh, I have,' he said, still angry. 'It's three bear shifters; one of them is the ringleader.'

'Bear shifters? Has Yanni spoken to them?'

'The girls don't want that – they want to stand up for themselves. Plus, the bullies are polar bears and not from Yanni's line.'

That was when it clicked and I realised why Ezra had come to see me. 'You want me to teach the girls self-defence?'

'Absolutely. These bullies are only cubs. They're not exactly petite, but I reckon if the twins can show them that they won't be pushed around – literally – then they'll back off. Obviously, I'd pay you for your time.'

'You don't have to do that,' I said. 'You're family.'

I didn't miss his almost imperceptible wince. 'Any self-respecting member of your family would tell you that you have to earn money, so I'm paying you and that's that.' He paused. 'Assuming you'll help?'

My heart warmed. I really did love him, even if it was just as a friend. 'Of course I will!'

'When are you free?' he asked. 'Obviously they have school, and it's a full moon tonight, so they'll want to be out with the pack. You're not going to want to teach them while they're in wolf form!'

I'd wanted to fight Ezra in wolf form when I was a kid just to prove I could beat him, but my parents had forbidden it. The wolf's primary defence is its teeth; the last thing I needed now was a wolf bite to make my situation even more complicated.

'Tomorrow?' I suggested. 'Before we go to Lorenz's?'

'Perfect. Sounds like a date – with the girls, obviously,' he added hastily.

'You never give up, do you?'

He grinned. 'You can't keep this werewolf down. Besides, it's fun winding you up.'

He was such a git but I loved him and I knew he'd make some other woman very, very happy one day. I just needed to find that woman. Maybe that was something else I could put on my to-do list while I was officially unemployed: find the Flame, get Ezra a girlfriend, and get Fraser Banks out of my head.

Sadly, only one of those three actually felt possible, but I'd definitely be giving the others a go.

Chapter Seven

Given that I was having my first proper day off since arriving in Witchlight Cove, I decided to give my long-suffering retriever a proper walk. 'I think you'll like the woods,' I told her. 'But remember what Ezra just said about it being a full moon tonight? We're not going too far. Okay?'

Eva barked and wagged her tail, and I felt a flurry of excitement cascade from her. It wasn't just about the walk; it was about the two of us having some time together. Eva was definitely a people dog, and the more people she had around to love her the better, but it had obviously been hard for her having to share my attention with so many others. When we were in London, it had just been the two of us.

I felt the same: there was nothing better than some solitude with my bestie – except maybe the addition of a good thriller and... 'Actually, before we go for a walk, how about we grab one of Sonny's coffees?' I suggested.

She gave me a look which in a human would have been an eyeroll, but then she relented, wagged her tail and barked. She didn't want me spending too long there when I'd promised her the scents and sounds of the woods to enjoy. 'I'll be quick,' I wheedled.

She huffed but set off happily by my side towards Sonny's.

By pure luck, I timed my arrival between the breakfast and lunchtime rushes, so there were only two people ahead of me in the queue. Sonny's coffee was insanely good and people would often wait for an hour for one of his cappuccinos.

Feeling like fate was on my side, I stepped into the café. Immediately a strange prickling travelled the length of my spine, as if I were being watched. I knew instantly whose eyes were on me and yes, I was aware that it was weird that I didn't need to turn around to check. That knowledge led to something that felt remarkably like a thousand butterflies swarming in my stomach.

I glanced to the side and, just as I'd expected – *known,* Fraser Banks was there. As if he felt my gaze, he looked up and a welcoming smile curved across his features.

'Hey, Beatrix,' he said before turning to the waitress. 'Kaz.' He waved his hand to catch the attention of the female vampire. 'Put whatever Bea wants on my tab.' He turned his gaze to me. 'Would you like to join me? No pressure,' he added hastily. 'You can grab the coffee and go. Don't feel obliged.'

I found myself smiling; he was rambling and it was surprisingly cute. 'I'd love to,' I said, my lips moving before my brain had a chance to think about his offer; my mouth was clearly running an independent operation, much like Eva who'd already abandoned me for a better prospect. She was sitting by Fraser's feet, resting her head on his lap. So much for thinking she was craving *my* attention.

Kaz flashed me a smile. 'What would you like?' she asked warmly. She was the polar opposite of Sonny's usual 'charm', and probably the reason he still did a roaring trade despite his sour disposition.

'A mocha, please. Double shot.'

'No problem. I'll bring it over.' She started bustling around the coffee machine, grinding fresh beans and tamping them down expertly.

I left her to it and looked around the café. I immediately spotted a glowering vampire in one of the booths; I knew he was a vamp because he was flashing his fangs as he sipped his coffee and he had a daylight tattoo on his neck. He wasn't trying to hide who or what he was, and I kind of liked that. None of us should need to hide who we are.

I met his eyes and gave him a friendly smile. After a beat he acknowledged my existence with a jerk of his head then pointedly turned back to his coffee. O-kay, interaction over, I guessed. A shiver ran through me. I was good at reading people but I got *nothing* from this guy; it was like he was emotionless. Totally creepy.

When I walked over to Fraser's table, he rose – displacing Eva's head – and pulled out a chair for me. The fluttering in my stomach intensified and my pulse spiked as if I'd just run a half-marathon. Of *course* he was a total gentleman: the damned selkie didn't have a single flaw – other than his flawlessness. But maybe that just showed I didn't know him yet. Everyone has flaws, some worse than others. Weirdly, I found I was looking forward to discovering his.

'How are you feeling?' he asked carefully as he sat down again. 'After yesterday? Is everything okay?'

I felt his nervousness so acutely that I had to push my barriers up another notch. All that time in the non-magical world had accustomed me to maintaining a much lower barrier because I hadn't needed to work so hard to block out emotions, but lately it felt like I was battling them all the time. If my powers remained on the blink like this, I'd have to spend a serious amount of my unemployed time working on strengthening my shields.

As the barrier kicked in, I wondered if I'd misjudged what I'd been feeling. Surely Fraser couldn't possibly be nervous about speaking to me? We'd had conversations before and I was nothing to be scared of. And yet I *knew* he was nervous, which annoyingly made my own tension increase. Those damned nerves were contagious, multiplying like tribbles.

I felt conflicted. Part of me had wanted to sit with him before he'd even offered, as if I'd been drawn by some unseen force, but the other part of me wanted to hold back. Still, I couldn't ignore the sense that he *needed* to talk to me.

I realised I'd been silent for too long. 'Well, it's been a lot to deal with,' I blurted.

'Yes, I can imagine. How is Maddie? Is she all right?'

I loved how his eyes lit with genuine concern. 'I think she will be. She's going to work with Ernie – Old Jacobson. He says he can help her.'

'That's good, I suppose.' He frowned. 'I don't know him well. Is he trustworthy?'

That was a big question. Ernie had chucked Fraser around this very café, so I could see why he'd be ambivalent about him despite his helping Maddie.

I snorted. 'Define trustworthy. On a scale from "would lend you a fiver" to "won't sell your soul to the highest bidder", he's somewhere in the middle.' I paused. 'It's complicated. I discovered some things last night about Ernie. About me.' I didn't know why I was holding back because the urge to share with Fraser was strong. He'd all-but bared his soul to me a couple of days ago and it felt like it was my turn to reciprocate.

'One double-shot mocha,' Kaz said as she placed a cup in front of me.

'Thank you.' I flashed her a smile, then waited until she'd walked away before dropping my voice and continuing. 'It turns out that Ernie is my grandfather.'

Fraser blinked. 'Your grandfather? And you had no idea?'

I shook my head. 'Not a clue.'

He reached over the table and squeezed my hand. 'That's a lot to deal with. Is there anything I can do to help?'

'No – but thank you. I just need to find my feet again.' I smiled wryly. 'Like I've been trying to do ever since I arrived back in Witchlight.'

I hadn't specifically asked but Kaz had placed my coffee in a takeaway cup. At that moment it felt like a sign from those fates that I totally didn't believe in, a nudge that I shouldn't stay there getting closer and closer to Fraser.

I picked up the cup. 'I should get going.' I moved to stand, only to stop. 'Oh, wait – you said you wanted to talk to me. I'm sorry, I completely forgot. What was it about?'

Fraser tilted his head. 'I don't think I did,' he replied slowly, his gaze holding mine. 'I asked you to join me, but there wasn't a specific reason.'

I felt sure he was lying. 'Are you sure?' I asked. I'd been so sure he wanted to speak to me about something specific, and it had felt ... essential. Desperate. But now ... nothing.

'Beatrix, is everything alright?' Fraser touched my hand. 'Are you okay?'

'I'm—'

The flash hit me like a bolt of lightning: the same vision I'd had before I'd fallen asleep the previous night of him sitting in a green armchair, a glass of whisky in his hand. Only this time it felt even more vivid; it wasn't just the whisky I could smell; I could sense the aroma of the leather chair in my nostrils and see his wet coat, the one he'd placed around me, lying across its arm next to him.

The coat wasn't in the form of a leather jacket like it had been when he'd saved me, it was more natural than that. It was a pelt, and there was magic buzzing from it – magic that was drawing me in.

With a jolt, I freed myself from the vision and backed out of my seat, practically knocking over my chair. My hands and knees were trembling. *His pelt*: he'd wrapped his pelt around me. 'Come on, Eva,' I blurted, not daring to look at Fraser. 'We're going!'

With my heart racing, I sprinted out of the cafe only realizing once I was on the pavement that I'd left my coffee. Again.

I groaned. One day, I would actually have a normal drink at Sonny's.

Chapter Eight

When I got home from walking Eva a couple of hours later, I'd calmed down. The vision obviously wasn't *real*, it was just some sort of trauma response. I wasn't powerful enough to have *real* visions so it must have been my imagination going crazy. If it had felt super real and I could still smell the smoky, peaty tang of whisky on the air – well, I had a good imagination, that was all.

The house was empty and cold, and the absence of the Eternal Flame rankled. This house shouldn't *be* cool, it should be sweltering. Seeing the empty fireplace made my heart sink and my guilt rise up. Some Guardian I was.

To divert myself, I dug out my lockpick set and an old padlock hoping they might provide some challenge. They didn't – the lock popped open almost instantly. At least if my magic didn't pan out, I could always become a career criminal. It was always good to have a Plan B.

I picked up my current book but before long I realised I'd read the same page three times: even my thriller wasn't thrilling me. I felt flat and weird, and I didn't know why.

It was a relief when Maddie bounced in from her shift. 'Guess what?' she asked, eyes sparkling with mischief.

'You're going to have to give me a clue,' I replied. 'You're working at the police station in a magical town, so literally anything could have happened.'

She snorted. 'Fine then, I'll tell you.' She was clearly too excited to continue her guessing game. 'The head of the Order of the Nightshade came into the station today. Her name is Candice, and she's phenomenal – terrifying but phenomenal. And the heels she was wearing! They were red soled. Louboutin's, obviously. Everything she was wearing was designer – her bag was Chanel. Vintage.'

I nodded sagely. 'Yes, nothing says "secret assassin organisation" like a bold fashion statement.'

Maddie rolled her eyes. 'Honestly, she looked so kick ass!'

'I thought the Order was meant to be secretive and nobody was supposed to know they're here?' I said, cutting Maddie off before she gave me every single detail of the vampire's outfit. Still, the smouldering vampire at Sonny's hadn't been subtle either, and I had no doubt he was part of the Nightshades; something about him had screamed deadly.

Maddie dropped onto the sofa. 'I spoke to Dove about that. We think the idea is that they don't let anyone know where they've been *after* they've swept in and assassinated someone,' she said. 'When they're on the job they're ghosts, but as an organisation they want people to know they exist so that their reputation spreads. And they let the charities they donate to know who they are – apparently they even hold a charity ball once a year.'

That probably made it easier for them to find clients, but it still felt odd. I'd hate to imagine what would happen if a fight broke out at an assassin's party. 'What did Candice want?' I asked nosily. 'I assume she came to speak to Yanni?'

'Yeah. She wanted to reassure the police that the Order are here purely for administrative business and their visit shouldn't bring anyone any harm or distress.' Maddie's tone indicated she was quoting Yanni.

'I'm not sure that's reassuring when it's coming from a professional murderer.'

'Apparently there are some grudges going back years with various shifter groups. She wanted Yanni to be aware of that, and said she'd told her vamps to park any resentment. Oh, and she asked for a list of local charities because they always donate to the town where they hold their AGM.'

Part of me wished I'd been at the police station to see Candice so I could get her measure myself, although I clearly wouldn't have got half the thrill from the designer clothes.

'What about you?' Maddie tucked her feet under her. 'Did you get up to much today?'

For a second I considered telling her about the walk with Eva, the moment with Fraser in the coffee shop and the flash that had felt almost like a vision. But … I didn't. There was something else I wanted to bring up instead, something more important than the churning in my gut every time I thought of Fraser.

'I think my powers are getting stronger,' I blurted out.

She stared at me. 'Wait – what? Really? How do you know?'

'It's subtle things, like feelings. You know how I can generally pick up supernatural people's emotions?'

'Yes, of course.'

'Well, that's changed. I've always been able to pick up one dominant emotion, maybe two, but now I can unravel a whole bundle of them. When Ezra came round, I wasn't just feeling his strong emotions but the slight ones, too. I could feel how upset Ezra was about his nieces and how guilty he felt that he hadn't done more to help them.'

'Perhaps it's a sign of a bond growing between you and Ezra?'

I glared at her.

'What?' Maddie replied, with faux-innocence. Then she sobered. 'Bea, I hate to rain on your parade but I don't know how this is different. You've always been able to feel our emotions because you're close to us.'

'Not like this,' I insisted. 'This is different.'

Her eyes were sympathetic. 'Are you sure you're not reading into it because you *want* your powers to grow?'

I considered her question carefully. Could this just be in my head? No, it definitely wasn't; I knew my magic – limited though it was – and it had definitely changed since I'd been shot. 'Honestly, I think this is really different.'

'Maybe it's something to do with the Flame disappearing,' Maddie suggested. 'It is part of your family, after all.'

'I don't know.' I wouldn't have been surprised if the Eternal Flame had just wandered off in search of a better guardian. It was that thought that kept my stomach churning in the small hours of the night.

With everything that had happened in the last twenty-four hours, the missing Eternal Flame had been pushed way down my list of priorities but it couldn't stay there. I had to drag it to the top – it was the whole reason I'd returned to Witchlight Cove.

'It's weird, because the wards around the town haven't fallen so the Flame might not be in this house but it *must* still be local. I should probably do some digging, maybe find other places that have Witchlights.' I was speaking my thoughts aloud. 'I could see if there are records of anything similar happening.'

'Sounds like a good idea,' Maddie said. 'How easy do you think it will be to locate another Eternal Flame?'

'Not easy at all,' I admitted with a rueful smile. 'Fancy giving me a hand in the library?'

'Sure.' She uncurled her legs, though she paused before she stood up and opened her mouth as if she wanted to say something. A moment later, she closed it again.

'What?' I asked.

'Nothing.' She avoided my eyes.

'You were going to say something. What was it?' I knew my best friend and I wasn't going to let her keep anything from me again, not after the way it had ended last time.

She pressed her lips tightly together before she said, 'I wondered if you were going to ask about how my session with Ernie went today or if he'd asked anything about you. But it doesn't matter. I know how difficult it is for you.'

Another shard of guilt stabbed me: of course I should have asked about her time with Ernie. Just because he was an uncomfortable topic for me didn't mean I had to be selfish. 'Sorry, Mads. This afternoon was hectic and it slipped my mind to ask.' I was rusty at this whole friendship thing. 'Sorry,' I repeated. 'How *did* it go?'

'Well, for what it's worth, I think he's a really good guy.' Maddie still sounded a little huffy. 'He was telling me about his youth, how he put a protection spell over a whole village of elves so they couldn't be found, which was a really lovely thing to do. And he mentioned several times that he really wants to get to know you.' She shifted and started playing with the toggle of her hoodie jumper.

I frowned. 'You didn't say anything about me, did you?'

She shook her head quickly – too quickly. 'No, of course not. You told me not to.'

I felt a flicker of nervousness radiating from her. I decided to press her; there had already been enough lies between us and I wanted them to stop. 'Maddie, what are you not telling me?'

The tense silence that followed said everything. A moment later, she broke. 'I didn't tell him anything he didn't already know,' she protested. 'Only that you're a great person and family is a touchy subject for you. Honestly, that's all I said.'

My gaze softened. Those weren't exactly military secrets, and besides I couldn't be mad at her because everything she did for me came from a place of love. Even this. 'If you could avoid telling him any more, I'd really appreciate it,' I said. If I was going to build a relationship with my grandfather, I wanted him to learn about me from me.

She nodded rapidly. 'Okay, but you should know that he really wants to get to know you. He seems incredibly lonely. He loved a woman who broke his heart, so he threw himself into work because he couldn't cope with getting his heart broken again. Then he discovered he had a son with this woman – who he probably knew was insane – and she'd used him in the most horrible way. He did everything he could to find his child but only succeeded because his son had died. That's got to be a bit of a mindfuck, right?'

Thinking about it that way, I could definitely understand where he was coming from.

'Maybe you could come to one of my sessions,' Mads said gently. 'I'm not saying you need to be alone with him but maybe he can help us with the Witchlight. He's incredibly powerful, Bea. And if something is going on with your powers, he might be help with that, too.'

There were so many reasons why talking to Ernie Jacobson was a good idea – apart from the fact that I wasn't sure my heart could take it if I grew close to him and lost him too...

I was pretty sure it would destroy me to lose someone else. It didn't take Freud to tell me that pushing away Maddie, Ezra and Yanni had been a defensive reaction. Now that I was back home, I could see how futile it had been because if anything had happened to them, I would still have been devastated. I still loved them and they loved me; all I'd succeeded in doing was not having them in my life for a decade.

Maybe I was making the same mistake with Ernie.

'I'll think about it,' I said aloud. 'For now, I'm going to look in the library for all things Eternal Flame. Are you joining me?'

'Sure, but I probably won't last long. I'm knackered.'

'You and me both,' I said wryly. I was tired, ridiculously so, but I needed answers. It was time to get bookish.

Chapter Nine

Our library had been my dad's favourite room in the house. It wasn't big; if there hadn't been so many books spilling off the shelves and onto the floor, you might just have squeezed a double bed in there, but every inch of it was crammed. Books of every size, from little pocket notebooks to massive, heavy tomes filled every nook and cranny, and they made me think instantly of my father.

Greg Stonehaven had been a complete bibliophile. He used to say books were his one true love – until Mum cleared her throat and reminded him she was standing right there. The memory made my heart ache; they'd loved each other so much. For the first time, I found myself wanting that same love for myself.

I gave myself a shake and inhaled the scent of the room. I love books too, but I'm not really an encyclopaedia girl: thrillers, murder mysteries, anything with a bit of action, are my go-to. When I was a kid wading through these dusty pages full of ancient spells and magical histories and artifacts had only served to remind me of the powers I didn't have. There were so many stories about great witches and wizards to whom I would never compare, thousands of charms and incantations I'd never be capable of casting, and they had made me feel so inadequate. As a future Guardian of the Flame, I was expected to learn them all without ever being able to use them; I had to know it to pass it down to the next generation.

Mum had told me that it was my responsibility to wed and bed as soon as I was of an age to do so. She'd made it sound like a royal decree – though with little chance of being whisked away by a handsome prince and far more chance of awkward small talk over breakfast. She'd wanted me to marry for love but she'd also hoped I'd find a strong wizard who would spawn another powerful generation of Guardians.

Unlike me. I pushed the bitter thought aside and focused on the books around me.

I'd always felt a sense of frustration walking into this room, as if the room itself was responsible for my shortcomings, and it had saddened Dad that his sanctuary had been my purgatory. Now it was different: I was going in there with determination and a purpose.

‘Where do you think we should start?’ Maddie was standing on tiptoes peering at the shelves. ‘There must be at least a thousand books in here.’

‘At least,’ I agreed. ‘And I don’t know the best place to begin. Dad always kept the ones he read most often on his desk.’ I pointed to the plain oak table beneath the window. ‘Maybe we should start there.’

‘Sounds good,’ she said. ‘I bagsy the comfiest chair.’

Three hours later, Eva was snoring softly while my eyes were so heavy I feared they’d fall out of my head. I’d read about various paranormal creatures and astral realms. I’d read about spells that could block powers, hide locations or do things to your anatomy that would put plastic surgeons out of business in a heartbeat. One spell had promised ‘eternal youth with just three drops of moonlit water’, which seemed a very vague unit of measurement. How big were these drops? How much moonlight? I didn’t buy it; clearly there’d been scammers selling people obscene beauty standards centuries before beauty magazines had made us all feel inadequate.

But despite the plethora of books we’d dived into, there was nothing about the Witchlight; apparently, it hadn’t been on Dad’s ‘recently read’ list.

One theme did come up more than the others, though: sorcery. Every time I saw a reference to the dark invasive magic, it made me shudder. Dad had known what his mother was practising and what she was capable of. I looked at the piles of books and wondered if he'd feared his mother's return. Of course he must have; that was why he'd restricted his own magic use.

Had Mum known about my grandmother? Had she married Dad with her eyes wide open to the dangers he brought with him? It hurt that I didn't know the answers to those questions and I never would.

'I'm sorry.' Maddie yawned so widely I could see all the way down the back of her throat. 'I have to go to bed. Nana's got me on the early shift tomorrow – I asked for it so we can get to Lorenz's early. I hear there's going to be quite a queue. Have you chosen what you're wearing yet?'

'Jeans,' I mumbled instinctively. She sighed. 'What?' I asked defensively. 'That's pretty much all I packed. And I've got some nice jeans.'

'At least wear heels with them?' she pleaded.

I grinned. 'You think I brought heels?'

The look she gave me was the one she reserved for someone who had just admitted they didn't like cake. She leaned down and kissed Eva on the top of her furry head. 'I'll see what I can dig out. Sleep well, you two.'

'You too,' I said. 'And Maddie?'

'Yeah?'

'Thanks.' I gestured at the piles of books we'd looked through.

She smiled softly. 'No problem.'

I picked up another volume, but when I could no longer focus on the words I called it a day. My concentration was shot and I needed some down time, so I went upstairs with Eva and soaked in the bathtub.

Baths have always been my refuge when I'm not quite ready to sleep but I want to close my eyes and switch off from the world. However, when I closed my eyes the vision that filled my head was anything but relaxing; instead it triggered something dark within me – my altercation with Gilbert.

It was like watching a film in slow motion, though the perspective was off. Instead of being on the boat, I was in the water staring up at a massive white object: the yacht. As I continued to bob there something appeared at the top of my vision: me.

Watching myself was dizzying and confusing but I forced myself to stay with the vision. Keeping my eyes locked on Boat-Beatrix, Watery-Me moved closer to the edge of the boat. Even though I knew what was about to happen, the gun blast that shot through my memory – and into my side – reverberated through me. Panic shot through Watery-Me as Boat-Beatrix fell backwards towards the depths of the Mother Ocean.

I jolted up in the bath, splashing water everywhere. Great. Now the floor was also having a bath.

Fuck! That was just … so real. And so weird.

My heart was racing. 'You're okay, Bea. Everything's okay,' I said to myself.

I placed a hand on the spot where I'd been shot, not that there was any evidence of the injury; whatever spell or potion Fraser had used on me hadn't left so much as a mark, let alone a scar. I could feel my heart pounding through my ribs.

How long had the whole thing lasted for? The water was cool now and I started to shiver. I cast around for a towel and climbed out of the bath.

I told myself it was all part of that same trauma response, and it was natural that my mind would want to return to the moment. After all, the shooting had only happened twenty-four hours ago. But why was I seeing it from that point of view, as if I'd been in the water?

It was *Fraser*'s point of view.

Maybe my subconscious was obsessed with Fraser and that little Daniel Craig scene on the beach was doing a number on my subconscious. I hadn't had sex in a while and my basic id urges were focusing on the sexy property developer. That was all it was.

I mopped up the water on the floor and wrapped a fresh towel around me as my phone buzzed on the toilet cistern. Without looking, I knew who it was; I *knew* it was Fraser. Okay, maybe I didn't *know* know; it was a reflex because I'd been thinking about him.

God, what the hell was wrong with me?

My hand trembled as I reached for the phone. Did I want to see his message? Why was I so worried about it? He was just a guy – an attractive guy, sure, but still just a guy. I had other attractive guy friends in the non-magical world, but something about Fraser was different. Something about how I felt around him was different.

Sure enough, the message was from Fraser. *Hey Beatrix, I hope you're okay. Maybe we could find time in the week to meet up. You were right – there is something I want to talk to you about.*

The tone of the message was serious, which made my stomach twist into knots. Serious wasn't something I wanted to deal with right now. I couldn't give in to my feelings for Fraser: he was a complication and a distraction I couldn't afford. And anyway, I didn't do relationships, and I wasn't going to start now.

I fired a message back. *Pretty busy. Will let you know.*

I regretted it the moment I hit send. I'd just given him the world's least convincing brush-off and my flippancy made the knots inside me tighten with guilt. He didn't deserve my shit. My baggage wasn't his fault.

I dressed in jammies then, figuring I deserved a little more suffering for being such an idiot, I headed back to Dad's library. I read until the words blurred again, then crawled into bed next to Eva.

On the plus side, the next day I was holding my first self-defence class, and I was genuinely looking forward to it. I was desperately missing teaching; I loved helping others and I was eager to help Ezra's nieces. Their bullies wouldn't know what had hit them.

Chapter Ten

'Okay, so what's the aim here?' I asked the girls.

Ezra's nieces were standing in front of me. Aged ten, they weren't the youngest students I'd ever taught but they *were* my first set of identical twins – and they were completely identical, even down to their hairstyles and the way they posed with one foot crossed over the other as if they were both a little nervous. Thankfully, they were wearing different coloured tops, otherwise, I'd have had no chance of knowing who was who.

I'd lost count of the number of Ezra's relatives – the cousins alone had hit double digits back when we were kids, and it wouldn't have surprised me if it was in the twenties by now. I wouldn't have been shocked to find an entire secret village made up of just his relatives. But I definitely hadn't met these two nieces before because I'd left around the time that they were born.

I could tell from how they were staring at me transfixed, that they weren't sure what to make of Ezra's recently returned friend.

'They're kids – the bullies, that is,' Ezra said, when it became clear that the twins were too nervous to respond. 'So I guess the aim is to deter them rather than hurt them.'

'No!' Roz said, putting her hands on her hips. 'The aim is *definitely* to hurt them! When Dallas tripped Hallie the other day, she hit a tree and she had a black eye all week! And he just laughed. She was bleeding, and all he said was that she shouldn't be so clumsy.'

My jaw tightened and Ezra gave a low snarl.

I refrained from calling their bullies names, but only just: these bullies were little twats.

Obviously the bullies didn't care about physically hurting the girls. That little outburst was the first time either of the twins had spoken and it was a clear sign of how upset the situation was making them.

'Well, the thing about self-defence is that you *are* going to hurt your attacker,' I admitted. 'That's how you make them stop. But ... and this is a big but ... you've got to make sure you don't *start* anything. I'm not here to teach people how to start fights, okay?'

'We never do. Ever.' That was Hallie. '*We're* not the troublemakers.'

'Good. I'm glad to hear it. Now tell me, do they ever pull your hair?'

'Yes!' Roz said indignantly. 'All the time, especially if I've got a coloured hairband.' She glared. 'And if you tell me it's their way of telling me they like me—'

'No way!' I interrupted her. 'Normalising anyone hurting someone else by explaining it away as "they like them" is how kids grow up to be abusers. Physical harm never equals attraction, so get that out of your heads right now. This is not your fault, and it is *not* okay.'

I watched as the tension left their small frames. They were finally accepting that I was on their side and this was a safe space for them.

'We're going to start with hair pulling and how to get out of that situation. What I'm going to show you is called a "pendulum swing". The only thing is ... I'll need someone to practise on. Someone who doesn't mind getting beaten up a bit or thrown around.'

As I glanced to the side and let a smile creep across my lips, the girls' eyes lit up; they knew exactly who I was talking about, although it took Ezra a moment longer to catch on.

He looked amused. 'You probably won't be able to hurt me, you know that, don't you?' he said. 'It's different from when we were kids. I'm double your size now!'

'Yeah?' I looked back at the girls. 'Did your uncle ever tell you how I used to beat him up when we were kids? Purely for training purposes, of course.'

'Yes,' Hallie said. 'He told us you were amazingly strong and super smart. And really pretty, too.'

Ezra's cheeks coloured. 'I'm not sure I said *that*...'

'Oh, don't be shy, Ezra. If you want to add "graceful, witty and an unparalleled genius", I won't stop you.' His blush deepened and I took mercy on him. 'Come on, let's see how quickly I can mop the floor with you this time.' I moved away from the girls into an open space.

'You're going to be disappointed,' he smirked.

'Really? Are you doubting how effective a teacher I am?'

'No, but—'

'Right, then. Stand there.'

I turned to the girls. 'Ezra's my attacker and he's going to grab my hair. I'm guessing Dallas generally comes from behind you?'

'Yup,' Hallie said. 'If we see him coming, we always turn and walk the other way.'

'That's good. You should avoid a confrontation when you can. If a situation upsets you, always think of LACH. Can you L – leave? Can you A – accept? Or should you CH – change? There's no accepting this situation, so that option is out. Where possible, we'd do L, but if he starts something then we're doing CH – we're changing you from feeling like victims to asserting and saving yourselves. So let's see what we can do to change the situation next time Dallas grabs your hair.'

I pulled a hairband off my wrist and tied my hair into a ponytail. 'Now, grab my hair,' I said to Ezra, who did as instructed. 'When I swing my arm, I'm going to let it go straight through his legs like a pendulum. I want you to watch the movement,' I said to the girls. 'See how I swing from the shoulder. Are you ready?'

Although I was asking the girls, it was Ezra who replied. His cockiness had faded substantially. 'Erm ... how badly is this going to hurt?'

'I'll be gentle with you,' I promised. 'As gentle as I can be, anyway,' I amended.

A moment later, I swung my arm straight between his legs. The goal of a pendulum swing is to use your entire arm to strike to increase the force of the hit; it also creates a larger striking area for you to use, so there's less chance of missing.

Even though I kept the action light it was still aimed at a sensitive place and Ezra stumbled back with a gasp. 'You ... are... a terrible friend,' he wheezed.

'Shush! You're the one who asked for help. I'm helping.'

He groaned again and doubled over. 'If you do that to this Dallas kid,' he whispered to the twins, 'he's going to avoid taking you two on again. That's for sure.'

I turned back to the girls. 'Now, I want you to practise getting the movement right – you don't need to actually hit your uncle like I did.'

'When did I become the crash test dummy?' Ezra objected.

I grinned. 'The moment you agreed to be helpful. No backsies.'

For the next twenty minutes, I showed the girls defensive moves. Although the aim was to remove them safely from situations with their tormentor rather than cause physical injury, they were also sending a clear message that they weren't to be messed with.

At the end of the session, the girls were red-faced, grinning and standing confidently. It was a pleasure to witness the transformation. 'That was amazing,' Roz beamed. 'I can't wait for Monday. That'll be the last time anyone picks on us for sure.'

'But we're not the only kids they pick on,' Hallie said. 'They bully others in different year groups, too. Do you think if we talked to the teacher, you could come in and do self-defence classes for everyone?'

Even though I was looking at the girls, I could feel the pride radiating from Ezra. Whether it was for me or his nieces, I wasn't sure, but I didn't hesitate to answer. 'I'd love to.'

'And we can do this again next week?' Hallie said. 'I'd like to practise more.'

'Of course. We need to build up those neural pathways so the action becomes automatic if you're in danger. Same time next week, girls.'

As they disappeared arm in arm, giggling to each other, Ezra pulled out his wallet. 'How much do I owe you?' he asked.

That made me feel uncomfortable; I wanted to help the girls because it was the right thing to do, not because of a pay check. 'You don't need to pay me.'

'I damn well do,' he said firmly. 'Like I said, I'm employing you properly.' He fished out two twenties and pressed them into my hands.

'That's too much. It's usually £10 a session each.'

'But don't you usually work with a much larger class size?'

'I do,' I admitted uncomfortably.

'Well, then. I'll give you forty a session – and even that's a bargain. I owe you more than that for giving these girls some confidence. I'll get you a drink at Lorenz's tonight, too.' He held up a hand before I could object. 'I want to – my way of saying thanks. Plus you'll get to see what a big-deal guy I am now.'

I snickered. 'Big deal, huh?'

'Oh yeah. Maybe I could take you to dinner sometime, too? Just to catch up. As friends.'

There was no doubt that I really enjoyed spending time with Ezra like this; there was no awkwardness, just good old friendship. But I didn't want him to get the wrong idea.

'Maybe,' I said vaguely. 'Anyway, I'd better go.' I turned tail and walked away before I needed to reject him outright. Although he might talk about friendship, his eyes had a speculative look that I didn't like. Not when I couldn't stop thinking about bloody Fraser Banks.

'I'll see you tonight,' he called after me.

'Not if I see you first,' I replied over my shoulder, just as I had when we were teenagers. He laughed.

It was starting to feel like I'd never left Witchlight Cove at all.

Chapter Eleven

'Are you sure Yanni won't mind?' I asked as we left the house.

Going out for a night out with Ezra and Maddie meant leaving Eva on her own, and that wasn't something I'd ever done: she was usually glued to my hip and both of us liked it that way. Still, it was going to be a fairly boozy night and I didn't expect to be home until after midnight. I really didn't want her to be alone that long.

Thankfully, Maddie had rung her grandmother, who was more than happy to dog sit – though I didn't know how much coercion had been involved on Maddie's part.

'Are you kidding?' she said. 'Nana mentioned today how much she misses Eva. She's even thinking about getting a station dog.'

'Really? That would be lovely.'

'Maybe,' Maddie said. 'But I know who'll end up picking up the poo.' She pointed to herself. 'Muggins here.

Anyway, we need to get going. One of the sirens I used to tattoo messaged and said the queue is already massive.'

'You did tattoos for sirens?' I was intrigued. I could understand werewolves needing tattoos for full-moon issues and vampires needing them for daylight ones, but I couldn't for the life of me think why a siren would need magical tattoos.

'It's for when they're dating,' she explained. 'You know how a siren never knows if a guy actually likes them or if they're inadvertently using their magic on him? They get tattoos when they're dating so there's no mix-up. Or at least, they used to.' She bit her lip.

'How are you finding it?' I asked gently. 'Not being able to do your alchemy, I mean. I know how much your tattoos meant to you.'

'It's not easy,' she admitted. 'Ernie thinks there's a way he can help me. Actually, I'm sure he already knows how, but he doesn't want to try anything until he's sure there's no trace of dark magic left in me. If there is, apparently it might try to draw me in again.'

'That sounds sensible, but it must be frustrating for you.' When you love what you do, you never work a day in your life, and Mads had obviously adored her tattooing.

'Yeah, it is, but it's better than being in a magical coma.' She smiled but I could feel disappointment radiating from her.

Like me, Maddie hadn't fit in with her family. Whilst most of her relatives were shifters, she'd inherited some recessive magic-weaving gene together with alchemical powers. It had taken her years to discover her talent and then, like me, she'd had no one other than my parents to support her. After years of struggling, she'd finally found her place tattooing wards; now that security had been taken from her. I could only imagine how hard that was.

It wasn't the time to push the subject: if Maddie wanted to talk she would, but she probably didn't want to bare her soul just before a night out. Neither did I. This was a night for renewing friendships, and I was ready to drink and dance and laugh. Definitely *not* obsess over the colour of Fraser's eyes. Or the shape of his broad shoulders. Or the way his smirk did weird things to my insides. No obsessing here. This was an obsess-free zone.

'Hello, beautiful girl!' Yanni opened the door and immediately knelt down to fuss over Eva. 'How's the smartest little dog out there? Are you ready to have a night in with Auntie Yanni?'

'Auntie Yanni?' I giggled. I handed over a bag of Eva's things, which included her bowl and some food, a lead and the grey cuddly bunny that she always slept with.

'While you two are having a fun night out, we're having an evening on the sofa.' Yanni continued fussing over Eva and ignored my comment about her self-chosen moniker. 'I may have even bought a couple of pigs' ears for treats.'

Eva wagged her tail then turned her wide eyes to me, silently asking permission to go inside and enjoy the rest of her night. 'Looks like you're going to be spoiled rotten.' I leaned down to kiss her on the head before saying to Yanni, 'I'll pick her up in the morning, if that's okay.'

'Of course it is. She'll probably be with me at the station – I'm guessing you won't be up early.'

I laughed; one of these days, I might become a morning person just to prove everyone wrong. Then again, maybe that would be more effort than it was worth.

I leaned in to Yanni. 'Just hide your keys,' I murmured. 'She loves stealing keys. House keys, car keys – keep them hidden from her.'

Yanni looked fascinated. I could already tell that she wouldn't heed my advice and then she'd spend an hour searching for her keys. Well, I had warned her.

As we headed into town, we could see the queue stretching from the top of the hill. 'This is going to take forever,' Maddie harrumphed. 'Luckily, I brought us a little something.' She pulled a hip flask out of her bag and waggled it triumphantly. 'Tequila Rose?'

She handed me the flask, though I didn't immediately take a sip. 'Are you sure you should be drinking?' I asked carefully. 'You know, after everything?'

'I checked, don't worry, *Mum*. Ernie said drinking isn't dark magic – not the kind I'm not allowed to mess with, anyway. It's absolutely fine. Now, let's see if we can find anyone fun.'

No sooner had she said the words than a familiar figure stepped out from near the front of the queue and beckoned us over. 'Pepper's working,' Ezra called. 'She said we can queue-jump.' Pepper was another of Ezra's cousins. She was only a year or so younger than us and I could easily imagine her working in a bar.

'That's fantastic,' Maddie said. 'I'm all for equality, but in this case I'm more than willing to roll with some nepotism. There's no way this drink will last that queue – and these heels are a killer. They look amazing, but the sooner I can sit down the better.'

She turned towards the door. Two enormous brutes stood outside, dressed in black: bouncers. And by the looks of things, they were part giant.

I was just about to follow Maddie in when I noticed Ezra wasn't moving. His attention was fixed behind us with an expression I couldn't quite read. I dropped my barriers for a moment and let his emotions filter in; a mixture of anger, annoyance and curiosity were radiating from him in waves. I'd picked up three emotions crystal clear in a single moment – three! My powers were definitely getting stronger.

'Ez, is everything alright?' I asked.

'Yeah, I just wasn't expecting to see bloody Archer Arden here.'

'Archer?'

He gestured to a broad man with pale blond hair in the queue near us. He looked younger than us, maybe early twenties, and had a definite swagger to his step.

'He's one of the pack,' Ezra murmured to me. 'But he's also the reason Pepper had to work tonight because he got sacked.'

'What did he do?'

Ezra shook his head. I wanted to sift through his emotions again but I didn't want to invade his privacy just because I was insatiably nosey.

'It doesn't matter,' he said after a moment, except that it clearly did.

Judging by the way his jaw was twitching, I had a feeling tonight was about to get a whole lot more interesting.

Chapter Twelve

The doors opened straight into an open area with dozens of low tables and chairs, all occupied, and a long bar that was surrounded two deep by customers.

'At least we've got this while we're waiting.' Maddie passed her hip flask around. I'd never been much of a Tequila Rose fan – it's far too sweet – and I felt a little bad about us drinking our own liquor, but it wasn't like we wouldn't spend plenty if we actually got to the bar first.

As we inched forward, I told Ezra about how I'd come across Eva and she'd helped me defeat a demon and free half a dozen captive elves within twenty-four hours, all while she was still a pup. 'She's a pretty incredible pooch,' he said.

'She is! Just don't call her a pooch to her face. She's very particular about being called by her given name.'

He laughed, obviously assuming I was joking. I wasn't; when I'd first met Eva, I hadn't wanted to name her because it had felt like too big a commitment, then she'd been more than a little annoyed at some of the suggestions I'd offered. Let's just say 'Princess Barkington' was not well received.

I was about to tell Ezra as much when we reached the front of the bar. Pepper came up behind us. 'Hey. Glad you made it.' Like the rest of the staff, she was wearing a white shirt with dark-green braces and a matching bow tie, but unlike everyone else she had a coat slung over her arm.

'Thanks for helping us with the queue jump.' Maddie kissed her cheek. 'You have to let us get you a drink to say thank you.'

Pepper smiled appreciatively. 'I'd love to, but I'm actually heading off and I've got a long journey ahead of me.'

'I thought you were working all night?' Ezra queried.

'Lorenz found someone to cover for me, thank God,' she said. 'Bloody Archer. I got tickets to this gig in London six months ago. Paul would have been furious if Archer was the reason we couldn't go.'

'What did Archer do?' Maddie asked.

'He just couldn't keep his mouth shut.' Pepper lowered her voice and stepped closer to us. 'He was saying how the water shifters are running amok because Lorenz is too busy building his empire to support his people – basically he was blaming Lorenz for what Gilbert did. I don't know why he felt the need to stir shit when it's nothing to do with him.'

'Is Lorenz the head of the water shifters?' I asked.

'Yep.'

I thought of Fraser ... of course I did. I knew he was second in charge of the water shifters, and I wondered if he and Lorenz saw eye to eye.

When I'd lived in Witchlight Cove, I'd had little to do with the water shifters and so far my experiences with them hadn't been particularly positive. After all, it was Gilbert the eel-shifter who had shot me, and that had really affected my fondness for seafood.

Pepper glanced at her watch. 'I'd better go. Have a good night.' She leaned up and kissed Ezra's cheek. 'You know I'll be calling in a favour for this queue-jump, don't you?'

'What is it with this town and favours?' he complained. 'I feel like I'm accidentally signing up for a magical mafia every time I accept a drink.' He sighed. 'Yeah, whatever, Pep. Have fun and stay safe. Say hi to Paul.'

She grinned then disappeared into the crowd.

'It's seriously vibey here,' Maddie said. 'I wonder what it'll do to Shady's if this becomes *the* place to go to at night.'

'Surely there's enough space in Witchlight Cove for more than one bar?' I said, thinking of how Fraser had renovated the Smuggler's Rest to cater to a different clientele. 'The town has grown a lot since I was last here.'

'True,' she said. 'Sometimes Shady's gets so rammed you can't get in for *hours*.'

Talking of Shady's reminded me of the Order of the Nightshade. Would they be drinking blood there? As far as I knew, all the pubs in Witchlight served regular alcohol and soft drinks; if you wanted anything different you had to drink it at home before going out. Then again, Shady *was* a vampire so it seemed likely he'd have blood on hand.

Maddie's brain was evidently working in a similar direction because she asked, 'What do you think assassins talk about when they get together? Do you think they give feedback on their kills? Mark each other out of ten?'

'Maybe they share jobs,' I suggested. 'Divvy them out.'

A voice behind us snorted. 'They don't hand out assignments at the AGMs, they just go on and on about the *rules*.' We turned to see who had spoken, only to find ourselves entirely too close to a clearly inebriated vampire.

'No killing during AGMs.' He wagged a finger at us. 'No killing in public. No killing in front of children.' He swayed. 'For an organisation of cold-blooded killers, they really love their rules. I didn't know that when I signed up,' he said grumpily. 'If I had, I'd have stayed out of it. Vlad the Impaler, a lone wolf, you know? But vampire.'

Vlad looked as far from a cold-blooded killer as you could get. Round and flabby, he was wearing an ill-fitting suit and had a day's worth of blond stubble. He looked like someone's favourite uncle – someone's *drunk* favourite uncle.

Maddie and I were temporarily speechless, and Ezra was busy at the bar. 'Huh,' I said finally. 'Who knew?'

'I just wish I could rampage, like in the good old days,' Vlad said mournfully.

The brooding vampire from Sonny's was suddenly there, moving fast enough to make my heart race. Dressed in black with a crimson tie and a matching crimson pocket square, he looked sharp, sexy and dangerous. 'Vlad, you never rampaged,' he said dismissively. I realised how tall he was; he'd been sitting at Sonny's, but now he was towering over me. 'Candice is most displeased with your little disappearing trick.'

'What can I say, Lestat?' Vlad waved around a glass of clear liquid. 'I want to be where the pulses are.'

'Lestat?' I tried not to laugh. 'So you're Vlad and he's Lestat? Were all the non-clichéd names taken?'

'We each get a terrifying code name when we join the Nightshades,' Vlad hiccupped. 'It helps foster our scary reputation. Except for our girl Candy, she needs to be "friendly" and "accessible". Changing her name from

Drusilla was one of the hottest debates in our AGM five years ago.'

'I dare you to call her Candy to her face,' Lestat said drily.

Vlad blanched. 'I'd be grateful if you could not mention that particular nickname to our beloved and well-respected leader.'

'And what do I get in exchange?' Lestat asked.

'My unwavering affection?' He reached out and stroked Lestat's bulging bicep. Lestat glared at the offending hand and Vlad whipped it away before it was forcibly removed.

Lestat sighed. 'Come on. You're at the wrong party.'

'I *like* this party,' Vlad whined.

'Complain to Candice.' Lestat's tone made it clear exactly how successful he thought that endeavour would be. 'Move.' He jerked his head towards the exit.

Vlad downed the remains of his drink and slumped away. Lestat turned to us, his eyes lingering on Maddie. 'Ladies,' he murmured before turning on his heel and marching out.

'Well,' Maddie said. 'That was ... something.' She brightened. 'Lestat was totally sexy though, wasn't he?'

I couldn't help laughing. 'A hundred times sexier than rampaging Vlad.'

Ezra finally joined us and handed me a glass of red wine. My nose crinkled involuntarily. 'You're not a red wine drinker?' he asked as he read my expression. 'Shit, sorry. I should've asked. I'm just used to— Never mind. Sorry!'

'It's fine,' I said. 'I'm more of a white wine person, but I can drink red.' I took a sip to show willing. Ugh: it was oaky and strong, like drinking disappointment in a glass. I kept the distaste off my face as best I could and took another sip; the quicker I drank it, the quicker I could get something I actually liked.

'Shall we find somewhere to sit?' I suggested.

'Seems unlikely,' Maddy replied looking around. 'But let's give it a go.'

As we moved away from the bar, I saw a silver-haired man in a dark-green suit kissing cheeks, offering deep hugs and throaty laughs. 'That must be Lorenz,' I said. Now that I knew he was a water shifter, I tried to figure out what he might shift into: the grey in his eyes made me think shark, but the softness in his smile didn't quite fit. Dolphin, maybe? Or whale? Or, given the way he was schmoozing, possibly a very charming otter.

As if he sensed me staring, he turned and made a beeline for us. 'Madeleine! Ezra!' he said, hugging them both tightly. Then his gaze fell on me. 'And ... sorry, I don't believe we've met.'

'Lorenz, this is my good friend Trixie,' Ezra said. 'Trixie, this is Lorenz Matheson.'

'Beatrix,' I corrected. 'Beatrix Stonehaven. Ezra's the only one who calls me Trixie.' As I'd anticipated, my name elicited a flicker of recognition in his eyes, though it was subtle, and I appreciated that he didn't visibly recoil.

'Well, thank you so much for coming, Beatrix. You know it's half-price on all drinks until midnight?'

'Is that so?' I glanced teasingly at Ezra. 'Well, Mr Big Bucks here definitely owes me another then!'

'I agree.' Lorenz grinned. 'Enjoy your night. Thanks again for coming – all of you.'

Maddie beamed at him. 'Thanks, Lorenz.'

I didn't know whether he was good at managing the water shifters or not, but he was perfectly polite and clearly a wonderful host.

Any other thoughts I had about him or anything else disappeared when I caught sight of someone else across the room. I shouldn't have been surprised to see him there, but somehow I was. 'Fraser,' I murmured his name before I could stop myself.

Maddie followed my gaze. 'Let me guess. You want to go and speak to your potion-wielding saviour.'

'No,' I said weakly. 'No,' I repeated more firmly. 'This is a night for friends.'

She eyed me. 'Hmmm. I think we'd better get this over with.' She hooked arms with Ezra and me and practically dragged us across the room before I could object.

It looked like I was going to speak to Fraser after all.

Chapter Thirteen

I'd never seen Fraser socialising, talking to people, smiling. He had a ridiculously infectious smile, one that seemed to glitter in his eyes like he was a freaking movie star. He was definitely hot enough to be one.

I had it bad. This was getting ridiculous.

There was something about him that said *power.* He commanded the room and people were circling around him like planets stuck in his orbit. Women were simpering and trying to get his attention, which I was pathetically pleased to see he seemed to ignore.

We were still a good few feet apart when he turned and his eyes locked onto mine. Just as had happened in the café, he'd somehow known I was there just as I'd seemed to know that he was there. We had some sort of cosmic connection that, quite frankly, freaked me out.

I watched him murmur his apologies to the person he was talking to and walk toward us – me. His smile was more restrained than it had been moments before, but it felt like this one was meant for me alone. I tried to ignore the warmth spreading through my chest.

'Fraser.' Maddie stepped in front of me and broke the moment. 'I need to thank you for the other night, for taking me to Jacobson's. And for staying quiet about the other thing.' She gave an exaggerated wink. My best friend didn't have a subtle bone in her body.

Fraser's eyes flicked between Maddie and me, then shifted to Ezra where they flashed with caution. 'It's fine,' I said, sensing his reservation was because he was protective of our secret. 'Ezra knows – he's our oldest friend. But maybe it's not something we should discuss here.'

'Agreed.' Ezra stepped forward and extended his hand. 'Ezra Bentley. You must be the selkie who's been spending all this time with my betrothed.'

'Betrothed?' The colour drained from Fraser's face as his gaze darted between Ezra and me, and even with my shields up I could feel his panic.

'He's joking,' I said hurriedly. 'We're not betrothed.' I hit Ezra, and this time I didn't pull my punch.

'Well,' Ezra wheezed, 'I think some might say we're married. That ceremony was pretty official – we had witnesses and everything.'

Fraser was still looking worried until Maddie stepped in with an explanation. 'It was in primary school,' she said. She shot Ezra a glare.

'I even stole my mum's ring,' Ezra added. 'A proper diamond one. And we made a certificate saying we were married. Mum was furious about the ring, and I think if it had been anyone else she'd have gone berserk, but she's always had a bit of a soft spot for Trixie.' He turned to me. 'You really should come and see her. You know she'd love that. Dad, too.'

'Yes, I will,' I promised, smiling at the thought. Mrs Bentley was one of the warmest matriarchs around and I missed her gentle touches as she bustled around doing twenty things at once. She was always busy, yet she'd always made me feel welcome and wanted.

'And of course,' Maddie stated firmly, eyes on Fraser, 'you saved our Beatrix's life with a potion too. We owe you.' Her comment seemed rather pointed and I didn't miss Fraser's slight wince. What was I missing?

This was uncomfortable. I wanted a moment alone with Fraser, but I didn't want to be that person who brushes off her friends at the first sign of a sexy guy, even if he did look like he'd been sculpted by the gods as their personal apology for the existence of Mondays. I shot Fraser an apologetic smile.

Thankfully Maddie seemed to read the situation. 'Come on.' She tugged Ezra's arm. 'This red wine isn't doing it for me and Bea's barely taken a sip, so there's no way I can finish hers as well. Let's get something else. You'll wait here for us, Bea?'

'Sure.'

As they disappeared into the crowd, I became acutely aware that my hands were almost aching to reach out and take Fraser's, but I stopped myself as I remembered the flash I'd experienced the last time we'd touched.

'Sorry for messaging you last night,' he said, shoving his hands in his pockets and looking as awkward as I felt.

'No, it's fine. I'm sorry if my response was brusque. It had been a really long day.'

'Right.'

Silence swelled between us. I wanted him to break it, but my mind wasn't working properly and all I could think about was him coming out of the damned sea.

Fraser cleared his throat. 'Yeah, it's just... There are some things about that night when you fell into the water that I really need to talk to you about.'

I nodded though I was unsure what he wanted to discuss. Then again, he was second-in-command of the water shifters and he probably had plenty of questions about Gilbert, a sect police report to prepare, that sort of thing.

'And it's not something you can tell me now?' I pressed.

He glanced around. 'It'd probably be best if we were alone.'

'Right.'

I could feel myself involuntarily leaning toward him. 'Is this about your coat?' I asked. 'Your pelt?' In my vision previous night, magic had swirled around the jacket.

His eyes widened slightly. 'Yes. You know?'

'Is it...?' I lowered my voice and stepped closer to speak directly into his ear. 'Using selkie magic on a witch is probably frowned on, isn't it? Is that what you want to talk about? You want me to keep it to myself?'

He coughed nervously. 'It's not that exactly. The thing is—'

Whatever the thing was, I didn't find out because at that moment a scream tore through the air.

'He's dead!' someone screamed. 'He's been murdered!'

Panic rippled through the crowd like wildfire. *Who is it? Who's dead? Where's Lorenz?*

Fraser and Ezra jumped into action. 'Ladies and gentlemen, the bar is officially closed,' Fraser announced firmly as Ezra ran over to the member of staff who'd screamed. As they gave orders, the staff leapt into action.

I was confused: obviously they'd obey Fraser – but Ezra? 'What's going on?' I asked Maddie. 'Why are they listening to Ezra?' It wasn't just wolves: there were people in the club from all sorts of magical sects and not a single one of them was questioning his and Fraser's leadership.

'Well, he *is* second-in-command of the werewolves.' Maddie's tone was matter of fact. 'That ranks him pretty highly.'

'Wait – what? Ezra's beta?' I blinked in surprise. He'd told me he was a big deal but I'd had no idea he'd moved up the ranks to become *numero dos* to his father's *numero uno*. And Mr Bentley was a stickler for making your own way in life; if Ezra was beta of the whole pack, he'd earned the position.

'The other second died nearly a year ago and they chose Ezra to be his successor. He was already beta of his family's pack, which is the most respected pack in Witchlight.'

Ezra was second of the entire werewolf sect in Witchlight Cove. Who knew?

I picked up whispers as I watched him and Fraser work the crowd. *Lorenz*: they were saying the dead guy was Lorenz. I hoped it wasn't – I'd liked him.

By the time Yanni walked through the door with Dove and Eva at her heels, Ezra and Fraser had secured the area.

She came over to me. 'You weren't lying about the keys,' she muttered. 'I would have been here sooner if your dog hadn't hidden them.'

Eva's tail went between her legs and Yanni sighed. 'It's okay, I forgive you – after all, you did help me find them again.' She sent me a flat look. 'She'd put them in my boots.'

Despite the stressful situation, I smiled. 'I *did* warn you.'

'You did. Lesson learned.' She handed me Eva's lead and went into the back room, leaving me with Dove and Maddie.

'Hey cheeky girl,' I said quietly. Eva wagged her tail once, an acknowledgment that she was happy to see me but knew this wasn't the moment to jump up and greet me with a shit-tonne of spittle. Her sense of propriety was stronger than some humans; she certainly had more self-control than I did when I was presented with free cake.

'Any chance you could give me a hand clearing the crowd?' Dove asked. 'Fraser and Ezra have done a great job in keeping them back, but we need to take names and contact details then get them home.'

For a second, I thought she was talking to me, but she was looking at Maddie. A pang of disappointment that I wasn't part of the police team hit me, but then I realised that gave me the freedom to observe without being tied to Yanni's professional standards. I could sneak and delve in ways they couldn't.

With Eva at my side, I moved closer to where Yanni, Ezra and Fraser were talking to the employee who had screamed. I must not have been as subtle in my approach as I thought because they all turned to look at me. I decided not to beat around the bush. 'Is it true? Is it Lorenz?'

They exchanged glances then Fraser looked at Yanni. 'You know we can trust her.'

She nodded. 'Of course – and anyway, there's no keeping a lid on it. Yes, Bea, it's Lorenz.'

It seemed insane that only half an hour earlier, I'd spoken to him and now he was dead. 'Do you know how he was killed?' I asked briskly, trying to keep my tone professional.

As I looked at Yanni, her voice echoed in my head. *Soon everyone will know it's a vampire bite. No point trying to cover it up.*

I blinked rapidly. Had she just said that out loud? I'd heard her voice clear as day but her lips hadn't moved. 'Did you say it was a vampire bite?' I asked.

Yanni looked startled. 'I didn't say anything,' she said slowly. 'How do you know that?' She was looking at me like she'd seen a ghost.

I faltered; clearly I couldn't say I'd heard her because even in Witchlight Cove having voices in your head wasn't a good thing. 'I must have overheard you,' I said weakly.

Fraser's gaze lingered on me and his eyes narrowed slightly. He knew something was off about my explanation, even if he didn't know what.

Yanni chewed her lip before she spoke. 'I need the coroner's report. We're leaving the body where it is until Dove can conduct a proper forensic sweep, but there did appear to be bite marks on his neck.'

'Bite marks?' I repeated. 'The day after the Order of the Nightshades arrived in Witchlight?'

Her expression hardened. 'Don't make assumptions, Beatrix – I've told you that before. And definitely don't make assumptions about people like the Nightshades because it won't end well for you. Do you understand?'

I nodded. Yes, the Order had made it clear when they arrived that they were here for an AGM and not for a job, but that could have been no more than a smokescreen. We had an influx of vampires and a powerful sect leader dead from a vampire bite. Plus Vlad had been talking about the good old days and wanting to kill people… I'd tell Yanni about that when she took my statement. At the moment, she was clearly in defensive mode and I didn't want her to dismiss my comments out of hand.

I did my best to shield myself from the emotions swirling around the room but it was difficult. The place was saturated with grief, anger and shock, feelings that would have impacted anyone – and especially an empath. I needed to lock this shit down tight. I raised my psychological walls then turned back to Yanni. 'There's CCTV covering the area, isn't there?' I gestured to a camera near the ceiling in a corner of the room. 'Surely Lorenz had one of those in his office, too?'

'As soon as the place is cleared, I'll look into it,' Yanni replied grimly. 'You go home now. I'll take your statement tomorrow – I know where you live.' It rankled to be dismissed, but she was totally within her rights to send me away. I didn't work with her any longer, so the murder didn't concern me.

Eva nudged my hand with her nose and when I looked down at her, she gave a wide yawn. Sometimes my dog was less subtle than a toddler, but I couldn't help loving her for it. 'Sure. I'd better take Eva home anyway,' I said.

Yanni winced. 'I'm sorry – I forgot to bring her things.'

'It's no problem,' I said with an easy smile. 'I'll pop by the station tomorrow and collect them. We can do my statement then.'

I looked at the three of them: Yanni, the formidable chief of police and my best friend's grandmother; Ezra, my oldest friend and now the beta of the werewolves, and Fraser, the man who seemed to call to me in ways that I couldn't explain. I didn't know how it had happened, but I was tangled in their lives now. And I *wanted* to be.

The chances of me leaving Witchlight Cove anytime soon were getting slimmer by the hour.

Chapter Fourteen

I didn't go to bed until Maddie got home and it wasn't just because Eva was whining about not having her grey bunny to sleep with. Even if she'd settled, I doubted I'd have slept because the itch to know what was going on was as strong as ever. Besides, I needed to know Maddie was okay. Only the day before I had been in Maddie's position, employed to 'answer phones', and it had quickly turned into much, much more – including me getting shot. The thought that anything similar could happen to Maddie was more effective in keeping me awake than three double espressos.

More than once I considered returning to the bar but I didn't want to complicate the situation when people had jobs to do, especially now my powers were acting up. It wasn't just the emotions that were flooding me; twice I'd been certain someone had spoken to me, only to realise that they hadn't. If that continued, I'd have to start politely responding to imaginary conversations and that was the slippery slope to full-on eccentricity. Next stop, talking to pigeons in the park.

And then there was the vision I'd had when I touched Fraser...

Needing to occupy my mind, I used the time to look through more books in the library. This time I wasn't looking for information about the Eternal Flame but something that would help explain what was happening with my magic. I found one piece of information about a witch developing her powers in her later years but it was tied to incantations, blood magic, and drawing powers from her ancestors, none of which applied to me. Another talked about a young witch's magic being blocked because she'd suffered a childhood trauma, but to my knowledge I'd experienced no trauma until my parents' deaths and my magic should have manifested before that.

There was a final reference to a witch whose mother had died during childbirth and who had needed to grow up with her father in the non-magical world. Her dad had asked a witch to bind her and the child had only accessed her magic some forty years later when she'd stumbled across a coven that had told her what she was and had undone the bind. There was a lot of hatred for both her father and the witch who had placed the original bind in that account, though I sympathised with her dad. If he knew nothing about magic and wanted his daughter to be safe, it seemed like a pretty sensible thing to do. But I had grown up in the magical world with magical parents, so I ruled that out, too.

I stored all the information away for future reference and was about to open another book when the front door opened. Relief flooded through me.

'Hey, I didn't expect you to be awake,' Maddie said when she saw me.

Impulsively, I ran over and hugged her tightly. When I drew back, I saw that she was tired but other than that she looked okay. I released her awkwardly. 'Sorry, I was worried about you. Is it definitely murder? I'm guessing Yanni hasn't arrested anyone?'

'No.' Maddie shook her head. 'But I saw the body and it's definitely a vampire bite. Weirdly, though it doesn't look like the blood was consumed. It was just ... there.' She shuddered, 'Pooling all around him.' She licked her lips. 'So much blood.'

'Let's get you a hot chocolate,' I said firmly. 'You sound a little shocky, and you don't need that when you've already been through so much.' I sat her down and wrapped a blanket around her shoulders, then bustled to the kitchen to make her an extra-sweet drink.

'Here,' I said as I handed it to her a minute later. 'I cooled it with milk so it should be perfect drinking temperature.' She sent me a grateful smile.

Now that I'd taken care of Mads, I considered Lorenz's death. I'd studied vampires as part of my guardianship training and I knew that biting and not drinking blood were rare. It would have taken a vampire a fair bit of restraint to walk away, given how much they craved blood when they scented it in the air – unless they'd been trained to kill like that, the way an assassin would be.

Which begged the question: was our killer a highly disciplined vampire or a very sloppy one?

'What about the CCTV?' I asked. 'Did you get anything from that?'

'No, that was weird as well,' Maddie replied. 'The plug for the CCTV system had been pulled out, which Nana assumed the killer did before they killed Lorenz – but when she got it back online, the last two days' footage had been wiped.'

'So are we thinking it's someone who visited Lorenz before his death?' But dozens of people must have gone in and out of the bar during those two days to make deliveries and do last-minute jobs. That was a big pool of suspects to fish through.

I was about to say as much to Maddie when Eva gave a strange whine. 'What's wrong, girl?' Maddie asked, sounding concerned. 'You're normally curled up asleep by now.'

I rolled my eyes. 'She should be, only I gave Yanni her bunny because she was meant to be staying overnight with her. Eva's whining because she has to sleep without it.'

Maddie laugh. 'You're a total one-off,' she said to my dog. 'I've got a couple of cuddlies in my room. Come on, let's have a look – maybe you can pick one you like.'

Eva followed her upstairs. Two minutes later they returned with a fluffy yellow duck in her mouth. 'You do know that'll come back covered in slobber?' I asked.

Maddie shrugged. 'It's alright, I've outgrown cuddly toys. She can keep it.' That duck had been her favourite toy when she was a kid and I knew that it wasn't nothing for her to give it to Eva. My heart swelled: she was the best.

'Thank you so much, Mads.'

She ruffled Eva's head. 'I'd better get to bed. I suspect the phones will be busy tomorrow with everyone convinced they'll be the next victim of the Order of the Nightshades.'

'If there's anything I can do, let me know,' I said. Even if she didn't, I decided I might do a little digging; after all, I couldn't have a mystery on my doorstep and *not* try to solve it.

I pulled out my laptop and navigated my way to the dark web. I'd once paid a magical hacker called Donovan an eye-watering sum to get me banking access codes and encryption keys; using the portal he'd created for me I could pretty much log into any bank I wanted from anywhere in the world. I logged in and searched for Lorenz Matheson's financials. He had a mortgage on a modest house, and a business loan for his new venture that made me wince. He had chump change in his bank, but it looked like he'd sunk everything he had into the business. Whatever motive someone had for killing him, we could rule out money.

A yawn cracked my face. I put the laptop back on the coffee table. It was very late and I was in need of a good sleep and – ideally – a very long lie-in. Given that I didn't have a job to go to, I couldn't see any reason why that shouldn't happen. Then again, I should have known better than to assume anything would go to plan in Witchlight Cove.

Chapter Fifteen

Eva didn't let me have a lie-in; in fact, she didn't even let me get a good night's sleep. Although she held the tattered yellow duck beneath her chin as she slept, waves of annoyance and sadness continued to emanate from her. I'd never experienced anything like it – I woke up crying from *her* sadness. I was going to have to be one of those parents who bought three versions of the same teddy in case their beloved child lost their favourite – only I'd be doing it for a dog. This was officially my life now: sleep-deprived and emotionally manipulated by a canine.

I'd never realised how much she loved that fluffy bunny, and I wasn't even sure where it had come from – maybe one of my old students had given it to her. Thinking about my students reminded me of the twins. They had a full weekend to practise what I'd taught them before school started on Monday, and I could only hope it helped. Sometimes, it wasn't about the skills or the fighting, it was about the confidence the training gave them. That *don't mess with me* energy they'd carry into every room. And if Dallas wasn't smart enough to pick up on their new vibe, he'd definitely get what was coming to him.

By 8am, I'd had enough of Eva's wriggling and whining. 'Come on, then,' I finally snapped. 'Let's go to the station and get your damned bunny.' Her tail wagged so hard it whipped my side.

As I opened my bedroom door, I was surprised to see Maddie. 'Are you only just going into work?' I asked.

She nodded. 'Nana said Dove and I could come in an hour later after we worked so late last night.'

'In that case, we'll walk in with you. Eva likes her new duck, but apparently it's not Bunny.'

Maddie gave Eva a kiss. 'Sorry Ducky didn't fit the bill.' Clearly proud of her joke, she grinned. Then she sobered. 'I can't believe there's been another murder in Witchlight Cove. Poor Jennifer probably hasn't even had a chance to get her head around her dad and Toby dying, and now they're old news. I was thinking about it before I fell asleep – the Nightshades arriving and the murder feels too coincidental. I told Nana about Vlad and Lestat, and she said she'd talk to them although they'd left before the murder happened.'

'It does feel like more than a coincidence,' I agreed. 'But you know what Yanni says?'

'Don't make assumptions.'

'Right.' It was easier said than done.

When we reached the front doors to the police station, Maddie went to open them but I stopped short. There was a strange tingling on my skin and the feeling seemed to be coming from inside the building. It was the feeling of a presence: *his* presence.

'Bea? Is everything okay?' Maddie asked.

I wanted to tell her that Fraser Banks was in the police station but I didn't because I didn't know how I knew. I could sense him, not his emotions but *him*. It unnerved the hell out of me.

Eva looked up at me and barked as if she knew something was happening.

I shook my head and forced a smile. 'It just feels weird going into the police station when I don't work here anymore. Come on, let's get Eva's bunny.' I pushed aside my agitation. I was actually grateful for this strange sixth sense that had alerted me to Fraser's presence; that way I wouldn't be surprised to see him there.

It looked like he hadn't gone home: he was wearing the same shirt from last night, his hair was tousled and a dense stubble covered his cheeks and chin. My fingers twitched with the sudden urge to touch it. Nope, nope. All the nopes.

'Beatrix,' he said, his voice low. 'Everything okay?'

'Yes,' I said quickly. 'Eva just needs her toys. Yanni said she'd bring them in for her. Is she in her office?'

'No, she went out this morning.' He paused. 'She got a tip-off last night.'

'Really?' Maddie said as she came up to me. 'And she's gone alone?' She sounded both exasperated and panicked. 'Nana should have waited for someone else. She could be in danger! Beatrix got *shot,* for goodness' sake.'

I couldn't blame her for panicking because Gilbert had fired his gun at Yanni as well as me when we were on the boat. Luckily he'd missed, but I'd told Maddie what had happened and maybe I should have omitted the shots. 'Hasn't Dove gone with her?' I asked.

Fraser shook his head. 'No, she went home. I offered to go with Yanni but she asked me to hang on here until Maddie came.'

'I'm going to check her office and see if I can find out where she's gone,' Maddie said.

She disappeared, leaving Fraser and me on our own. For a second I thought about telling him how I'd sensed him when I was still outside the building, but I realised that could come across weird and stalkerish. 'Hi, I can feel you in my bones' wasn't exactly a casual icebreaker.

'How does the water shifters' hierarchy work?' I asked suddenly, remembering something we'd been discussing the night before. 'Now that Lorenz is dead, what happens in terms of leadership?'

'I'm the new leader.' Fraser's tone was grim. 'There was a magical bind between us. If something happens to the leader, the second-in-command automatically takes their place.'

'You don't have a choice?' I asked. 'I'm guessing being leader will be really different from being the second-in-command.'

'Yes, it's very different – and no, I don't have a choice now. I did willingly accept the bind at the time though.'

I could feel the burden of expectation pressing down on him. For a second I wanted to lower my guard and let his emotions flow into me, to truly know him, but Mum had always been super strict about me reading someone out of curiosity, so I didn't. Stupid morals.

'Is that why you came here today? Because of the shifter leader thing?' I said instead.

'Yes – and there are still a few things to clear up from Gilbert's case. It's been sent to the magical council and there are forms to sign, but something pinged through about half an hour ago and Yanni bolted out of here.' He paused. 'I don't want to leave until I'm sure she's okay. You don't mind, do you?'

I blinked. 'Of course I don't – but I don't actually work here now, so you don't need *my* permission to stay. I'm not leaving either until I see her.'

'Maybe we can wait together?' he suggested.

'Sounds good,' I replied, trying to ignore the way my mouth was suddenly so dry.

If I'd been the relationship type, I'd have looked for someone like him in a heartbeat – but I wasn't. And even if I had been, a selfless selkie and a witch with powers that didn't work properly didn't seem like a good match.

As I stood there, I recalled the flashes I'd seen when he'd touched me in Sonny's cafe. What if my powers weren't on the blink? What if selkies could psychically transfer images when they touched someone? That would certainly make more sense than my powers suddenly manifesting a couple of years before I turned thirty.

I was considering how to ask him about it when I was hit by a wall of emotion so strong it doubled me over.

'Beatrix?' Fraser was at my side, reaching for me.

Stumbling backwards, I waved him away. Another vision was the last thing I could handle. Nausea swept through me as emotions surged again and again: agony, grief. Someone was outside the building, someone whose heart was broken.

Strengthening my barriers to their full extent, I straightened up as the door swung open and Yanni strode in. Her suspect was in cuffs beside her and he looked miserable.

I'd found the source of the agony and you could have knocked me over with a pixie wing. The one feeling such grief was Sonny.

Chapter Sixteen

The surly vampire had certainly made an impression on me since I'd come back to Witchlight Cove, though not the most positive one. He probably wasn't my biggest fan either, given that my grandfather had thrown Fraser across the floor of his café and I'd bolted out of the place more than once without paying for my drinks.

Nobody seemed to have a kind word to say about Sonny beyond praising his coffee. His brother Shady, who ran the cocktail bar, supposedly had far better people skills though I'd yet to meet him.

But at that moment as I struggled to keep my mental blocks in place, I wasn't thinking about what I'd heard or seen; all that mattered were the emotions that Sonny was radiating in waves: grief, loss, disbelief – and a bit of underlying irritation, though I assumed that was just his default state.

I took a moment to steady myself before I finally tuned in to what Sonny was saying to Yanni. 'You have to believe me,' he pleaded. 'I wouldn't want Lorenz to die. I don't know what evidence you've got but whatever it is, it's not what you think!'

'Sonny, wait until we're in the interview room where everything will be recorded. You don't want to have to go over it all again,' Yanni said wearily. I'd have bet good money that Sonny had been protesting his innocence since she'd arrested him and her legendary patience was wearing thin.

'You shouldn't be questioning me at all!' Sonny yelled. 'I'm not behind this – I'd never harm Lorenz! You're wasting time, letting the real killer get away! This is absolute bullshit!' His eyes scanned the room clearly searching for someone to back him up. His gaze landed on me.

'She's a witch, isn't she?' He pointed at me. 'Get her to put a truth spell on me. I didn't kill him! It must be one of the Nightshades. We know they're in town – why the hell are you protecting those bastards? Do your fucking job, let me go and find the *real* killer!' He flashed his fangs and venom dripped from them.

Instinctively I shifted into a fighting stance, but before I could do more Fraser had moved in front of me, his body shielding mine just as he'd done when Ernie had lost his shit. I didn't know whether to feel annoyed that he thought I couldn't defend myself or flattered that he'd put himself in harm's way for me again, so I settled on a bit of both.

Yanni gave a low, warning growl; if my eyes had been closed, I'd have sworn she'd shifted into bear form to make that threatening rumble. 'You need to calm down,' she said coolly. 'I'm not talking to you until you do. For now, I'm putting you in a cell. We'll talk when you've had time to settle.'

Sonny ran his tongue over his fangs, retracted them and looked defeated. 'I didn't kill him,' he muttered.

I could still feel his emotions and they didn't feel like those of a murderer. Sonny was grieving in a similar way to how I had grieved when my parents had died. That edge of bemused disbelief cinched it for me: he hadn't killed Lorenz.

He remained silent as Yanni escorted him to the cells. When she returned I asked, 'You really think Sonny killed Lorenz?'

'The evidence is pretty damning. The two of them had a massive row yesterday evening before opening.'

Evidence was key in any investigation – but I'd felt Sonny's emotions and they couldn't be faked.

'What about a truth spell? Can't you do that?' I asked. 'Not with me, obviously.' We both knew my lacklustre skills didn't extend that far.

Yanni pinched the bridge of her nose in frustration. 'We used to have a magic-weaver who did them, but we discovered that the magic could be easily manipulated. A few years back, a witch used a truth spell to try and get her friend out of trouble. Let's just say I never want to deal with a pile of paperwork like that again. Unless I had someone I trusted to perform it here, I wouldn't use one.'

If magic couldn't be used, maybe science could help. 'Can you get DNA from the bite?' I asked. 'Surely that would tell you whether it was Sonny or not?'

Yanni shook her head. 'Vampires don't work like that. Their cells are dead, which means their DNA is destroyed when they turn. Any test would be a waste of police time and funds, and we barely have enough of those as it is.'

'We should leave Yanni to it,' Fraser said gruffly, reminding me that he was still there. 'Perhaps you and I could have that talk I mentioned?'

But I couldn't let it go. I pressed my lips together and looked Yanni square in the eye. 'Do you mind if I talk to him? In the cell?'

Yanni's eyes narrowed. 'Why? What are you thinking?'

'That he's innocent,' I said. 'And I want to prove it.'

Yanni was aware that my stubbornness knew no bounds. She could forbid me from seeing Sonny, but she recognised that if she did I'd try something rash, like sneaking in when she went for her lunch break.

'If you're right and he's guilty,' I wheedled, 'I won't be able to prove he's innocent. But if you're wrong...' I paused. 'How certain are you?'

'I'm not certain,' she admitted. 'The evidence stacks up.'

'I'm sure it does – but did someone else do the stacking?' I let the question hang for a moment before I continued. 'I'm an empath, Yanni, and lately my power has been stronger than ever. You can't fake Sonny's grief – I know real grief and that was it.' I thumbed in his direction.

Her eyes softened. 'You have no official capacity,' she pointed out gently. 'No legal reason to be involved.'

'No, I don't, but I'm a PI and a good one. Sonny can hire me and then you'll have an extra pair of eyes. I won't step on your toes, I promise – I'm good at working with the local police.' I pulled out my phone. 'Look, I've got a couple of friends in the Met – that's the Metropolitan Police Force, the non-magical police in London.'

'I *know* what the Met is, thank you, Beatrix,' Yanni said flatly. 'Next you'll be explaining how to shift.'

Whoops! 'Why don't you speak to one of the officers I know? Get some reassurance from someone who's worked with me.' I paused. 'On more than answering phones, I mean.'

I scrolled through the names on my phone. I could have called Gazza or Tanya, but my finger stopped on Dean's name; he was the most senior of my police buddies, and I was sure he'd put in a positive word, if only because he had a bit of a crush on me.

Before I could press dial, Yanni stopped me. 'I don't need to speak to anyone to know that I can trust you,' she said gruffly. 'I think you're wasting your time, but it's your time to waste. You've got five minutes with him – and I'll be listening in.'

I wasn't his lawyer so I didn't get client confidentiality. 'Of course. I wouldn't expect anything less.' I flashed her a smile. I turned to leave but stopped when someone called my name.

'Beatrix,' Fraser said. 'I'd still like to speak to you. Properly.'

'Yes, of course,' I said, not sure how else to respond. 'But now's not a great time.'

'No problem,' he said. 'But it's important. Maybe tonight? I've got to deal with the sect council at some point,' he added, his voice heavy. 'Though I'm not sure when they'll want to meet. Maybe I can call you when I have a better idea?'

'Is it alright if *I* call *you*?' I asked.

Fraser smiled. 'I'd like that.'

'Okay,' I said, my cheeks turning pink. 'I'll speak to you later then.'

He nodded goodbye, gave Eva a last stroke and left the office. I gave myself a full three seconds to appreciate the view before forcing myself back to reality. The man had a lot on his plate, and here I was admiring the fit of his trousers.

'If you've finished drooling...' Yanni teased, her tone amused.

I cleared my throat. 'I was just making sure he was gone before we discussed business with Sonny.'

'Of course.' She smirked. 'That's *definitely* all you were doing.' The smirk didn't last long and she glanced towards the cells. 'Come on,' she said. 'I've said I'll let you talk to the vampire, so let's get it over and done with.'

Given what I already knew about Sonny, I wasn't expecting a warm welcome so it was no surprise when he didn't even acknowledge my presence. His head was slumped forward on his knees and, had I not known better, I'd have assumed he hadn't heard me come in. I knew that wasn't the case, though, because vampires have incredible hearing.

From the doorway, Yanni caught my eye and lifted an eyebrow, tacitly asking if I wanted her to come in with me. I shook my head. The sight of a police officer can make even innocent people clam up and I was sure she'd have that effect here. I needed Sonny to see me as an ally, or at the very least a neutral party.

'Sonny,' I said softly.

His head jerked up and he hastily wiped his cheeks, but not quickly enough for me to miss the tears streaking down his face. For vampires to cry was rare; tears weren't as deadly as sunlight to them, but they were uncomfortable as hell and they hurt. He'd need some blood to help him heal.

'I didn't hurt Lorenz.' His voice trembled.

'I believe you.'

'I would never have hurt him,' he insisted. 'Never.'

He swallowed. I accepted that he hadn't hurt Lorenz, but I could tell he was holding back something important, something I needed to know. 'Sonny,' I started gently, 'Yanni says she has some evidence that suggests you're responsible. Someone called in with a tip-off about you.'

'I would *never—*'

'I get that.' I cut him short. If Yanni was going to be strict about me only having five minutes , then the last thing I wanted was Sonny pleading his innocence over and over again. I needed more than that, and so did he. 'I believe you. I need you to focus. Someone said they had evidence that you'd argued with Lorenz.'

He nodded tersely. 'We had a fight,' he admitted. 'It got … heated, but in the end, we made up.'

'Can you tell me what the fight was about?'

He bit his lip; whatever it was, he really didn't want to share. I lowered my shields; under all that grief and loss there was now an undercurrent of fear – fear he'd be wrongly charged, or something more?

'Sonny, what is it?' I asked. 'I can feel that you're afraid of something. What is it? I'm trying to help you, but I need you to tell me the truth. What aren't you telling me?'

He stared at the ground. Finally he said, 'If you knew, I'm not sure you'd still want to help me.'

'Why don't you let me be the judge of that?'

His dark eyes met mine and it was like staring at pieces of onyx: complete, absolute blackness.

'Okay, Beatrix. Time's up,' Yanni said, appearing next to me.

I was about to protest that it hadn't been five minutes when I realised what she was doing. She was subtly applying pressure on Sonny, making it crunch time so it was now or never for him to tell me the truth.

'In my flat,' Sonny blurted. 'If you go into my flat, you'll see. But I don't have the keys – I don't even remember where I left them. I was working when I heard about Lorenz and I locked up and I think… I don't know where they are.'

'I can get past missing keys,' I said confidently. 'As long I have your permission to pick the lock.'

He scoffed. 'You can burn my whole flat down if it means finding out who killed him.' His eyes met mine again, as if he were willing me to see what he was too afraid to vocalise.

'I'll go to your flat,' I promised. 'And then I'll be back.'

As I left, Yanni was handing him a blood bag and reading him his rights before she started the formal interview.

I thought about Sonny telling me I could burn down his flat if it meant finding out who had killed Lorenz. My respect for the grumpy coffee shop owner was growing; under that crotchety exterior was someone who valued justice, and I could relate to that.

Chapter Seventeen

After stuffing Eva's grey bunny into my bag, I headed straight for the coffee shop. It was well known that Sonny lived above the cafe which was why it was open such crazy hours – that and the fact that neither he nor his staff technically needed to sleep.

As I walked, I patted my pocket to double-check I had my lock-pick set. I was looking forward to picking an actual lock, rather than just practising at home with a padlock. The thrill was slightly abated by Sonny giving me permission to pick it, but the challenge was still there.

When I reached the coffee shop, Kaz was outside scrubbing at graffiti on the window. *KILLER* had been sprayed in red paint across the glass. 'When did this happen?' It was less than an hour since Yanni had brought Sonny in. Sometimes it was scary how fast news travelled in this gossipy town. The reminder felt timely, considering I was currently harbouring my own secret about the Eternal Flame having disappeared.

'Not long ago,' Kaz replied. She was clearly distressed: her normally tidy hair was splayed across her face, her fingers were red from all the scrubbing, and her nails looked like they'd had a run-in with a cheese grater.

'I was still inside. I tried to close up straight away after Yanni came in, but there was a queue and people were getting cross. I didn't know what to do – it's Sonny's business, and after everything he's done for me I want to keep it going for him – but I should have just shut up shop.'

'You should report it.' I frowned at the graffiti. 'Whoever did this should be held to account. This is *not* okay.'

Eva growled as she sniffed at the paint; she was obviously as annoyed at the pieces of shit that had done this as I was.

'Why bother?' Kaz muttered. 'Whatever group it was will cover for each other. But I'm sure it was the water shifters – their leader was the one who was killed, and there were a couple of young ones in the café when the police chief took Sonny away.'

'If that's the case, I'll talk to Fraser.'

Kaz studied me. 'Why are you here? We're closed.'

'I know,' I said quickly. 'Sonny asked me to help him.'

'So you think he's innocent?' she asked.

'I do,' I said, noting the certainty in her tone. 'There's no doubt in your mind, is there?'

She was silent for a while. 'I don't know,' she said finally. 'I'd like to think he is because he's been my boss – and friend – for years. But he does have a temper.' She bit her lip.

'Is that right?' I asked. My attention was stolen by a small group of people walking past, tutting. I couldn't tell whether they were tutting at the word on the window or the act of vandalism.

'Can you tell me about Sonny?' I asked. 'The more I know about him, the more I can help him – though perhaps we should go inside.'

'Sure.' She picked up the bucket. 'Though I'm not sure I can tell you anything helpful.'

Eva and I followed her into the coffee shop; I'd never seen the place so empty before and it felt eerie, as though someone had died – which, of course, they had.

As Kaz dropped into a seat, I took the bucket. 'I'll get you some fresh water,' I offered. 'You sit for a moment – this must be horribly stressful for you.'

'Thank you.' She put her head in her hands. 'I know I said he has a temper, but I honestly can't believe he killed Lorenz.'

As I moved around the counter to empty the bucket, I noticed a laptop open by the coffee grinders. I immediately recognised what was on the screen: a monitoring feed that kept track of who came in and out of Witchlight Cove. It was useful if you worked for the police but I struggled to see why a coffee shop would have a system that extended so far beyond its own premises.

'Are you and Sonny doing a bit of surveillance?' I asked, gesturing at the laptop.

Kaz shook her head. 'Not really. It was one of Sonny's ideas to make us more efficient – he said we could use it to help us predict when we'd get rushes. We've been getting these massive parties coming in from beyond village – covens, wolf packs on road trips, that sort of thing. Dozens of them arrive unannounced and it's chaos. I know my way around computers, so I realised we could access the barrier info. I thought monitoring road activity might help us prepare – and if they were coming for something other than coffee, at least we wouldn't be blindsided.'

It was a surprisingly sensible idea, and I liked the use of technology with magic. Too many people feared combining the two, but I was sure they could work together. Dad had loved to combine magic and science. Now I wondered if that had been just one more way for him to fly under his mother's radar but still get shit done.

I emptied the bucket and refilled it then I carried it back and sat opposite Kaz. Eva had headed for one of the couches and was sprawled on her back. 'Eva!' I chastened. 'Get down!'

'It's fine.' Kaz laughed. 'She looks happy.'

'Are you sure? She leaves hair everywhere,' I warned.

'You wouldn't believe what I've found on those couches,' Kaz commented 'A little dog hair is fine.'

Ew. 'You and Sonny go way back, right?' I asked

'Way, way back,' she confirmed with an affectionate smile. 'I met him when I was human and he was stealing blood from a hospital.'

'Really?' I'd assumed Sonny had moved to Witchlight Cove from another magical community, but apparently not. It said something positive about his morals that he was the type of vampire to steal blood bags rather than going straight for someone's jugular.

'How come you were at the hospital?' I asked. '

She gave a wan smile. 'I was eighteen and I was sick. I didn't know it then, but I was dying.' Her eyes grew distant.

'I'm sorry,' I murmured. 'That must have been terrifying.' I couldn't even imagine dealing with a terminal illness at such a young age.

She shrugged, clearly not ready to discuss the experience in any detail. 'Anyway, I saw Sonny and he looked horrified that he'd been caught. He started panicking about rules and councils – I thought he was crazy until his fangs pinged out of his gums. Have you seen his fangs? They're really impressive.' The warmth in her smile told me their bond was deeper than that of employer and employee.

'I have,' I admitted with considerably less relish.

'The hospital was his main source of blood and he was terrified that if I told someone what I'd seen, they'd increase their security and he'd have to go out hunting. You know,' she lowered her voice even though no one else was around, 'hunting humans.'

I suppressed a smile and nodded.

'Once I realised what he was and that it wasn't some sick joke, I made him promise that if the doctors couldn't cure me and my illness was terminal he'd turn me before it was too late.'

'And he kept that promise.'

'He did,' she said. 'Three years later, after we'd exhausted chemo and radiotherapy and I'd even been on an experimental drug. Although the treatments had given me extra time, I was still dying and I was all out of options.' She looked faintly sick as she remembered and I was grateful I'd kept my shields fully in place; I couldn't cope with this on top of Sonny's emotions – and my own.

'I called the number Sonny had given me not expecting him to answer – by that point, I honestly thought I'd had some sort of hallucination. But he answered.' Her relief was obvious. 'Sonny had set up the coffee shop a few months earlier and he gave me a job and a home.' She looked at me with grief-stricken eyes. 'I owe him everything and here I am doubting him! It's inexcusable.' She shook her head angrily.

'Unless you were there and you saw who killed Lorenz,' I said firmly, 'of *course* you'd doubt Sonny. He's been arrested as a suspect. None of us can truly know the thoughts and minds of another.' Except maybe me, if my powers kept growing.

That thought was shocking; I'd had rarely thought positively about my powers, but the ability to tell what someone was thinking or feeling was actually a huge advantage. It was a total paradigm shift.

I sat there, feeling a little dumbfounded. Could my magic actually be an asset?

Chapter Eighteen

Kaz was looking at me weirdly and I realised I'd been quiet for too long. I cleared my throat 'So the question is, did someone kill Lorenz because they had an issue with him or were they trying to frame Sonny? The anonymous tip-off can't be a coincidence – it has to have come from the killer to make him look like the culprit.'

'Why can't it be both?' she asked. 'From what I've heard, Lorenz could be fiery too – he sacked a werewolf last night. And with the Order of the Nightshades in town, someone could easily have hired one of them to kill him.'

She was right. I needed to speak to the Order, or at least question Lestat and Vlad, but that wasn't a proposition that thrilled me. Maddie might have liked Candice's fashion choices but Yanni had made it clear that the Nightshades were not to be messed with.

I stood up. 'Sonny said I could go into his flat. I'll let myself in. Thanks for talking to me.'

She looked surprised. 'That's strange – he doesn't let anyone in his flat. He's super private.'

'Not even you?'

'I lived there when I first came to Witchlight but only until I found my feet. It was a bit much living above the place you work, and I needed some distance from it. Sonny keeps crazy hours and he never expected me to do the same, but it's hard not to help out when you're upstairs and you can feel the queue building up.'

I nodded. 'Well, thanks for your time.' I called Eva, and Kaz picked up the clean bucket of water. A thought struck me. 'Why don't you ask a witch to help with this?' I gestured at the graffiti. 'They could probably clean it up a lot more quickly.'

'Witches don't help vampires at the best of times – and this isn't the best of times,' she scoffed.

I grimaced; she was right. Supernatural politics were a nightmare and situations like this only made things worse. 'I know someone who'll help,' I promised. 'Go home, you have enough to deal with. I'll sort out the graffiti and talk to Fraser Banks – he's the head of the water shifters now. If the culprit was one of them, he'll make sure whoever was responsible is held accountable. As for Sonny, he's innocent until proven guilty.'

'Thank you.' She pulled me into a hug.

That was when the flash happened again. I saw Kaz lying in a hospital bed, an IV in her arm, and Sonny leaning over her with a faint smile on his lips as she nodded bravely. His fangs extended from his gums and she knew what he was about to do – I could feel it as if her emotions were my own.

The image started to blur and another flash followed: Kaz and Sonny were driving into Witchlight Cove and I felt her nervous excitement, an apprehensive thrill about her future now that she had one. As I tried to pick up on everything I could, the edges of the image began to blur and I knew I was going to be taken somewhere else, to another of Kaz's very private memories.

Oh heck! 'Oh,' I yelled aloud, pulling back from Kaz's embrace and yanking myself out of the moment.

She looked at me wide-eyed. 'Is everything okay?'

Thankfully I'd broken the connection before I'd seen anything I'd need to scrub out of my eyes. 'Yes,' I said hastily. 'Sorry. I'm weird about hugs,' I offered lamely.

'I should have checked. Not everyone is touchy-feely.' She looked contrite.

'Totally my problem,' I reassured her. 'Sorry for being weird.'

She flashed me a relieved smile. 'Not at all. It's fine, honestly.'

It wasn't fine at all: I had invaded her memories and my pulse was racing at quadruple pace. I did my best to act normally, as if I just hadn't peered inside her head like a peeking pixie. 'Is the door to Sonny's flat around the side?'

'Yes.'

'Great. Thank you. And sorry – about the hug and the graffiti. And Sonny.' I was babbling. 'I'll see you soon – and I'll sort out the graffiti.' I swung open the café door and raced around the building; only when I was out of sight did I flop against the wall.

So much for thinking Fraser might be to blame for my hinky powers; they were a hundred percent on the blink and I needed to do something about them. Soon. I couldn't just blunder into people's minds willy-nilly – that sort of thing was frowned on.

Eva was looking at me oddly. Knowing I needed some reassurance, she pressed against me and her love rolled over me like a balm to my soul. I crouched down and gave her a full body stroke. 'Something happened to me in there,' I admitted. 'I think … I think I had a vision. And not of Fraser this time.'

My magic was evolving. I could feel emotions more strongly than ever and now I was having visions. I knew from my work with my dad that there were dozens of types, depending on the type of witch and the magic involved. Bloodline visions were common but those wouldn't have come into play when I touched Kaz and Fraser unless we were related, so the chances of me being a bloodline witch were pretty much zero. And what I'd seen had been in the past, not a prophetic vision of the future, so I wasn't a seer. So what the hell was I?

This was where I needed a coven. It was all well and good being part of an elite family and Guardian to the Eternal Flame, but that had excluded me from the covens and now I didn't have anyone I could – or wanted to – turn to.

The covens had been welcoming and kind when my mother was alive because she was incredibly powerful and the Flame had raised her standing even further. But when she'd died, and they'd discovered my deadly sorceress grandmother, they'd given me the widest berth possible. They'd even cut their ties with the Eternal Flame, as if I had corrupted its magic to harm them.

I didn't trust them now, and the feeling was mutual. If I told them about my issues, no doubt they'd assume my newly manifested magics were malevolent talents inherited from Dear Old Grandmother.

There was only one person I could speak to: Ernie Jacobson. That prospect scared me, because if I spent time with him – if I let him in – then one day he'd hurt me.

One day he would die, and I'd spent the last decade doing anything I could to never feel grief like that again.

Even so, the surges of emotion were getting stronger and more frequent. It was time to risk my heart and talk to the only person who might be able to help me. Plus I'd told Kaz I'd help her with the graffiti and my grandfather was the only witch I knew who could handle that. After I was done at Sonny's, I'd go to see Ernie.

Decision made, I felt like a weight had been lifted off me. I pulled my phone out of my pocket and called Maddie. 'Hey,' I said when she answered. 'Do you have Ernie's number?'

'I do!' She rattled it off. 'Are you going to call him?'

I grinned. 'That's generally what one does with a phone number.'

I could sense her eyeroll. 'Are you taking on Sonny's case?' she murmured.

'I think so.' I tried to sound noncommittal, even though I'd already decided I would – unless the evidence in Sonny's flat made me run in the opposite direction.

A pause followed, and I suspected Maddie was wondering if she should try to talk me out of it; she didn't want me to wade into murderous waters, PI or no. She didn't, though; instead she said, 'Okay. Well, just take care.' She paused. 'I love you, you know,' Her voice cracked and I realised those words had been hard for her to say.

I swallowed the sudden lump in my throat. 'I love you too, Mads,' I blurted back. 'I never stopped loving you.' I hung up because talking about my decade-long disappearance was still a risky move.

Before I could change my mind, I called Ernie. 'Hello?'

'Ernie, it's Beatrix.'

'Beatrix!' There was genuine joy in his voice, mixed with delighted surprise, which made me smile despite myself.

'How are you?' I asked politely, not wanting to dive straight in and ask for a favour.

'Better for the call,' he said honestly. 'How can I help you?'

I winced; he'd recognised that I wasn't calling for chit-chat. 'Sonny has been arrested for Lorenz's death and someone has vandalised the coffee shop. Is there any chance you could come by and help Kaz clear it up?'

He didn't hesitate. 'Of course. I just need to finish something here, but I'll be there as soon as I can.'

'Thanks. I appreciate it.' I paused. 'And maybe sometime soon we could .... talk? About my parents and my magic?'

'I'd like that very much,' he said warmly.

'Right. See you around.' My shoulders loosened as I hung up. I rolled them back a few times as I looked at Sonny's door. 'What do you think, girl?' I asked Eva absently. 'A simple enough lock?'

She barked as I pulled the lockpick set from my pocket. I put the tension wrench in place first and applied just the right amount of pressure: too little and the pins would fall back into place when depressed, too much and the lock could jam. Holding the wrench in the right place, I went for a rake pick. I wasn't in the mood to find each individual pin and press them down and raking the lock was quicker and easier, albeit way less technically skilled.

Finally it clicked. Once all the pins were flush, I used the wrench like a key and turned it. 'Nailed it,' I murmured to Eva as I pushed the door inwards. I held it open for her and we went into Sonny's flat.

I looked around. 'This is *not* what I had expected.'

I knew Sonny had daylight tattoos from Maddie so he could enjoy the sun like a regular human, but I'd still expected the flat to be dim with closed shutters or at least heavy curtains. Instead, gossamer-thin drapes allowed sunlight to pour into the very tidy one-bedroom flat. Everything was neatly arranged and the cream carpet looked recently vacuumed.

I slipped off my shoes. 'You stay here, girl,' I told Eva, pointing to the mat. We hadn't been on any particularly muddy walks but dogs and cream carpets didn't go together. With a huff, she sat her butt neatly on the matt. 'Good girl,' I praised. 'I promise I won't be long.'

I moved further inside. Warmth radiated from the room, not just from the sunlight but from the paintings in yellows, oranges and pinks that hung on the walls. They were vivid, happy colours that evoked the idea of 'sunny', even if that was very much the opposite of the impression Sonny gave in person.

I didn't have a clue why Sonny thought coming here would change anything but then I spotted three photographs on a small table. I picked one up: it was of Sonny with his arm around a man of similar height with the same dark hair and sharp jawline. The man's style was sharper than Sonny's – he was dressed in a dark shirt with sunglasses perched on his head – but they had matching tattoos which were probably Maddie's work. This had to be Shady, Sonny's brother.

The next photo was of Sonny, Shady and an older man. Though he was shorter than the brothers, his jawline and deep-set eyes were unmistakable: it must be their father.

I picked up the final picture and froze. Once again, Sonny had his arm around another man but they weren't looking at the camera, they were looking at each other. Sonny's smile was wide, radiant and filled with love.

I recognised the other man immediately, even though I'd only met him once: Lorenz. The way they were gazing at each other made it clear that they were a couple and I frowned. Sonny had said that once I knew, I might not want to work for him. What? Because he was gay?

'He can't be serious,' I muttered. 'It's the twenty-first century!' I'd lived in London not far from Soho and I'd regularly gone for nights out on Old Compton Street where the vibe was always friendly and fun and you didn't get hit on non-stop. As if Sonny being gay would stop me from taking on his case!

All that agony now made so much more sense. Sonny had *loved* Lorenz and now someone had taken him – and worse, framed him as his lover's killer.

I took a picture of the photo on my phone and marched back to the door. 'Come on, Eva,' I called. 'We have a vampire to save.'

Next stop, the station. Yanni needed to know about this development because it changed everything.

Chapter Nineteen

'You're back fast,' Yanni said when she saw me marching through the office. 'Everything okay?'

'It will be,' I said forcefully. 'I need a couple of minutes with my client.'

She sighed. 'He's not being open with me so maybe you'll get something more from him. Maybe you could tell him that co-operating with the police is the way forward.'

'Believe me, we're going to have words about being open and honest.'

Yanni buzzed me in. When I walked into the cell, Sonny lifted his head; he looked utterly miserable. 'You loved him,' I said without preamble. 'And he loved you.'

Tears filled his eyes. 'Yes,' he choked out. 'We kept our relationship secret.'

'Why?' I asked, genuinely bewildered.

'It's complicated.'

'No, it's not. Talk me through this.'

'We were in love,' Sonny said simply. 'And it's all very well for you to come in here with this "nobody cares" attitude, but that's not the world *I* grew up in. I was raised in a time where being gay was a sin. Forgive me if it hasn't been easy to be open about my sexuality.'

'Why don't you want people to know?' I asked softly. 'It's part of who you are. You can't believe that people will have a problem with that, not in this day and age?'

He snorted. 'Are you really so naïve as to believe that everyone in this world is so accepting? A lot of vampires are old, Beatrix, and they were raised in a different century. They're already ashamed of me – a vampire running a *coffee house*.' He said it with the same disdain most people would use for a brothel. 'They'd be less embarrassed if I ran an underground fight club – especially if I was laundering money through it.'

He sighed. 'If he – if *certain* people found out...' His voice faltered as if the words physically pained him.

I thought about the other photos. 'Your father? Your brother? That's why you kept this hidden. They don't know?' I ventured.

Sonny shook his head. 'I'm already the biggest disappointment in the family. Everything I do is a screw-up. Vampires are supposed to have suave professions – be club owners or antique dealers – and they're meant at least to like the idea of feeding from humans, even if they have the self-respect not to do it. They're charming, charismatic, everything I'm not. Shady would probably have been happier if I'd been a bloody drug dealer rather than a barista. Add this particular insult to injury…' his voice cracked '…and I'd be disowned. It'd be the nail in my metaphorical coffin.'

My heart ached for him; I knew full well what it felt like to feel that you were a disappointment to those around you.

We sat in silence for a moment then I said, 'Sonny, I don't care who you love – in fact, your relationship with Lorenz convinces me even more that you didn't kill him. Others won't care either. You need to tell Yanni the truth.' He started to protest and I held up my hand. 'We'll circle back to that. For now, tell me about the evidence. Do you know what it is?'

'Footage of us fighting, apparently. We had a big fight yesterday.'

His regret hit me like a bloody bulldozer. I drew in a breath, trying to filter out Sonny's emotions the best I could before I asked my next question. 'Where were you?'

'We were in the office at his bar. It was before the staff had arrived for the opening night, so I didn't think anyone was in but I guess I was wrong.'

Archer hadn't been fired then; he could have heard the fight, and he may well have had access to the security camera footage. Archer was definitely on my radar, but he was a werewolf; if he'd killed Lorenz, it was with vampire help.

If he was behind this, I'd need to link him to the Nightshades and that probably wouldn't be easy. I was pretty sure that trained assassins were damned good at hiding their tracks. Was there a reason why Vlad and Lestat had been at the bar? Were they scoping it out or interfering with the CCTV equipment?

I pulled my thoughts back to the miserable man in front of me. 'Can you tell me what the fight was about?'

'He wanted me to come to his bar opening, for us to be there *together* as a couple. I said it was too dangerous.'

'For you or for him?'

'Both,' he admitted. 'The water shifters weren't pleased with him. They thought he'd dropped the ball after the Gilbert fiasco.'

Fiasco: that was a wonderfully understated way to describe murder and attempted murder, right up there with 'a bit of a mess' and 'an oopsie'.

'And people were blaming Lorenz for Gilbert's actions?' I asked, frowning.

'Not directly, but they think that if he'd had a better grip on the sect he'd have known that something was up with Gilbert. They're saying the bar renovation distracted him, but I think...' He hesitated. 'I think it was me. It was hard for us to carve out time together, especially with all the meetings and responsibilities Lorenz had. Maybe he *did* drop the ball. Maybe it was my fault.'

His voice cracked again. 'I didn't want to give people another reason to think he was incapable of doing his job. Even if we hadn't been gay, me being a vampire would have been enough to make people think ill of him. But he just didn't see it that way.'

His eyes shifted to his lap and I got the feeling there was another detail he was missing out. I hazarded a guess as to what it was. 'He thought you didn't want people to find out about you? That was why the fight got so bad?'

'He thought that was the only reason I didn't want to be there – but it wasn't! I can't deny that I didn't want to come out to the entire town when I hadn't even told my family, and I know I should have told them by now. I loved Lorenz – I was going to propose to him when we went away next week. I'd bought a ring and everything. I knew that meant my friends and family would find out, but I wanted this for us first. I couldn't tell him that without ruining the surprise.' His hand moved to his chest as though he could somehow hold his breaking heart together.

'Did he know that you were going to ask him to marry you?'

He shook his head. 'No. He died thinking that I'd never tell Shady. Lorenz thought I'd be the one to break his heart.' Sonny's voice became a whisper. 'But I was all in. And now … now I can't even tell him that. He died thinking—'

'No, he didn't,' I interrupted firmly. 'You said you made up after the fight, right?'

'Yes. But the fight must have looked bad if it was enough for Yanni to haul me in and think I'm capable of murder.'

'We'll sort this out,' I said firmly. 'I promise.'

A flicker of hope crossed his face but faded almost immediately. 'How?' His voice was laced with despair.

I glanced towards the office. 'I'm going to tell Yanni the truth.'

'You can't!' he blurted. 'Not until I've told Shady! He deserves to hear the truth from me, not in the rumourville.'

I stared at him. 'You do realise you're being held under suspicion of murder, right?'

'Please?'

I sighed. 'Fine. I'll take a look at the tip-off tape then I'll ask Shady to visit you. You're going to tell him the truth, then I'll tell Yanni. If coming out of the closet helps clear you of murder, it's time to do it.'

Sonny gave me a shaky nod then his shoulders sagged. 'It's past time.'

'You can rectify that now.'

'I can, but it's still too late for Lorenz.'

I didn't respond because he was right.

Chapter Twenty

Yanni's lips were pinched. 'You can't see that video, Beatrix. It's police evidence and you are not police.'

Ugh. 'Okay, so how about this? I'll tell you what I know, then you can clarify how it ends for me. How about that?'

She frowned. 'I'm not sure I understand.'

'You will, trust me. The video is of Sonny and Lorenz having an argument in Lorenz's office at the bar. Initially Lorenz is angry and Sonny looks like he's pleading, upset rather than cross.' I paused. 'I'm right so far, yes?'

She grimaced. 'Yes,' she admitted reluctantly.

'Right. Lorenz is the one who is angry and I'm guessing Sonny is trying to placate him. Is that correct?'

'Initially.'

'Sonny gets mad, too, and I bet his fangs popped out before the video suddenly cut off. You don't see Sonny or Lorenz leave the room and you don't see if they reconcile after the argument.'

Yanni's frown deepened and I knew I'd hit on something important.

'Don't you think that's a little suspicious?' I pressed. 'If Sonny really had been to blame, would the video not have shown him lashing out? Wouldn't it have shown one of them storming out? I also bet the timestamp has been scrubbed so you can't tell what time of day it is – though I can tell you it happened in the morning, hours before Lorenz was killed. But there's none of that, is there? And do you know why?'

She stayed silent though her lips tightened.

'Because the killer didn't want you to see what happened next because if you did, it would wipe out any suspicion that Sonny could have been responsible for Lorenz's murder.'

Yanni was still frowning. 'Why? What did it show?'

Shit: I didn't want to out Sonny after promising that I wouldn't, so I tried to be subtle. 'They made up, hugged. Trust me, those two were close. Sonny is devastated – I'm an empath and I can feel his pain.' I looked at her entreatingly and she nodded grudgingly. I appreciated that she didn't point out that my empath skills were usually weak at best.

'Yanni, you can't use that video as evidence when there *is* no actual evidence, especially without the timestamp.

That row could have happened days ago. People fight all the time. Let me show you something.'

I waved my hands above my head and gesticulated angrily at her. 'If you filmed me speaking to you like this, it would look like we were having a massive row. But we're not – it's just smoke and mirrors.'

'It's not just that, though, is it?' she said pointedly. 'Sonny is a vampire, Beatrix, and he doesn't have an alibi for last night. The coffee shop was closed and all he's said is that he was home alone. He can kill in the way in which Lorenz was killed, and there is some evidence that they fought. I'm not saying I don't believe you, but right now Sonny is our main suspect and he's not talking.'

'Okay, but the Order of the Nightshades is here and they're all vampires – vampires who can be paid to kill. Did Maddie tell you about Vlad and Lestat being at the club?'

'Yes, but they have alibis, Beatrix. They returned to Shady's before the time of death.'

Dammit. 'So it's not them – but someone else from the Order could have done it. Apparently the water shifters are furious at Lorenz because of the whole Gilbert situation, plus he sacked one of his employees a couple of hours before his murder. Anyone could have hired a Nightshade. There are definitely avenues to explore and I'll explore them with or without you.'

I expected her to be angry but instead she looked amused and rather approving. 'You weren't joking about being good at this PI business, were you?' she said.

'Nope.'

'And how are you doing?' she asked carefully. 'After being shot?'

I blinked. Was she worried I wasn't at full capacity? 'I'm fine. Whatever Fraser did healed me completely.'

'About that – have you spoken to him yet?'

'No.'

Her smile was strained. 'You might want to get round to that.' She studied me. 'It's probably not professional for me to say this, but I suspect I'm going to enjoy watching you dig into this case. It's good to see you in your element. If you get anything concrete, bring it to me. Don't put yourself in any danger. Do you understand?'

'Yes, ma'am,' I replied, giving a mock-salute.

I think we both knew I was fibbing.

Archer was now my main suspect – people could get fiery about being fired, plus I needed to set Yanni's sights on someone other than Sonny – so I rang Ezra to get the man's address.

'I didn't actually get you a drink that you liked last night,' he said when he answered. 'Any chance you're free later?'

'Sorry, I've got a lot on my plate at the minute,' I said truthfully.

'Lots on your plate could either be really positive or really negative.'

'I'm not sure which it is at the moment,' I joked.

Ezra gave a warm chuckle. 'The girls have already written a letter to the school about you giving self-defence lessons so I'm fairly sure you'll get a call soon.'

'That would be amazing,' I said gratefully. 'Thank you so much.'

'It was your great teaching that did all the work.'

'Thank you, Ez. That means a lot,' I admitted, and it did. 'How are the girls getting on?'

I heard the grin in his voice. 'Let's just say, Dallas isn't bothering them any more.'

I beamed. 'I'm glad to hear it. Anyway, the reason I'm ringing is to do with Archer. I was wondering if you could give me his address.'

'Archer?' Ezra groaned. 'Trixie, please tell me you're not sticking your nose into Lorenz's death?'

'I'm not sticking my nose into anything,' I protested. 'Whatever I do is in a professional capacity only.' Although technically Sonny hadn't hired me since we hadn't discussed a contract or terms.

He sighed huffily. 'Do you want me there while you question Archer? It might help having a senior member of the pack with you.'

'It's fine,' I said. 'Trust me, I've done enough of these interviews. Archer might even open up a little more if a pack member *isn't* there.'

Ezra grunted acknowledgement. 'I'll ping the address over to you – but let me know how it goes. If I don't hear from you in an hour or two, I'll be there.'

'Guns blazing?' I teased.

'Claws sharpening,' he corrected his tone serious.

'I'll let you know,' I promised. 'You're the best.'

'Just not good enough to go on a date with?' He said it with humour though his tone was a little resigned.

'Ez, you're like family,' I started.

'Don't worry, I'm only winding you up. Just call me after you've seen Archer and stay safe, Trixie. We've only just got you back. Be sensible.'

'Sensible is my middle name,' I lied. 'Don't worry. And Ez? I'm not going anywhere right now,' I hung up, grateful he hadn't taken my rejection badly.

Archer's address was on Nutwood Lane, not far from where Ezra's parents lived and I remembered I'd promised to drop in and say hi to his mum. Like Ezra, Alice had been a huge support after I'd lost my parents and I definitely owed her a visit, but I only had ten minutes to spare and she deserved more than that. I put visiting her on my to-do list.

There were several routes to Archer's address but I didn't want to go around the forest and get Eva dirty in case we returned to Sonny's flat later. The last thing I wanted was to trample mud into his pristine carpets. Instead, we went through the centre of town and past the coffee shop.

Standing in front of it, with his hands against the window and a soft, yellow glow rising from them, was Ernie Jacobson. My grandfather. It was still weird to think that. As he turned, he saw me and lifted his hand to wave. A blast of light shot from his palm and he looked embarrassed, which made me grin.

'Thank you for doing this.' I nodded at the clean pane of glass.

'It wasn't much of a job, if I'm honest – and I felt bad for Sonny. I come here a lot for my coffee – it's just about the only time I leave my house – so it seemed fitting I should help.'

I felt a twinge of sadness. If a daily coffee was the only time he saw other people, I couldn't imagine how lonely he had been. I'd been fairly solitary in the non-magical world, but I'd still worked with clients and police officers, not to mention my students. Ernie's situation took loneliness to a whole new level.

'How have you been?' he asked. 'I'm sorry about how I told you about your father and me. I've been thinking about it a lot. There was probably a better way.'

'I don't think there was a good way to tell me,' I admitted.

He shook his head. 'I don't know. I thought you'd be pleased to have some family, but now I see how silly that was. You don't know me from Adam.'

Ernie was old, and although he might be long-lived, I didn't know how much time we'd have left together. Was I really going to waste it? 'Of course you're family,' I said. 'But we're starting from scratch. Learning that you'd known about me for such a long time and not managed to find me hurt, but I'm trying to move past it. It wasn't your fault you couldn't find me, and I know you were hurting too.'

'I'm sorry, Beatrix. I really am.'

He looked so morose that I felt the need to offer an olive branch. 'I was planning to come and see you. I wondered if you could offer me some guidance ... with my powers.'

His gaze intensified and I wondered for a second if he was psychic. Had I inherited those weird flashes from him?

He lowered his voice. 'I don't mean to be insensitive, but I gather you didn't inherit much of your parents' skill.'

It really said something when news of your uselessness had reached your reclusive grandfather. 'Oddly enough, they seem to be growing.' I cleared my throat. 'But right now I'm going to question a suspect and Ezra will worry if I take too long. Maybe I could come and talk to you later in the week.' I could ask him about the Eternal Flame, too.

He smiled. 'I'd like that very much.'

'I'll ring you.'

'Of course. Any time, day or night.'

I gave an awkward wave and walked on. Talking to him had settled something spikey in my heart and I felt much less anxious, which was good because I was about to speak to someone who might have commissioned Lorenz's murder.

Chapter Twenty-One

It's a well-known fact in the magical community that teenage werewolf boys can be a little ... difficult. Yes, Ezra was pretty much always a delight but I never hung out with any of his brothers or cousins because they were as irritating as hell.

There was an arrogance that came with being an adolescent werewolf that set them apart from other sects. At that age they started going out on runs with the rest of the pack at full moon and wondering if they'd ever have a chance to become an alpha or beta. They'd check out the competition and look for ways to put them down. Apparently with someone like Archer that attitude lasted into their early twenties, too.

He opened the door a slice, peering out. I could see why, he was wearing only a pair of boxer shorts. 'Hey,' he said as he scoured my body with his eyes. From what I could see, his body was toned enough but it wasn't a patch on Fraser's.

It was only when he cleared his throat and smirked that I realised I'd drifted off into thoughts about Fraser. Annoyingly, Archer clearly thought *he* was the reason for my daydreams. 'I know. Whole package, if you get what I mean.' He raised his eyebrows.

What a jerk. 'I'm Beatrix Stonehaven – I'm a private investigator,' I said briskly. 'I have a few questions for you. I understand you used to work for Lorenz, but he recently let you go. Is that right?'

His smirk dropped for a second but returned in full force. 'Yeah, but I didn't need that crappy job. Being at home gives me plenty of time to enjoy myself, if you know what I mean. Why don't you come in? I can show you what I get up to.'

Eva let out a low threatening growl and he blanched. He might have been a werewolf but a bite from a dog would still hurt like hell – not to mention the embarrassment factor.

'We're fine where we are, thank you,' I said firmly. 'I just want to talk to you about Lorenz Matheson's death.'

Archer sneered. 'I don't know why anyone would care. The guy was a prick.' Apparently he hadn't been taught not to speak ill of the dead.

'Was he really? Or are you just pissed off that he fired you? Because most people have very positive things to say about him.'

The smirk was well and truly gone; now Archer was glaring. 'I wasn't alone in disliking Lorenz – all the water shifters thought he was a dud but they were too afraid to say so because he was their leader. His focus has been way off for the last year. There was a whole faction trying to persuade Fraser Banks to stage a coup.'

'So why did you turn up at Lorenz's launch party if you hated the guy?'

'He'd promised free booze for the staff.' He sniffed. 'I wasn't missing out on that just because I didn't like him.'

'Even though you weren't staff because you'd been fired? And you'd made extra work for your friends and the pack because they had to cover your shifts?'

He groaned aloud. 'Oh God, Pepper's not still going on about that, is she? I don't know why she's whingeing – she only had to cover a few extra hours and she got to that damned gig in London. She's such a whiner.'

'You're right, she did go to her gig – but you still haven't explained why you turned up at the very place you'd been sacked from. Did you really expect Lorenz to offer you free drinks?'

'Only after closing time, obviously.' He sniffed. 'But he went and got himself killed, so we never had our promised lock-in.'

Obviously Lorenz hadn't wanted staff to drink when they were working but he must have said they could stay on after closing time for a private party. I could feel Archer's annoyance that it hadn't happened. Lorenz had lost his life and Archer was pissed off because he'd missed a few quids' worth of free booze. He had the empathy of a teaspoon.

Annoyingly, though, I was pretty sure he was telling the truth. I needed to speak to Fraser about Lorenz's relationship with his pack.

The over-developed man-child in front of me wasn't a vampire so he hadn't killed Lorenz – but could he have hired the Order of the Nightshades? He didn't seem angry so much as inconvenienced and annoyed, but even so I dug a little further. 'You didn't stay long, did you?' I asked. 'I didn't see you inside.'

Archer shrugged. 'When I saw the Big B there, I thought it wouldn't be wise to stay. He isn't too impressed with me. I was going to pop back after closing time.'

'The Big B?'

'The beta.'

'You mean Ezra?'

He nodded. 'Yeah.'

I could only imagine how overjoyed fourteen-year-old Ezra would have been to know that one day he'd be known as 'the Big B'. 'So you saw Ezra and you headed home?'

'I was going to. I thought about heading to Shady's and grabbing a drink there—'

'Shady's was closed,' I interrupted. For an event with the Order of the Nightshades... Maybe he *had* ventured there.

'I didn't need to go to Shady's. I got to the back of the queue and saw Agatha there. She's this mer chick – smoking hot.'

I was pretty sure that 'merwoman' or 'merperson' would have been more appropriate terms, but I knew there'd be no point trying to give Archer a lesson in non-sexist terminology. 'So what happened?' I pressed. 'With you and Agatha?'

'You wanna know all the details?' He did the sleazy eyebrow thing again. 'She came round to mine and she'll probably give you a blow-by-blow account, if you know what I mean.' He winked.

He was a complete prick and I couldn't even put it down to teenage werewolf hormones. 'And she'll verify this for you?' I said.

For the first time, his cockiness faltered. 'You're not the police.'

‘No, but I’m working with them. Can Agatha confirm she was with you, or do I need to ring Chief Inspector Greenridge and tell her I have a suspect?’

He pulled out his phone. ‘Jeez, there’s no need to play hardball. Here’s her number.’

I copied it into my own phone. ‘Thank you for your time.’ Just because he was so lacking in manners didn’t mean I had to copy him.

‘Sure. You sure you don’t want some more of it?’ He held up his hands. ‘These fingers are magic, baby.’

Somehow, I doubted it very much.

I spun on my heel and walked away. Yes, Archer was a dick but he wasn’t giving me killer vibes – which meant I was right back at square one.

Chapter Twenty-Two

I was exhausted. I'd been running around with no chance to recover after the battering I'd had from Sonny's emotions, and I knew I couldn't handle much more. I messaged Fraser to say I was too tired to meet that night and to wish him well for his meeting with the sect leaders.

Although I was tired, Eva needed a decent walk so we went into the forest before heading home. While she was happily sniffing for squirrels and barking loudly at the ones that taunted her from the branches above, I messaged Maddie to say that I'd pick up pizza; I wasn't in the mood for cooking, and I suspected she wouldn't be either. The smiley-faced and pink heart emojis she sent back told me I was right.

I phoned in the order and then rang Shady. He answered the phone with total silence. 'Shady?' I asked after a few moments.

'Talk,' he said brusquely.

And I'd thought *Sonny* was supposed to be the rude one. 'I'm Beatrix Stonehaven. I'm—'

'I know who you are,' he interrupted me. 'Talk quickly, Stonehaven. I'm in the middle of something.'

'I'm acting as a private investigator for your brother. I saw him earlier. He needs to see you. To talk.'

He grunted and hung up. What was with all the rudeness today? Shady might have been busy but would saying goodbye killed him? Maybe murder made people crabby but there was no reason to shoot the messenger. Feeling disgruntled, I trudged into the pizza shop and picked up my order.

'Maddie, I'm home!' I called as I walked into the house.

'In the lounge!' she hollered back.

'How was your day?' I said when I walked into the living room with two large boxes in my hand. 'You weren't in the office when I came by.'

'No, but I heard how you'd been causing chaos. I was feeling a little bit woozy so Nana sent me home for a nap.'

'You weren't feeling well? Why didn't anyone let me know? I'd have come back to make sure you were okay.' I put down the pizzas and reached out to touch her forehead to see if she was feverish, just like my mum had always done to me the second I'd declared myself ill.

Maddie smiled. 'Just dizzy – I'm fine, honestly. I was tired, that's all. It's like I'm suffering from a major energy shortage. My brain is ready to bounce back but my body isn't.'

'Shall I ring Ernie?'

'No. Honestly, it's okay. I don't need mothering.'

She did, and I was volunteering for the role. I vowed to stay by her side until she looked brighter. The first hint of glowing fingertips and I was calling Ernie.

'I just wish I hadn't done it,' she said quietly. 'I wish we could forget it ever happened.'

I needed to distract her. 'Well, I'm back to proper PI work today, and I'm sure Sonny is innocent. So with that job and a couple more self-defence classes, plus your work at the station, money shouldn't be a problem for us.'

'That's great, Bea. How much is Sonny paying you?'

I shrugged. 'We'll get down to the specifics later.'

Maddie stared at me flatly. 'Beatrix Stonehaven, you know better than that! You need to work out charges up front and get a retainer.'

She was right and usually I did, but my working methods had been totally thrown by coming to Witchlight. I'd find my new normal soon. 'Look at you, Miss Business Savvy.' I smiled at my wan-faced bestie. 'I'm so proud of you.'

‘Thank you. And you’re right – that’s one less thing to worry about if we can afford our food and bills.’ She cast around for a way to change the subject. ‘So how are things with you and Fraser?’

‘What do you mean?’ I tried to look nonchalant, but even hearing his name raised my pulse. ‘There are no “things” between me and Fraser.’

Maddie gave an unladylike snort. ‘Like heck there aren’t,’ she said firmly. ‘I see the way he looks at you. And then there was all that stuff he said about wanting to talk and having some alone time.’

She stretched out the word *alone* so that the second vowel lasted four times longer than necessary. I wouldn’t have been surprised if she’d started making kissing noises, too. As if she’d heard my thoughts, she sang, ‘Beatrix and Fraser, sitting in a tree, K-I-S-S-I—’

‘Don’t you *dare*,’ I said.

She lifted her hands as if admitting defeat; more importantly, she stopped singing that damned song. ‘Look, I might not have been the guy’s biggest fan, but he saved your life with a potion and he seems very interested in you.’ She shot me a mischievous grin. ‘And you’d make a seriously hot couple.’

‘It’s not what you think. He’s only checking up on me after I was shot, and I really should thank him properly.

I've been thinking about it a lot and I'm pretty sure he didn't use a potion on me. I didn't come to with a funny taste in my mouth or anything like that, and in my dreams I keep remembering the feeling of warmth and a beautiful light... I think he used his selkie coat to save me.'

Maddie's smile faded. 'What do you mean, his coat?'

'He put his coat over me when I'd been shot. It was wrapped around me when I regained consciousness.'

Her eyes were wide, her mouth hanging so far open I wouldn't have been surprised if it had dislocated her jaw. I'd rarely seen Maddie lost for words and unease skittered through me. I was clearly missing something, something big.

'Are you *sure*?' she finally spluttered.

'I was definitely wearing it later because I offered it back to him and he told me to keep it. And it was weird because the jacket fit me perfectly, as if it had been made for me – but Fraser's shoulders are really broad and it fits him perfectly, too. I guess it magically resizes or something.'

Maddie's expression hadn't changed and her mouth was still open. Exhausted as I was, I allowed myself to feel a smidgin of her emotions – and was met by shock. That wasn't good. What did she know that I didn't?

'I must have told you he lent me his jacket?' I said faintly.

Her jaw closed with a clack. 'No, you absolutely didn't. There is *no way* I would have forgotten you saying Fraser put his coat around you,' she said emphatically.

Apprehension was trickling down my spine but I tried to stay calm. 'So he used his magic to save me. That's fine, isn't it?'

When Maddie finally replied, her voice was shaky. 'He's a selkie, Bea, and he gave you his coat.' My expression remained confused, so she continued. 'Hon, that means you're bound to him... Eternally.'

Now it was my jaw that dropped. Surely Fraser would have mentioned if we had some sort of bond? I felt faintly ill.

'Bound to him as in—?'

'As in you're Fraser Banks's freaking *wife*!'

Fuck.

Chapter Twenty-Three

Momentarily rendered mute, I stood up before turning and marching out of the door. 'Where are you going?' Maddie called after me.

I didn't reply. She knew where I was going. Eva trotted at my heels as we marched towards Fraser Banks' home.

Maddie had to be wrong – there had to be another explanation. Fraser would have told me if we were. But then I thought uneasily that he *had* wanted to talk to me privately. He'd chickened out at Sonny's, even though I'd felt sure it was important; he'd chickened out because what he had to say to me was a huge fucking deal.

I struggled to wrap my brain around the idea. The longest relationship I'd had in the last decade was with my favourite pizza delivery man, and that relationship had advantages: I got extra toppings and to use my vouchers even when they were out of date. But this was a very different situation. To start with, I'd *chosen* that particular pizza place. And I sure as hell hadn't chosen Fraser Banks.

'It's important to choose your pizza supplier – and your mate,' I said aloud to Eva. She slid me a sidelong glance that suggested she thought I was a little unhinged. 'Well, you know what?' I said. 'You find out you may be accidentally married without your consent and we'll see how hinged you are.'

She gave me a sympathetic nuzzle and nearly tripped me up. 'I appreciate the support,' I told her, 'but maybe nuzzle me when we're stationary?'

Fraser's *wife*? My brain was shouting the phrase over and over like an old record player stuck on a loop.

Though I'd never been to Fraser's house, he had pointed it out to me and told me I was welcome anytime. He'd even told me there was a key under the mat, so I knew that I could get in.

I was still a fair distance away when I saw that the lights were on and people were moving around inside; Fraser wasn't alone and I couldn't very well march in there like a deranged psychopath when half – okay, *most* – of the town was already scared of me.

I tried to calm myself and consider his visitors, but it turned out I really didn't care about making a scene when my free will was in question. This was more important.

I didn't slow my pace until I reached the gates. There was no other way to get inside the perimeter wall; when Fraser had said I was welcome anytime, he hadn't mentioned that the grounds were impenetrable When he'd pointed out his house to me the gates had been open, as they probably were most of the time, but he must have closed them while he hosted his meeting with the sect leaders.

I scruffled Eva's ears and that small action helped calm me. 'I'm sorry, girl, but unless you can find a way in you'll have to wait here,' I said. I'd need to scale the wall and although Eva had a lot of crazy skills, climbing eight-feet stone walls wasn't one of them.

She whined but sat down obediently. After blowing her a kiss, I gave myself a run up and jumped at the wall. It had been a while since I'd needed to get over anything that high but my arms and legs held well and I got over it with relative ease. A spot of rage really helped.

I dropped down on the other side and landed in a crouch, stood up again and headed towards the house. At any other time, I'd have been impressed at how well the building blended with its surroundings; the architect had mixed warm deep timbers and a lot of glass to produce something quite exceptional. If there was a divorce, maybe I'd make him give it to me as part of the settlement.

My feet crunched on the gravel as I marched to the steps leading up to the front door. Letting myself in with the key under the mat seemed churlish when Fraser had guests, so I hammered my fist instead. Way less churlish.

He opened the door. 'Hel— Beatrix!' He didn't ask why I was there. He didn't need to; his expression said everything. 'Let me explain,' he started.

'Is this a joke?' I demanded. 'The pelt thing? Is it real?'

Rather than responding, Fraser glanced behind him. 'Look, I have the heads of the sects here. Let me ask them to leave.'

That was a reasonable request even though reason had totally fled from my brain. I nodded tightly. 'Fine. Do it quickly.'

'Two minutes. I know I've got a lot of explaining to do, but please understand that I can't throw these people out. These are the movers and shakers of Witchlight! Give me two minutes to explain that something important has come up and then I'm all yours, I promise.'

'And am I?' I demanded.

'Are you what?'

'Important.'

His gaze softened. 'Of course you are, Beatrix Stonehaven. You couldn't be more so.' Surely it was a good sign that he hadn't called me Beatrix Banks? He held the door wide. 'Come in. You can wait in my office.' He pointed to a door on the right of us. 'I won't keep you long.'

Before I could go through it, I noticed several people glancing into the hallway, one of whom I recognised. He was a man in his mid-fifties, almost as broad as he was tall; every inch of him was pure muscle. A surprised smile creased his face, only to change into a mock frown. 'Stonehaven! I heard you were back, and you haven't been to see us yet!'

'Mr. Bentley,' I said, shoving down my turmoil at the sight of Ezra's dad. 'What are you doing here?' I added before realising I already knew the answer. 'Of course, you're here for the sect leaders meeting.'

Jonah Bentley had been made alpha at a fairly young age but I'd never thought of Ezra's dad as head of the werewolves; yes, his authority had been intimidating but the man himself had never been. He had never been less than welcoming, and his wife Alice had mothered me.

'You should pop round for dinner some time. Alice would love to hear your stories about the non-magical world.'

'I'd like that,' I said, meaning it.

‘I’m sorry, but I have to deal with something urgent,’ Fraser told him. ‘I’m afraid we’ll need to cut the rest of the meeting short, but I believe we’ve covered the main issues.’

‘Short meetings, a man after my own heart.’ Ezra’s dad winked before shaking Fraser’s hand. ‘And we’ll catch up soon, Trixie,’ he added to me.

‘That would be lovely,’ I said. ‘Please send Alice my love.’

‘Will do.’

As he went to the door, several other people came into the hallway having heard Fraser’s announcement. While it was tricky to know what sect some of them were heads of, with others it was blindingly obvious.

The man with the giant black wings tucked neatly behind his shoulders was clearly the head of one of the Fae sects, and no doubt the woman who seemed to exude charisma and charm was a siren. But it was another female leader who held my attention the most. She was tall and slender; her hair deep brown at the roots, though it started to fade when it reached her shoulders and was bright platinum blonde by the time it reached her waist.

‘Julietta Cortez,’ she said, holding out her hand for me to shake. I took it; it was no surprise when her flesh was icy cold.

‘You’re the head of the vampire sect,’ I concluded.

'Indeed. And you're the little witch who has been talking to Sonny. You know, you shouldn't believe everything he tells you. He's a strange creature – and vampires are very good at lying.'

'If that's the case, does it mean I shouldn't believe everything you tell me, too?' I pointed out bullishly.

She smirked. 'Absolutely.'

'Do you know who killed Lorenz?' I asked as I lowered my shields.

Her smile widened but her eyes were cold. 'No, I do not.'

Annoyingly, I believed her. Her emotions were a mix of annoyance and frustration; she didn't know, and that was pissing her off despite the smile pasted on her face. Knowledge was power and she was raging that she had none.

'I'm sure I'll see you again soon, little witch.' Her tone was incredibly patronising. She turned to Fraser. 'Thank you for your hospitality. I'm sure we'll have things to talk about soon.' She laid a hand on his bicep and I had to resist the urge to rip it off him.

One by one the guests filtered out. As Fraser closed the door, I heard him take a deep breath as if he were preparing himself for whatever he was about to face. And rightly so: I needed answers, and I needed them now.

He turned to face me and his lips were parted as he prepared to speak.

My heart pounded. This was it. The moment of truth. 'You better start talking,' I hissed. 'Because you have some serious explaining to do.'

Chapter Twenty-Four

'It's not as bad as you think,' he said quickly. 'At least, I don't think it is. Look, would you like a drink? You might need one. Then we can sit down and talk properly.'

'I can talk properly now,' I said stiffly. 'I want answers. Are we married, Fraser? Am I bound to you forever?'

He licked his lips. 'There are things that... Look, it doesn't have to affect you at all. Please, can we have a drink – I sure as hell need one.' He shot me a wry smile that I didn't return.

There was a scratch at the door. Without asking his permission, I opened the door to Eva. I was acting like it was my home already. I tried to push down the hysterical laugh that was threatening to erupt; I was close to losing my shit.

I crouched down and cuddled my dog. 'Did you sneak in the gate when the sect leaders went out?' I asked. She wagged her tail so hard that her whole body shook. 'Clever girl.' I fussed over her for a minute longer until I felt a little calmer.

'Have you got white wine?' I asked as I stood up and looked at Fraser properly for the first time. His eyes were tired and he was obviously tense; he was right, he needed that drink.

'Normally the answer to that would be no, but I bought a bottle today – Oyster something. I don't know if it's any good.'

'You bought Oyster Bay?' I asked hopefully. The Australian Sauvignon Blanc was my go-to drink.

'Yes, I think that's it,' he said. He frowned. 'It was weird. I don't usually buy white wine so I'm not sure why the urge grabbed me today.'

I gritted my teeth. He *just* happened to pick up my favourite type of wine? Whatever magic was between us, it was obviously already doing its thing. As he opened the fridge I asked, 'Is everything alright with the sects?'

'It will be, but it will take some time. Transitions are always difficult. They put people on edge – and then there's the murder, too.'

'And one of Julietta Cortez's sect is a murderer,' I added. Not that she had looked on edge; she'd been totally calm and collected. I guessed it was easy to stay cool when your temperature never went above ten degrees.

'The murderer was a vampire but that doesn't mean it's one of her sect,' Fraser pointed out.

'Do you think it could be one of the Nightshades? That they were hired to kill Lorenz?'

'I didn't say that,' Fraser replied hastily, 'but I'm not ruling anything out. Julietta doesn't seem to think any of her vampires are involved, but then I'm pretty sure Lorenz would've said none of his shifters could have been murderers. And we know how that ended.'

Yes, with me being shot and accidentally donning a magical selkie jacket.

He handed me a very large, very cold glass of wine and I immediately took a long sip. There was no point talking about sects or murders; I was procrastinating, delaying the moment when I would find out just how screwed up my life was.

'However quickly that pelt helped me heal, you had no right to do that to me without my permission,' I said finally. My voice was quieter than when I'd burst into the house, but the anger and hurt were still there. I'd liked Fraser, more than I wanted to admit, and he'd taken away my free will. 'You had no right to place whatever this *bond* or spell is on me.'

'It's not a spell. It's older than that.' He cleared his throat. 'It's deeper – much deeper.'

'That doesn't make me feel any better.'

'I understand that. Come on. Let's sit down.' He nodded towards the chairs in a corner of the room. As I looked over, my stomach somersaulted. One of them was a green leather armchair, exactly the same as the one I'd seen Fraser sitting in before I'd fallen asleep. The pelt wasn't there, but there was a small side table on which was a bottle of whisky and a small tumbler, just like in my vision.

I'd been nowhere near Fraser at the time, so how the hell...? The bond, I realised belatedly; it had already been in play, even though I hadn't known about it. Because of the selkie skin, I'd been able to see him alone in an unguarded moment.

'We're linked, aren't we?' I said slowly. 'Can you see things about me, too? My memories? Can you feel my feelings?'

He shook his head. 'No. No, not at all. Well ... not consciously.' He hesitated. 'What do you mean "too"?'

I licked my lips. 'Let's deal with this first. What do you mean by not consciously?' I wasn't in the mood for evasive answers – despite the fact I was giving them.

'Is Oyster Bay your favourite wine?'

'Yes,' I replied cautiously.

'I've never had any desire to buy it before – no desire to get white wine at all. But I walked past it and felt that I needed to get a bottle.'

'So this *bond* tells you my favourite things?' I said waspishly. 'Bright copper kettles, warm woollen mittens, brown paper packages tied up with string?'

He shrugged helplessly. 'Honestly, I don't know. I've never been bonded before. From what I understand, it's generally fairly subtle and it depends on what you want me to know. I suspect I'd sense if you're having a bad day. But you can take action against the bond, put up barriers, if that's what you want. You don't have to open the bond between us if you don't want to.'

It was so much to take in. 'But we *are* bonded?' I asked.

He nodded slowly. 'Yes.'

'For how long?'

'Until death.'

Fuck. 'So, we're married?'

'No, nothing like that. It's a *bond* and you can accept or reject it. You won't be forced down the aisle, Beatrix.'

'Why did you put your coat over me if you knew this is what it would do? If you knew it would bond us until one of us dies?'

'Because it was the only way to save you,' he said simply. 'That bullet wound went straight through your vital organs and you'd have died before I could have got you to the hospital. The blood loss was so fast that you were already fading. I had to do something. I…' he hesitated. 'I either let you die or I used my pelt to save you.'

A huge chunk of my anger fell away. Without Fraser I would have died – it was that simple. I took a steadying sip of wine. 'So you bonded me to you instead?'

'It was the only option.'

'All right.' I blew out a long breath and tried to think clearly. 'We're bonded forever. What does that mean? Are you the only person I can have sex with? What happens if I want to have sex with someone else?'

He reached out and for a moment I thought he was going to touch me, but then he hesitated. 'It's not like that,' he said. 'Not for you, anyway.'

'Not for me?' I parroted.

His eyes shifted downwards. I wanted to get a reading from him, to know exactly what he was feeling, but I couldn't do that unless I lowered my barriers so, with a tentativeness that was close to fear, that's what I did.

The myriad emotions that struck me were the most complex I'd ever felt. There was heavy guilt and a heap of nervousness but there was something else: gratitude. Gratitude that I'd lived. One emotion was notably absent: regret. Fraser didn't regret saving me. And then I sensed hope that I wouldn't take this badly. And because that hope was so tentative, I took a deep breath and tried not to crush it.

'Fraser, I need the truth,' I insisted as I carefully raised my mental barriers again. 'What did you mean when you said "not for me"? How does the bond affect you?'

Wordlessly, he took the wineglass from my hand and took a massive gulp. I wasn't sure if I should be impressed or horrified; he was downing a good wine like it was water. He handed the glass back to me.

'The bond is supposed to be one way,' he said. 'I'm a selkie. When I put the coat on my chosen person, I'm saying that I will be with them for eternity. But you can reject being the chosen one. The power is in your hands, Beatrix, not mine.'

I stared at him. 'Do you mean you can't be with anyone else *ever?*'

'Be with them physically? No. Love them? No. That's it. I gave you my pelt. It's you or no one, for as long as I live.'

Chapter Twenty-Five

I needed to say something; he'd just told me that he had sacrificed the chance of ever finding true love for me but all I could do was stare at him with my mouth hanging open.

He took the empty wine glass and brought it back a moment later full to the brim. I still hadn't said anything – why weren't the words coming?

I took a long sip of wine and ordered myself to speak. 'You had to give up your chance of loving anybody but me in order to save my life? Is that what you're saying?'

'When you say it like that, it sounds pretty horrific.' He half-smiled.

'This isn't funny.' I knew he was attempting to lighten the mood but it wasn't working.

'I couldn't let you die.'

‘And I’m grateful for that, I really am. It may not seem like it right now because I’m so shocked, but I’m glad I’m not dead.’

‘Grateful? I guess there are worst places to start. Can I be honest with you? I suppose we might as well be honest because, you know…’

‘We’re bonded for life?’ I offered.

‘Yeah, that.’ His smile faltered and he picked up the whisky bottle from the side table and poured a good inch into the glass. Whatever he was about to say clearly wasn’t going to be easy for him. Finally he spoke. ‘I’m not a relationship person, Bea. I’m thirty-five, and I’ve had two serious relationships in my life. That’s it – two.’

‘That’s two more than me,’ I admitted involuntarily.

Fraser raised an eyebrow. I expected him to make a comment about it but he just nodded. ‘I have intimacy issues,’ I admitted flatly.

He sent me a wry glance. ‘Me too. This is going to be a fun combination, isn’t it? For me, it’s because of my parents – I never wanted anybody to feel trapped like my mother did, as if they were stuck with me forever. Giving my pelt to someone was never an issue because I knew I’d never do it. I never thought I’d find anyone who I’d *want* to offer it to. But,’ he took a gulp of his drink, ‘that was before I met you.’

'You mean before I was dying?'

'No. I mean before I *met* you.'

It took his words a moment to sink in, and when they did my skin burst into goosebumps. 'Fraser...'

'I'm not saying that to put any pressure on you – that's the last thing I want. I meant what I said about you ignoring the bond if you want to. But you asked me and I thought I should tell you the truth. From the moment I met you, I've been drawn to you.'

He hesitated. 'I'm so used to being in charge, but the first time we met you snarled at me, then you *demanded* I drive you to the hospital.'

'I'm not sure I demanded,' I said defensively.

He looked amused. 'Well, you certainly weren't taking no for an answer. That was the moment I knew I wanted to know you better – maybe just as a friend. Whatever. I wanted you in my life, but I wasn't going to hit on you, not with the whole Eternal Flame thing at play. And then slowly you undid me.'

He stopped and took another gulp of his whisky, then took a deep breath and blew it out harshly. 'I shouldn't have said anything. I'm sorry. This complicates matters, doesn't it?'

'I think it's already pretty complicated,' I replied honestly. Because I'd felt something towards him too, something more than simple attraction. I might not have wanted to admit it but it was definitely there. Yeah, it was complicated all right.

'Something shifted in me that night we talked on the beach,' Fraser continued. 'I could finally see why someone would offer up their coat and sign up to a lifetime together. Then, only hours later, I nearly lost you. I couldn't let that happen. We might not know each other well, but I'd rather have a world that I know you're in than one without you. I'm sorry if that makes you feel uncomfortable or pressured in any way. That was never my intention.'

Eva pressed against me sending wave after wave of love and reassurance to calm my stuttering heart. She was worth her weight in the finest kibble.

'Fraser, I…' I didn't know how to finish the sentence but I wanted to tell him I was sorry that by saving me he'd lost the chance to really explore what was between us. Now we were bound; if his initial attraction to me petered out, he was stuck with me.

He got in with an apology first. 'I should have told you sooner.' He shook his head. 'It was too important to delay but with you discovering your grandfather and Lorenz dying—'

'Oh God, while all this has been going on you've been dealing with taking over the sect, too,' I mumbled.

'It's okay,' he said. 'It's a lot, but I can cope with that. But I needed to speak to you.'

I had one last question, though I suspected I already knew the answer. 'I'm guessing there's no way to reverse the pelt's magic and break the bond?'

He shook his head. 'No. If there had been, I'd have broken it for my mother in a heartbeat.'

As we fell into silence, I pondered all the other things I wanted to know. I found I couldn't take my eyes off that green armchair. Since we were being brutally honest...

I gestured to his chair. 'I saw you sitting in that armchair the night after you saved me.

I thought it was just my imagination, but it wasn't, was it? You came here and sat in that chair and drank whisky.' I saw deep furrows form between his brows. 'Why are you looking like that? Shouldn't I have seen that? But isn't that what happens if we're bonded?'

'In theory, yes – but only if you're willing to accept the bond, if you *choose* me as your eternal mate.'

Had I understood him correctly? Did that vision mean that subconsciously I'd been considering Fraser as a partner *before* he'd draped his pelt over me? Another silence fell and this one was far less comfortable.

I picked up my glass and downed the contents. 'Thanks for saving my life and for telling me what's happened,' I flapped my hand between us as I stood up. 'I'm sorry for putting you in this position. I need time to think about it.'

'Beatrix, I didn't mean to make you feel awkward. You might've have seen me here because it had been a pretty intense night. It might not mean anything.'

'It probably does, though,' I admitted awkwardly. I didn't miss the flare of hope in his eyes. 'I'm exhausted – I've got a lot going on at the moment. I'll ... I'll be in touch.'

'Of course. I don't expect you to just accept what has happened.' He reached out his hand and after a slight hesitation, I took it.

This time, what I saw was more than just a flash – it was a whole slideshow. I saw all the moments since we'd first met: me opening the cottage door to him; him driving me to the hospital; the blast he'd taken when Ernie had lashed out in the coffee shop; the flood of emotion when we were talking on the beach. I could feel him falling for me, and I could see myself and the way I was looking at him. There was something in my eyes that I'd never seen before.

I couldn't lie to myself: I had been falling for him, too. But for ever? For ever was a lot without even a kiss or a date.

I was vaguely aware that my body was shaking with stress and Eva was barking.

'Beatrix! Beatrix!' As I opened my eyes, I realised that the movement I'd experienced wasn't in my mind: Fraser was shaking me. I was looking up at him, but something about the angle was wrong. Why was there a ceiling light behind him?

I was on the ground, the broken stem of my smashed wineglass still in my hand. Eva was barking frantically. 'Hey,' I managed to say to her. 'Shush now, love. I'm fine.' She quietened and nuzzled into my side.

'What happened?' Fraser asked as he helped me sit up. 'What was that?'

What was that indeed?

There was no way I'd admit to having had a vision of me falling in love with Fraser. Not a chance.

'Beatrix,' he pressed. 'What happened?'

The images had faded but the feelings lingered even though I tried to push them away. I wasn't ready to admit to what I'd seen.

I stood up shakily. 'It's fine. I was a bit lightheaded, that's all. I haven't eaten all day.' My stomach growled as if to confirm the lie. I remembered the pizza I'd left at home to come to Fraser's house and wished I'd grabbed a piece before I'd stormed out. Cold pizza was fine when you were hungover and needed a carb hit, but it wasn't a patch on fresh and piping hot.

'I should go. And I'm sorry for barging in the way I did.'

'You have nothing to apologise for. I understand. Look, I'll drive you home.'

I shook my head. 'No, it's okay. You've been drinking and the walk will do me good. Thank you for the offer, but I need some space.'

'You just passed out. I don't think you should—'

'I'm walking, Fraser,' I said with a strength to my voice that I really didn't feel. 'I'll be fine.'

He grimaced and I could see how much he wanted to fight me on this, how he didn't want to let me go. Even so, he nodded. 'Can you at least message me when you get back?'

'Of course,' I said. A text to say I'd got home safely after he'd given up his future to save my life? It was the least I could do.

'Thank you.' His eyes lingered on my face, igniting a thousand sparks inside me – all of which I tried to douse.

I grabbed Eva and left my bonded soulmate behind.

Chapter Twenty-Six

I get that life is more complicated when you grow up, and I never expected being an adult to be easy. Even when my parents were still alive, I saw the things they had to go through and how hard they worked. I knew there were responsibilities, things out of your control you had to deal with. But my current state of affairs was taking the piss.

So much was out of control that I didn't feel I had a say in anything in my life – except for taking on Sonny's case. I'd chosen to help him prove his innocence and find the person who'd killed Lorenz; maybe I'd get some karma credit for that and the powers-that-be would give me a break for a while. A girl could hope.

As I walked away from Fraser's house, I was surprised to find a figure lurking just beyond the gate – a figure I knew well. 'Ezra,' I said. 'What are you doing here?'

'Does it sound creepy if I say I was standing outside waiting for you to come out?'

'A bit,' I admitted, then smiled. 'How did you know I was here?'

'Dad rang me. He said you'd come to speak to Banks and you seemed pretty upset. He thought you might want an ear, someone to rant to.'

I shouldn't have been surprised because they were such a close-knit family. Of course his dad had rung him.

'What do you say we go back to mine?' he offered. 'I've got hot chocolate and marshmallows, and you can use me as a punchbag if you think it'll help.' He hesitated. 'It's a long time until the next full moon, though, so maybe don't go too hard on me.'

Despite all the things that were going on in my head, I couldn't help laughing. 'That sounds perfect,' I said. 'The marshmallows rather than using you as a punchbag – though that sounds pretty tempting too.'

He grinned easily and I could see it meant a lot to him that I'd accepted his offer. Maddie wasn't the only one I owed an apology to for leaving Witchlight Cove so abruptly. I'd apologised to Ezra but *saying* sorry and *showing* you were sorry were two different things.

'Hop on, then,' he said.

'Hop on?' It took me a moment to realise what he was talking about. Hidden in the shadows by the wall was a large motorbike with two helmets hanging from the handlebars. 'You got a motorbike?'

'I got a really *cool* motorbike. It's one of the perks of being beta of the wolf pack.'

'That reminds me – Big B? What a nickname.'

'I know, cool huh?' He offered me a wolfish grin before handing me a helmet. 'Are you getting on, or what?' He looked at Eva. 'It's not far. If we go slowly, can you run alongside us?'

Eve gave an enthusiastic bark, beyond thrilled at the prospect of a proper run.

I'd been to Ezra's house hundreds of times, but to my surprise we didn't veer off up the hill toward the forest; instead, we carried on along the waterfront with Eva running joyfully beside us. 'You moved?' I shouted over the rumble of the engine.

He called over his shoulder, 'I did. I got my own place when I was made beta. Maddie didn't tell you?'

I shook my head. 'No, she didn't but she's had a lot going on.'

He slowed at a stop sign, which made it easier to hear him. 'I guess the flame and stuff has really messed up her business.'

'It's not ideal.'

'I wish she'd come to me about it. I'm not sure how I could have helped, but she can't manage on her own. I don't know if it's a witch thing or because you're not part of a pack, but you two seem determined to solve all your problems on your own.'

As he accelerated away from the junction, I pondered his comment. Did I avoid asking for help because I didn't have a pack or a coven, or did I not want to burden the people I cared about?

'So, this is me.' Ezra pulled up outside a small apartment block that looked out over the water. 'Obviously, I got the penthouse.'

'Obviously.' I laughed.

'Just wait until you see the view. You're going to love it.'

Eva was panting but her tail was high and happy. 'Are you okay?' I asked her. She barked and chased her tail, and I felt the exuberance rolling off her; she was the poster child for the benefits of exercise.

We took the lift up to Ezra's apartment and it felt like I'd entered a different world. The penthouse took up the whole of the top floor and offered a 180-degree view of the village below. I'd never seen it like this before, with the waning moon reflected on the water and the twinkling lights of houses leading up towards the woods. It was strange to think that people were going about their lives in each of those houses, building their own magic-filled stories.

'It really is something, isn't it?' Ezra said from behind me.

'It is.' I turned to face him, only to find Eva looking up at me with her big brown eyes, pleading as she looked from me to the sofas and back again. 'Don't even think about it,' I said firmly. 'You need to stay off the furniture here.' I dreaded to think how filthy her paws were.

Ezra waved away the comment. 'Are you serious? This is a werewolf's home – she can go wherever she likes. That one's the comfiest, girl.' He pointing to a well-worn armchair angled towards the view; Eva didn't need to be told twice before she jumped onto it.

Ezra dumped his keys on the coffee table in front of her. 'Pick those up,' I ordered quickly.

'What?'

'Eva steals keys. Put them in a drawer or cupboard, or something she can't open.'

'Your dog steals *keys*?'

'Yeah. I think it's my fault. Because I pick locks, she thinks we need keys to help.'

He laughed. 'I like that.' Nevertheless, he put the keys in a drawer. Smart guy. 'And now that Eva's settled, it's time for hot chocolate.'

That was exactly what I needed: a hot drink and a sympathetic ear.

Ezra's penthouse was undeniably opulent with its underfloor heating and marble counters, but there were also homely aspects that I wouldn't have expected: colour-coordinated cushions and throws, candles on the coffee table. I hated to call it 'a woman's touch', but there were definitely soft feminine accents.

I wondered whether one of his family had made these additions – his mum, maybe – or if there had been a significant other in his life until recently. It pained me that I had distanced myself from him and Maddie to such an extent that I didn't know.

He filled a saucepan with milk, put it on to heat then turned to me. 'So, do you want to tell me what's going on?'

There were lots of things I wanted to tell him, and he knew I'd been upset when I'd arrived at Fraser's house. I could have lied but he deserved better than that. Even so, my bond with Fraser was raw and new and I didn't know how I felt about it, so I decided to skirt the truth. 'Fraser and I ... well, we might be kind of dating,' I admitted.

He stilled mid-stir. 'But he upset you?'

'He saved my life and I guess that accelerated things a little unnaturally.' I licked my lips, took the plunge and told him the truth. 'Fraser saved my life by giving me his pelt.'

Ezra's jaw literally dropped. He gaped at me for a long moment. 'Well, fuck,' he said finally.

'Yeah. It's a lot.'

'Of course it is. How do you feel about it?'

'Conflicted,' I admitted. 'I like him, but I don't like having my choice taken away from me.'

'You can still choose,' he pointed out.

'I know, but if I deny the man who saved my life I'm condemning him to a loveless – sexless – existence.'

Ezra blew out a long breath. 'That's hard.'

It was, and I needed to talk about something else for a moment. I looked at the feminine touches littering the room. 'You lived with someone?'

The spoon stalled again. 'Yes, I did.'

'It didn't work out?'

He sighed and turned to face me. 'My fault, I think. There were a few issues, and I ... I always wondered about you, Trix. You were the one that got away.' He shrugged awkwardly. 'I crushed on you for most of our teen years and I suppose I thought that one day...'

I swallowed hard as I suddenly remembered an almost-kiss on a summer's day that had been interrupted by Maddie's arrival. Back then, with the heat of teenage hormones, there had been something between us, even though I'd denied it ever since. But now? Attractive as he was, I just didn't feel that way about him. The intervening decade had solidified him firmly into the *family* category in my heart and memories, and there was no moving him out of there now.

He read my thoughts on my face and grinned. 'I know. There's zero chemistry now, isn't there?'

'Absolutely none,' I admitted ruefully. 'Sorry.'

'Don't be. I'm glad you're back and I'm glad I can let the romantic delusions slide back to where they belong in the past.'

'Maybe you can patch things up with... What was her name?'

'Nour. I'd like to,' he admitted. 'It turns out she's the *real* one that got away. I was too scared to commit before, but since we split up I think about her every moment of every day.' He didn't look happy with the admission that followed. 'I love her.'

I smiled. 'That's great.' I tried to ignore the fact that *my* brain thought about Fraser all the time.

Oh shit! He would be worrying because I'd promised to text when I was at home. I pulled out my phone.

Ezra picked me up. We're having hot chocolate at his. After a moment's thought I added, *As friends.* I hit send before I could second-guess myself.

Moments later Fraser replied, *I'm glad you're safe. And you don't owe me any explanations.*

And yet, I kind of do. Ez and I are friends, and I needed a friend after the revelations tonight.

'Texting Fraser?' Ezra asked as he poured the hot chocolate into mugs.

'Yeah.'

'You're smiling.' He was right; without any conscious thought, I was smiling dopily at the phone. 'You've got it bad,' he teased.

I sighed. 'So it would seem.'

'You said you had a lot going on. What else is bothering you?' Ezra asked. 'Not that that's not enough,' he added hastily as he sprayed whipped cream into our mugs then decorated the chocolate with mini marshmallows.

Tears pricked my eyes as I watched him choose the pink ones for me. My friends knew me so well; how the hell had I ever walked away from this caring man whose heart was at least as big as his biceps?

'You always have marshmallows?' I asked faintly.

'I always keep them in case you ever came back and needed them.'

‘Seriously?’

‘I needed to believe you’d come back one day and I wanted you to know you’ve always got a safe place here.’

His affection and quiet adoration were a balm to my soul. If Ezra loved and believed in me so much, things would definitely get better.

‘I know it’s only as a friend, but I do love you,’ I said. ‘You know that, don’t you?’

‘I do. And there’s nothing “only” about having a friend like you.’

He pulled me into a hug and for a moment I feared I’d get the same overwhelming flashes I’d had before – but that wasn’t what I got. Instead I was met with that same warmth and sense of safety; it was a wonderful place to be.

He drew back. ‘You’re tense. What else is bothering you?’

‘To be honest, something hinky is going on with my magic,’ I admitted. ‘Something new. For the first time in my life, I actually have some power.’

‘Seriously?’

I nodded. ‘My empath skills keep getting stronger, but it’s more than that. I can...’ I hesitated. ‘I can see things when I touch people.’

His eyes widened. ‘Dead people?’

I hit him. *The Sixth Sense* had been one of our favourite movies. He laughed. 'Okay, sorry. But seriously? Like visions or memories, or their thoughts?'

'I'm not sure.'

'Could you do it to me?' he asked, intrigued. 'Did anything happen when we hugged?'

'No, but I wasn't trying.'

'Okay, try again. I'm thinking of a colour. What is it?'

'It doesn't work like that!' At least, I didn't think it did.

'How do you know? If you want to test your powers, try them on me. Go on – I'm thinking of a number and a colour. Touch me and tell me what you can see.'

I wasn't sure I wanted to, but he was right: I needed to practise somewhere safe with someone I trusted, and that would be either Ez or Maddie. She was out of commission because of the whole accidental dark-magic thing, so that left the man standing in front of me.

'Fine.' I took a deep breath and placed my hand on top of his.

'Well? What is it?' he asked eagerly. 'Can you tell what they are?'

I couldn't, but then I'd had my empath barrier fully raised because I was desperate not to have my emotions or thoughts affected by Fraser's. As I focused on Ezra, I loosened it a fraction – and experienced a massive surge of excitement. Had I not known I was standing in front of Ezra, I could have believed it was Eva's emotions I was reading: there was the same unbridled optimism and pure good will. But as for colours or numbers, I couldn't see a damned thing, and there certainly weren't any flashing images like the ones I'd experienced with both Kaz and Fraser.

'Nothing.' I pulled my hand away. 'I didn't get anything other than your excitement.'

'Is that good or bad?' he asked.

'I don't know because I've no idea how this works. The only person I can talk to about it is Ernie Jacobson. I don't know if Maddie told you anything about my relationship with him, but it's complicated.' In for a penny, in for a pound. I took a deep breath. 'It turns out he's my dad's father – my grandfather. And he's been living here in Witchlight Cove for years, knowing that I exist and making no attempt to look for me.'

Ezra's outrage hit me, outrage aimed at Ernie. 'Are you kidding me?'

'I guess I'm not being entirely fair. He said he looked but he couldn't find me – it was as if I'd been blocked from his view. So he gave up and waited for me to come home.'

'Shit, Trixie – that's crazy. How do you feel about it?'

'Honestly? I don't have a clue. I'm hurt he gave up so easily, excited I could have some family to love, scared that he'll die.' I sniffed. 'And there's a lot more going on that is hard to deal with. I'm trying to prove Sonny is innocent – and my magic is haywire. I'm a bit of a mess,' I confessed.

Ezra's expression was grave. 'What is it?' I asked, concerned.

'You need another witch,' he said. 'Someone you can trust to talk with about your powers.'

'None of the covens want anything to do with me.'

'It doesn't have to be a full coven, does it? A single powerful witch might be enough to help you?'

'Other than my grandfather, I don't know one who would help.'

'You don't, but I do. I think I know just the person you need.'

Chapter Twenty-Seven

I shouldn't have been surprised to find Maddie waiting up for me. The moment I turned my key in the lock, she ran to the door and flung it open. 'Thank God you're back,' she said, wrapping her arms around me.

Again, I braced myself for a vision to hit me but there was nothing. No flashes of memory, no images from inside her head, nothing. It was just ... normal. The tension slid off me and I let myself enjoy the hug; it was a long time since hugs had been a normal part of life.

Finally she drew back and searched my face. 'How did it go? Are you okay? Are you married?'

'I'm sorry I took so long,' I apologised. 'It was all a bit much and afterwards I went back to Ezra's house to talk.'

Her eyes widened. 'And did you and Ezra...' I swear she almost leered.

'Knock it off, Mads,' I huffed. 'Neither Ezra nor I want anything more than friendship. He's in love with Nour.'

She clapped her hands excitedly. 'I *knew* it! I *knew* he just needed to see you to realise that you weren't his soulmate.'

'Hey!' I objected. 'So this whole time you were trying to push us together—'

She interrupted, 'So he'd realise Nour was the one for him? Yes! I'm an absolute genius.' She did a happy dance.

'An evil genius,' I shot back and she froze mid-boogie. 'Sorry!' I blurted. 'I didn't mean it like that! I just mean you're cunning, like Baldrick from *Blackadder*.' Ugh, foot into mouth. I hadn't meant to refer to her accidental use of dark magic.

She relaxed, although the happy dancing was over. 'I know you didn't. Anyway what about you and Fraser? Are you hitched?'

'It's not quite that simple.' I went into the kitchen and opened up a pizza box: cold pizza was better than no pizza at all. Between mouthfuls of soggy pepperoni, I relayed everything Fraser told me.

'So he can't be with anybody else?' Maddie exclaimed. 'But that's insane.'

'Apparently not.'

'How does that work? Will he not be attracted to anyone else?'

'I didn't ask the technical details. It was a lot to take in.'

'No wonder. It has to have reopened a wound for you.'

I blinked. 'How so?'

'You left here for a similar reason – your parents took away your free will. They didn't give you a choice when they gave up their lives for you, and to live with that guilt you detached yourself from society and avoided forming any new bonds so it couldn't happen again. But now it has – you'd only just started to like Fraser and now you're bonded without your consent. That's a lot to unpack. I can see why you'd struggle to wrap your head around it.'

I was absolutely floored; my best friend had psychoanalysed me and she was absolutely spot on. 'When did you get so insightful?' I asked finally.

'Oh, you know me.' She laughed and dodged the question. 'But judging from what Fraser said this will be tough for both of you, so have some patience, okay? And that means with yourself as well as him – you need to cut yourself some slack. You're completely justified in needing some time to get used to what has happened and if Fraser is half the man I think he is, he'll understand that.'

'I'm sorry,' I said, almost as stunned by her final comment as her previous Oscar-worthy speech. 'Did you just compliment Fraser Banks?'

She smiled slightly. 'What can I say? He saved my bestie, so he can't be all bad. Also, I'm shattered and my brain is obviously addled with tiredness. I'm sure I'll be back to insulting him in the morning.'

'Thank goodness,' I laughed and picked up another slice of pizza. 'Are you having any more?' I said, nodding at the box.

'No. Like I said, I'm exhausted. I'm going to head for my bed.'

'Thank you for waiting up for me,' I said softly. 'And I'm sorry for leaving you to worry.'

'You came back. That's what matters.'

My conscience pricked again as I thought about Ezra's words earlier that night.

As Maddie hugged me goodnight, I held her slightly longer than normal. Once again no visions struck, and I wasn't sure if I was relieved or disappointed. 'See you early in the morning,' I said when we broke apart. 'I'll come down to the police station.'

'To interview your suspect?'

'Client – he's a client.'

'Whatever. If you get up early enough, we can walk in together.' As soon as she finished the sentence, she snorted with laughter.

'It could happen!' I protested.

'We both know it won't. I'll see you when you stroll in at 10am.'

'I could be earlier! I've got a furry alarm clock these days. I'm sure I won't be late.'

I am so good at famous last words.

In Eva's defence I probably shouldn't have relied on her to wake me, but she almost always had me up by 9am. Obviously, though, when I needed to be up early she slept in, probably because of her run to Ezra's house.

As I stretched and opened my eyes, I was surprised to see she was still curled up at the end of my bed with her grey bunny wrapped tightly in her arms and a soft snore whistling from her big doggy lips. A quick glance at my clock told me it was already 10.30am; Maddie must have left for work over an hour ago. Crap. She'd been right.

'Wakey, wakey, Eva.' I stroked her face gently. 'We've got a big day ahead of us. We're going to see Sonny, then apparently Ezra is going to introduce us to a witch who doesn't think I'm bad news. Let's see how *that* goes.'

Eva opened one eye and looked at me with an unusually surly expression. Either she hadn't wanted to be woken up, or she didn't believe a single witch in Witchlight Cove would be willing to help me. Maybe it was a bit of both.

I made a cup of instant coffee that wasn't a patch on a cup of joe from Sonny's. I needed to prove him innocent if only to get a decent caffeine fix again. Now the graffiti had been cleaned off, I suspected that Kaz would open the shop and I couldn't blame her. It was bad enough that Sonny was behind bars for something he hadn't done; there was no need for her to suffer too.

Which reminded me that I'd forgotten to mention the graffiti to Fraser the night before. As I walked to the station, I decided to send him a quick text. That was easier said than done; trying to get the tone right after everything that had happened between us took me half a dozen rewrites. Finally I wrote:

Hey, — I started the text casually – *I forgot to mention there was some graffiti at Sonny's, and Kaz thought some of the young water shifters could be behind it. Any chance you could look into? Thanks in advance. And thank you for everything else too. x*

That last sentence and the single kiss took me ten minutes to decide on, but I was happy with the final message. I hit the send button just as I stepped into the police station.

'Hey, Dove. Hey, Mads,' I said, as Eva jumped into her usual place on the row of seats in the waiting area. 'Any chance I can speak to the innocent man you've got locked up here?'

Dove rolled her eyes, though a slight chuckle escaped her. 'You'll have to wait, I'm afraid. He's got someone else in there with him.'

'He has?' I said nosily. 'Who?'

'Shady,' Maddie told me.

I nodded, pleased that he had come. From what I knew about the brothers and their relationship, I'd half expected him not to visit despite my request. I felt a flutter of nerves; Sonny had been so worried about how Shady would react when he learned about his relationship with Lorenz, and until that cat was out of the bag, I couldn't tell Yanni the truth.

'Is Yanni in there with them?' I asked casually. 'Have you heard any fighting?'

Dove shook her head. 'No, it's all been very quiet. Yanni's up at the Watchtower Hotel – the owner's a little twitchy about having the Nightshades staying there, so he asked if she'd pop in. He wanted her to make it look like a casual visit but remind the vampires that there is law enforcement in town.'

I understood his nervousness: I could imagine how I'd feel hosting a group of deadly vampires, particularly ones with *their* murderous skill set.

'So what happened to the early morning start?' Maddie flashed me a teasing grin. 'Some things never change – you're virtually nocturnal.'

She wasn't wrong. 'Eva didn't want to get out of bed.'

'I can't believe you're blaming her,' Maddie said with mock horror. 'Especially when she's the most perfect dog in the whole world. Aren't you, girl?' Eva lifted her head and beat her tail wildly. 'See? What did I tell you? She's faultless.' She blew kisses to my retriever, who promptly climbed off the chairs to collect some real ones.

Eva loved a fuss and I didn't blame her; I wouldn't have minded some kisses and attention myself, though from a certain dark-haired selkie who'd bound us together forever.

After everything that had happened, I still wanted him. I decided that there must be something very wrong with me.

'I went to great lengths making sure my dog wasn't spoilt – and then I moved here,' I faux-huffed.

Maddie's eyebrows rose so high they were almost lost in her hairline. 'I'm sorry. Did you just say you *didn't* spoil your dog? Are we talking about the dog who wouldn't sleep without her grey bunny?'

'That's different,' I protested.

She and Dove started laughing, but before they could say any more the door to the cells opened and out walked a smartly dressed vampire. I couldn't tell whether the reddish tint in his eyes was natural or if he'd been crying, but he looked a little overwhelmed. He drew in a deep breath as if needing to centre himself then gazed around the room. His expression tightened when his eyes landed on me. 'Are you Beatrix Stonehaven?' he demanded.

'Yes.'

He marched over, only stopping when he was less than a foot away from me; all it would have taken was a tilt of his head and his fangs would have landed squarely on my neck. He didn't look mad – but he was definitely close enough to kill me.

I tried to control the drumming in my chest by thinking through all the logical reasons why he *wouldn't* kill me. We were in a police station. There were witnesses and cameras and—

'Thank you,' he said, cutting my reasoning short. 'Thank you for calling me, thank you for believing in Sonny and thank you for taking his case. Just – thank you. If you ever need anything, you come to me. And I apologise for the manner in which I spoke to you on the phone.' He gave a quick bow.

Whilst I was still blinking, he whirled around and stalked out of the building with a flourish that would have gone well with a cape.

'What was that about?' Maddie asked.

My lips were sealed until Sonny confirmed I could reveal the truth, so I smiled vaguely. 'If you don't mind, I need to speak to my client now.'

As I went into the cell, my pulse was still on overdrive. Given that Shady was supposedly the brother with the *good* bedside manner, I figured he needed lessons on how to show gratitude to someone without them nearly peeing themselves with fear. I was going to say as much to Sonny, but when I looked into the cell I stopped abruptly.

His face was a vision of happiness and relief. It was the first time I'd seen him smile genuinely and not maliciously. 'So you spoke to your brother,' I said. 'What did you tell him?'

'Everything. I told him how difficult I found it being a different type of vampire to him, and how the only time I'd felt okay being myself was with Lorenz. I told him we were together but I couldn't let anyone know because I didn't want Shady to be even more ashamed of me.'

'And what did your brother say?'

He beamed. 'That I was a fucking idiot for thinking me being gay would stop him loving me. He doesn't care who I want to be with, he just wants me to be happy.' The smile faded. 'I wish Lorenz could have seen this and known my family would have accepted him. If only I'd proposed sooner.' He was trying hard not to cry.

After a few moments, Sonny cleared his throat. 'Shady said he hated how much I've struggled to be a vampire and that's why he gets cross around me. He's always felt angry at himself for not being able to help me more.'

'So you two are okay now?' I asked optimistically.

'Probably the best we've ever been. It's a damned shame I had to be in here accused of murdering the love of my life to get closer to my brother.'

'I know,' I said softly. 'Can I tell Yanni the truth about you and Lorenz?'

He nodded soberly. 'Yes. Hopefully the truth will set me free.'

Chapter Twenty-Eight

The truth didn't set Sonny free. I called Yanni and, although she was grateful for the information, she rightly pointed out that lovers killed each other all the time; if anything, Sonny's relationship with Lorenz made her more suspicious of him, not less. I hung up feeling frustrated and restless.

I texted Ezra to let him know I was free to meet his mysterious witch and he replied immediately that he would swing by and pick me up.

Unlike the previous night, he wasn't on his motorbike; instead he was driving a large 4x4 pickup. His dad had a tree-surgery business, Bentley's Bark & Bite Tree Care; judging from the tools in the back, Ezra still worked there when he wasn't embroiled in pack business.

'Are you sure this is a good idea?' I asked as Eva hopped into the footwell and I climbed in. 'Do you remember what the witches were like to me after my grandmother showed up?'

'I do, but this one thought they were being harsh. She didn't have much of a voice to say anything back then but she's older now, less afraid of speaking up.'

'How old *is* she? And what sort of witch is she?' I asked. 'How do you even know her?'

I sensed a nervousness radiating from Ezra as he glanced at me. 'I'm taking you to meet Nour,' he confessed.

'Nour who you love? That Nour?'

'How many Nours do you think I know?' he grumbled and I grinned at his discomfort. 'Don't mention that I still love her, okay? I need to find a way to make it up to her – I wasn't the best boyfriend at the end.'

'Will it be awkward?'

He shook his head. 'It's fine. We ended on good terms. She's great – I think you two will really get along. And she's happy to help. To answer your question, she's a light witch. We met while I was out on a run in human form.'

I could just imagine the scene: topless, sweaty Ezra running through the forest, a beautiful light witch casting rainbows around herself. No wonder he was head over heels in love with her.

'So she definitely won't try to kill me afterwards?' I asked, only half-joking.

'I trust her as much as I trust you.' I knew how much that meant, and I stopped teasing him.

The house he drove us to was in a small row of stone and slate cottages. There were no immediate witchy vibes, no smoke billowing from the chimneys or familiars strolling in the street, though I'd never experienced enough of coven life to know if any of those stereotypes rang true.

'Does the whole coven live on this street?' I asked. Nour might be happy to help me, but that didn't mean the rest of her family would be overjoyed to see a Stonehaven on the street.

'No. All sorts of magical beings living here,' Ezra replied. 'You don't need to worry – I used to come and go all the time. You've nothing to be afraid of.'

'I'm not afraid,' I replied instantly. Even so, Nour was a witch living away from her coven and I didn't know if that was good news or not. However, Ezra trusted her – loved her – and for now that was more than enough for me.

When he knocked once on the door, the most beautiful girl opened it. 'Wow,' I muttered under my breath.

I wasn't sure what I'd expected from Ezra's ex-girlfriend, but it wasn't this. She was a little shorter than me – and much more curvaceous. Her dark hair fell in gentle waves around her jawline. Her nose was pierced, as were her eyebrows, and she had several studs running up her ears. Her fingers were covered in rings, and gold bangles adorned her arms. She was totally intimidating.

'Thanks for doing this, Nour.' Ezra gave her a lopsided grin.

'Don't be silly, it's fine. I'm honoured to get the chance to meet the amazing Trixie.' She gave me a warm grin. 'He used to talk about you non-stop.'

The tips of Ezra's ears turned red. 'I did *not*,' he protested.

'He did.' Nour winked at me. 'Don't worry, I won't embarrass you by telling her some of the stories from the time when she was gone.' Her grin widened. 'Or maybe just one or two of the good ones.'

With a look somewhere between amusement and anxiety, Ezra glanced back at me. 'On that slightly terrifying note, I'll leave you two to get acquainted. Give me a ring when you need picking up, Trix. I'm not going far.'

'Thank you,' I said. Eva was sitting at my heel, waiting for instructions. 'Are you alright if I bring my dog in?' I asked Nour. 'She can go with Ezra if you're not comfortable with her.'

'No, it's fine. I'm assuming she has a strong bond with you?'

'An incredible bond,' Ezra replied for me.

'In that case, she's very welcome.'

'Thank you.' I followed Nour inside and threw a quick goodbye glance over my shoulder at Ezra before the door closed. Fingers crossed, Ezra was right that I could trust her, otherwise I was about to find myself in a whole heap of trouble.

When I'd learned Nour was a light witch, I'd envisioned her home as having lots of mirrors and crystals; my mum had loved her mirrors and crystals. I'd imagined twinkling fairy-lights, and definitely hundreds of candles with aromas so thick and heavy they made it difficult to breathe.

Nour's home was nothing like that. The space was clean and filled with the aroma of baking from the kitchen. Yes, there were a couple of mirrors and crystals, but that was all. It looked like a well-kept, non-magical house.

'Can I get you a drink?' she enquired solicitously. 'I was just about to make a peppermint tea.'

'That would be great.' I followed her into the kitchen.

She definitely had her life more organised than I did; I could tell that from the tidy shelves and the to-do list pinned on a board beside her fridge.

'Does the rest of your coven live close by?' I asked to break the silence that had fallen as she bustled around the kitchen.

'No. I moved away from them. Technically they're still my coven and they still call me when they need me, but they didn't take too well to me dating a potential alpha wolf.'

'They didn't like you dating Ezra?' I had barely wrapped my brain around the idea that he was a beta; imagining him stepping into his father's shoes was impossible.

'They were worried that a werewolf husband would weaken our witch bloodline.' Her tone was matter of fact as she filled the kettle, then her expression turned grim. 'They tried to put spells on us to keep us apart.'

'I'm so sorry,' I exclaimed, genuinely shocked. 'That's awful.'

'It is.' She flashed me a tight smile. 'My sisters and I still get on – as much as you can when they've done something like that to you. And I have a good life now. I didn't realise how hectic coven life was until I moved away. It's peaceful here and I value that.'

I didn't think I'd have a kind word to say about anyone who tried to keep me and the person I loved apart. Immediately an image of Fraser rose in my mind, and for once it wasn't of him walking topless out of the sea.

I refocused on Nour. 'You didn't go back to the coven when ... you know?'

'When Ez and I broke up?' She shook her head. 'No. The move out wasn't really about him, it was about them. I realised that I didn't align with their beliefs anymore – maybe I never did. It was hard to step away but I'm glad I did. It was a toxic environment.'

She handed me a steaming cup of peppermint tea. 'Shall we sit in the living room? It's more comfortable in there. Then you can tell me what the problem is.'

I gathered that she wanted the conversation to move on from her and Ezra, which was fair enough. She was doing me a favour and the last thing I wanted was for her to feel that I was interrogating her about her love life. Her family had clearly done more than enough of that.

I shot Eva a look as I followed Nour into the living room and sat down, but I could tell she already knew: this was *not* the type of house where you were allowed to jump on the sofa. She shot me a begrudging look but curled up by my feet.

'Ezra said it's a problem with your magic,' Nour started.

'Kind of. The thing is, I don't usually *have* much magic.'

'What about the Eternal Flame magic?' she said. 'Can't you use that?'

'I've never been able to access it,' I admitted. There was no point in lying: Nour could only help me if I told her the truth, and it might set a few things straight with the older witches in her coven if she repeated what I told her.

'I *should* be able to,' I added. 'My mum was the Guardian, so technically I should be able to use it, but my powers never manifested properly except for weak empath skills. But recently, stranger – *stronger* – things have happened. I've had visions when I've touched a couple of people, though the experience isn't consistent.'

Nour nodded thoughtfully. 'When did the visions start?'

'In the last couple of days.' I hesitated. 'I nearly died, and I was saved by magic. I don't know if that has something to do with it.'

'What kind of magic saved you?'

I didn't know how to answer. No doubt that Nour would know exactly what a Selkie gifting his pelt meant. I suddenly realised that Yanni knew and that was why she'd been so cross with Fraser when he'd dragged me out of the water, why she'd asked me several times if I was okay and if I'd spoken to him yet.

I trusted Yanni, Maddie and Ezra – but could I trust Nour with the information? But if I wanted help, I couldn't lie. 'It was a selkie's pelt,' I admitted

'A selkie's pelt?' She blinked. 'Are you saying a selkie *gave* you his coat?'

'Yes – otherwise I would have died.'

'That's ... huge.'

'Yup.'

I sensed that she had a hundred questions whirring around her head but she didn't ask any of them; instead, she stuck to the task at hand. 'In terms of magic, a selkie's coat is incredibly strong.'

'Do you think that's why I'm getting these visions?' I asked anxiously. 'Do you think that's why my magic is getting stronger?'

'It could be. Let me see what I can find out. I'd like to do some magic on you, if that's okay.'

'Sure,' I said, trying to sound less nervous than I felt.

She smiled warmly and my tension eased a fraction. It was easy to see why Ezra had fallen for her; there was something incredibly calming about her presence as if she not only used light but projected it. 'What do you do exactly?' I asked. 'Light candles and chant?'

'That sort of thing,' she agreed. 'I'd like to take you into the garden and perform a couple of incantations. Obviously, the sun is our greatest source of light so I try to use it when I can.'

'Incantations involving me?' The nerves were back.

'When I'm performing the spells, I'll mostly be looking at how the sun reflects on your energy.'

'Okay, that sounds painless.'

'It is – or at least it should be,' she amended.

I really wished she hadn't qualified that.

Chapter Twenty-Nine

With Eva on my heels, I followed Nour to an area in the garden that she had already prepared. The pile of blankets and cushions were surrounded by crystals and mirrors that seemed to focus the sunlight directly onto me.

As I lay down, I instantly felt a charge in the air; although it was substantially weaker, it reminded me of the feeling I used to get around the Eternal Flame.

'I'm not making any promises,' she said. 'Every case is different, and obviously I don't have the bank of knowledge that I'd have if I was still with my coven.'

'Trust me – the fact that you can do this magic in any form is incredible,' I said.

'Just close your eyes and try to relax,' she told me.

'Right. Close my eyes and relax,' I repeated. I managed the first part of her request easily enough, but relax? It was hard to stop my thoughts from spiralling. What if this was a mistake? What if this destroyed the smidgen of magic I possessed?

Clenching my eyes as tightly as I could, I inhaled deeply and tried to settle. I could feel Nour moving around me and the sweet, soothing scent of incense filled the air. I felt safe around her, Eva felt safe around her and Ezra *loved* her. That was enough.

She was chanting, and at first her voice was so soft that it was almost too low to hear as it blended into the rustling of the trees. From beneath my closed eyelids, I felt the light changing, brightening then dimming, as if someone were moving a torch in front of me. There were colours flashing, too: purples, yellows and greens, just like I used to see in the Eternal Flame.

As I lay there, a tingling spread along my skin and it seemed to grow warmer with my every breath. At first it was a comfortable warmth, like the sun on a clear summer's day, but it didn't stop. I was too hot, way too hot. I was reaching the point where I needed to say something – but before I could, the images started.

Like before, these were images from the past but there was one clear difference: these images were *mine*. As I fought against the heat that was burning my arms and legs, I saw Mum and Dad in the garden, laughing as I swung between their arms. I was only about five or six years old.

Then there was another flash and I was sitting on Dad's lap as we looked at some of the books in the library. I must have been about four years old – I could recognise the occasional word but nothing more.

Each flash took me further back. Some memories were too old for me to remember—my dad hoisting me onto his shoulders, my mum rocking me to sleep in her arms – but they were all were filled with the same emotions: love and contentment.

The heat was so strong now that my muscles were shaking but I didn't want to stop. The images filled me with such joy. I had desperately missed seeing my parents and I didn't care if my body burned to a cinder if I got to steal these moments with them.

The heat intensified: whatever this next image was, it would be important.

As the flashback took me to the next scene, the feeling of love and contentment was gone. Something far darker had taken control: fear.

I was a newborn, laying in a crib and staring up at my parents. It wasn't love I could feel at that moment; it was paralysing terror. I could see it on their faces.

'We have to, Iris,' Dad said firmly, though regret coloured his tone. 'It's the only way to keep her safe.'

My body was on fire, but I couldn't stop. I had just heard my father's voice for the first time in a decade and I needed to hear my mother's too. I'd happily burn for it if I could hear her voice one more time.

A heartbeat later, I got my wish. 'At some point, we'll need to tell her,' Mum said, her voice laced with pain and guilt despite being as gentle as I remembered it. As my parents looked at each other in silence, I knew that hearing and seeing them again this one time would never be enough. I wanted to hear them again – *needed* to hear them again.

But the pain was taking over. I was on fire and I would surely die. 'Ahhhh!' The scream tore from my throat as I bolted upright.

The pain was gone instantly – but so were my parents.

Tears were streaming down my face. I had been so close to them only a second before and now they were lost to me again.

That realisation hurt more than the pain of the spell, and I sobbed my heart out.

'Beatrix! Beatrix, can you hear me? Are you okay? Talk to me!' Nour's voice was panicked, and I didn't blame her. This had been one cluster-fuck.

I felt her arms around me then she slid a pillow beneath my head. A grunting sound that may or may not have sounded like 'yes' came from my throat. 'Thank Hecate!' she breathed. 'I'll be one second. Don't move.'

As if I could. Next to me, Eva whined and dug her nose into my shoulder. My mind was still spinning, trying to make sense of everything I had just experienced. The heat had gone completely, leaving me shivering instead, but at least I wasn't still struggling with searing pain. That was something.

My phone blared into life: Fraser. I swiped to answer and brought the phone carefully to my ear. 'Beatrix! Are you okay? I felt pain!'

His voice soothed something in me even as I registered his panic. 'I'm fine,' I murmured. 'Some magic went astray.' I raised a heavy hand to stroke Eva's head.

'Tell me where you are,' he demanded. 'I'll bring my pelt to heal you.'

'No, I'm okay,' I said. 'You don't need to freak out.' I wished my voice wasn't quite so wobbly.

'I felt your pain!'

'It was temporary – it's already fading.' Which it was, thankfully. 'I'm fine.'

'You're not fine,' he growled. 'But I'm trying so damned hard to respect your privacy and your boundaries.' He released a harsh breath. 'Tell me again that you're okay.'

'I'm okay, Fraser,' I repeated, and this time my voice was firmer.

'All right. Call me if you need anything and I'll be there.'

He hung up before I could respond. Oh boy. I slid my eyes closed and did some deep breathing.

Nour bustled back to me. 'Okay, Beatrix, can you sit up?' She was standing over me, her face creased with concern.

'Sure,' I said, lying through my teeth.

'Take your time. I've got you.' As I inched myself upwards, she slipped an arm around me to help me sit up, then handed me a glass. 'Drink this,' she ordered.

I stared at the concoction. The tumbler was filled with black liquid in which thousands of small bubbles were hastily rising to the top. It looked gross. 'What is it?' I asked. 'Is it… Is it some kind of potion?'

She grinned. 'No, it's Coke. It's all I had, other than water. Have a sip – the sugar will help.'

It probably said something about my life that I assumed any liquid handed to me was some kind of mystic potion – but there again, Coke was pretty magical in my book.

My throat was dry and even though the heat in my body had faded, the memory of it hadn't so I was grateful for something cooling. When I finished sipping, Nour took the glass and set it aside. 'I take it that was another vision?'

she said. I nodded. 'And do they always happen like that?' she pressed.

I shook my head. 'God, no! I fainted once before but there was nothing like this. And it's always different because… because…'

I trailed off as the images I'd seen of my parents resurfaced. One in particular stood out, the first one of me swinging between their hands. There had been so much love in that vision.

'What was it?' Nour asked gently. 'What was different?'

'This time, it was me,' I said. '*My* memories. Normally when I touch someone I see visions from *their* lives from their perspective, but this was me. And it went all the way back to when I was really young. I was with my parents, and I kept getting younger and younger until – until…'

The last image resurfaced and I saw the fear on my parents' faces as they whispered over my crib.

'Beatrix,' Nour said softly. 'What is it? Did you see something? Did your parents do something to you when you were very small? Something that scared you?'

'Why would you say that?' I asked slowly. 'What did *you* see?'

She bit down on her bottom lip, worrying it with her teeth. 'I saw a lot of magical light coming from you,' she said finally. 'But it wasn't like it normally is with witches.

Usually when I see their magic, it's as an aura around them and light coming from every part of them. Yours is different.'

'How do you mean different?'

'It was there, but it was being covered by something like a shell. A very old shell, almost as old as you. But it's cracking – there were rifts in it that were letting your magic seep through.'

I went cold. I thought I knew the answer, but I needed her to say it. 'Which means what, Nour?'

She paused and looked at Eva, the way I often did when I needed the courage to tell someone something difficult. Slowly she drew a deep breath, and when she looked at me again her eyes were filled with such deep pity I felt almost sorry for her. But I knew that I was the one who needed sympathy.

'I think you already know what I believe I saw, Beatrix,' she said quietly. 'I think you saw the same thing.'

I wanted to tell her she was wrong, that I didn't know what she was implying, but I *did* know and it burned in my chest like the pain of heat that had only just faded.

'My parents... They placed a bind on my magic, didn't they?' I whispered, feeling a different type of heat behind my eyes. 'They bound me when I was young and made me think I was powerless.'

She nodded, her eyes still so horribly sympathetic. 'I believe so, yes.'

I didn't need to ask why because I knew. Dahlia fucking Bleakman. My grandmother.

Dad had always been cautious with his magic and, until the day he'd died, I'd assumed he wasn't powerful. But he hadn't been weak, he'd been *careful.* He could never have expected a child not to use their magic – it would have been better to ask a bird not to fly – so instead my parents had clipped my wings and grounded me to keep me hidden from my grandmother.

But all the same, she'd found me.

Nour stayed silent for a long time to let me process it in my own way. She sat by me, a hand placed gently on my arm to comfort me. It was obvious why Ezra had fallen for this woman: her compassion knew no bounds.

Finally, she spoke. 'I suspect the selkie's magic broke the bind. It healed *all* of you. Gifting the coat is hugely powerful, and I think its magic has let your birthright powers break through in the way they always should have done.'

'So what do I do now?'

'Do you want to be re-bound?' she asked.

'No,' I said instantly. 'No!' I'd wanted my magic my whole life. I'd been a dud for so long that having magic –

proper magic – would be an absolute gift. 'No, I want to be magical. I was *meant* to be magical.'

'Then it's a case of giving it time and waiting to see how it goes. The cracks are widening, the bind is breaking and soon it will shatter and fall away. But I'll tell you this much, Beatrix – from what I saw of the magic seeping through those cracks, there's a lot of it. I've never seen such a bright light – and that was with the shell covering you. Your parents may well have bound you because you are a very powerful witch. Very powerful indeed.'

Chapter Thirty

I'd dreamed about having proper magical powers for so long that I should have been excited by Nour's words but instead pure terror was coursing through me.

'You won't tell anybody, will you?' I asked anxiously. 'I need to work out what the hell is going on before I tell anyone.'

'I promise,' she said softly. 'I won't tell a soul, not even Ezra. I know you don't know me, but you can trust me. I always do my best to be a good person – and anyway, I'd never do anything to upset someone who is clearly so dear to Ezra.'

There was a wistfulness in her tone that made me feel hopeful for him. Maybe they would reconcile. I desperately needed to move the focus off myself, so I asked, 'What happened to you two?' I asked. 'He told me you dated for a while.'

'"Dated for a while"?' She gave a low whistle and shook her head. 'That's one way to describe the last four years of our lives.'

'Four years?'

'He didn't tell you that? Despite the time we were together, I always had the feeling that he wasn't quite all in and a part of him was still holding out for someone else.' There was no anger in her voice, just sadness, though her glance at me was pointed.

I winced. 'I love Ezra, but not in that way. He's my friend and I hope that I am his – and I think seeing me again has put to bed any teenage crush he may have had. I think you'd find now that he'd be all in.'

I hesitated. She deserved the truth and I knew Ezra wanted her back. I hoped a little more honesty would get them back on track. 'He told me he was dealing with some serious heartbreak and that you were "the right girl, wrong time".'

'He said that?' A glimmer of light shone in her eyes, only to be extinguished almost immediately. She sighed. 'I think it's too late now. I messed things up, got jealous. I don't know if you've seen many of the female werewolves he hangs out with, but those women are seriously hot, and they get the whole pack thing in a way that I never will. A witch dating a potential alpha might have been trouble for my coven, but a potential alpha dating a witch ... he was shooting himself in the foot by staying with me. Ending things was the right thing to do,' she said firmly.

So she'd left him because she didn't want him to miss out on his birthright even though she had already lost her family because she was dating him. If I hadn't already thought that Nour was a special person, now I knew it for sure.

'Who are you trying to convince?' I asked gently. 'Whatever there was between you, it's clearly still there. He thinks the world of you. He wouldn't have brought me to see you otherwise.'

She waved away the comment. 'He trusts me but that doesn't mean there's anything more to salvage between us.' She forced a smile. 'Anyway, you've got enough on your plate without matchmaking for me and Ezra. Let's sort you out first.'

She was right: getting the pair of them back together would be a great distraction but I had too much to deal with to be distracted, however much I might want to be. I sighed. 'I'm not sure how to handle this. It's not like I have a coven or family to talk it through with.'

I thought about Ernie, but we weren't at the 'sharing deep secrets' phase and it would take time for trust to grow between us. Besides, I wanted him to focus on Maddie; healing her was the priority.

'I can't imagine how hard it must be,' Nour said. 'At least I was still part of my coven when I got my powers. But you know I'm always here if you need me – and we only need one more witch. Three is a magic number and all that.'

I thought about that for a moment. 'Would you consider an alchemist as a type of witch? They *are* magic weavers.'

'Absolutely.'

I felt a flutter of excitement in my belly. 'Then maybe we should think about forming our own little coven with Maddie. I'm sure you must have met her.'

'Maddie?' She gave a wide smile. 'Yes, a few times. She's great.'

'She is – and we live together. Even if we can't form a coven, you could come over one night for a glass of wine.'

'A coven with wine.' Nour grinned. 'I'm liking the sound of this more and more.'

I grinned back and quietly ignored the warning voice that told me I shouldn't be putting down roots.

In some ways it had been a productive and positive session. I had discovered a lot about myself, like why I'd never had proper powers. I'd also learned that these visions weren't just some sporadic glitch but my own birth-given magic finally manifesting – and I might even have formed a new coven. But there had been a lot of darkness, too. My parents had been complicit in me having no power and they'd lied to me about it.

What with the bond to Fraser and Sonny's case to solve, I didn't have the head space to unpack it all, so I shoved the shit about my magic into a box in my mind and pushed it away. It would be Tomorrow Beatrix's problem.

'How did it go?' Ezra asked as I climbed into his car.

'Good!' I said. 'She was a great help – and I like her a lot.' I slid him a sidelong glance and embraced my meddling heart. 'She's obviously still crazy about you. You know that she ended things because she thought it would be best for you if you became alpha?'

Ezra groaned. 'I know, and I could see her point. Not that I didn't want her beside me, but it's a big commitment for anyone to become the beta's wife let alone the alpha's. My mum found it hard and she's a bloody werewolf, so I can't imagine how a witch would deal with it. I didn't want Nour to chain herself to me when I come with so much baggage.'

'Don't you think it should be her choice? If she was willing to go with it, surely that was all that mattered?'

He stared out of the car window directly into Nour's house. Something made me think she was standing there behind the curtains staring back at him. 'Maybe. Anyway, we're not talking about that right now. I need to do some work. Can I drop you somewhere?'

'Do you happen to know where Julietta Cortez lives?'

He stared at me. 'As in the head of the vampire sect?'

'That's the one.'

I needed to follow leads, and that meant finding another vampire who might be responsible for killing Lorenz.

'Julietta is the local real estate queen,' Ezra replied slowly. 'She's got an agency at the other end of town.'

'Will she be working today?' It was just gone midday and the sun was high – definitely not ideal vampire time.

'If she's not, someone can tell you where to find her.'

'Right,' I said. 'In that case, can you drop me and Eva there?'

'Will do.' Ezra squeezed my hand. 'I won't pry, but I hope that Nour helped with whatever is going on with your powers.'

'She gave me some insight, which was useful,' I said cautiously. I didn't want to share any more than that right now, not when I wasn't sure what it meant. And I didn't want Ezra to think badly of my parents.

'I'm glad. Well, good luck with Julietta. Dad likes her.'

The fact that Mr Bentley liked her carried some weight with me because he was a good judge of character, but with my increasing powers I suspected I could rely on my own opinions.

When Ezra stopped outside the building, I was sure he was in the wrong place. Yes, it was at the end of the high street, but it certainly didn't look like an estate agency. One of the joys of living in London was staring in windows at photographs of houses I could never afford to buy or rent but this place didn't have any of those: the large windows showed an area that looked like a living room.

'This is an estate agency?' I asked dubiously.

'A luxury one,' Ezra replied. 'For the rich and famous only.'

'We have rich and famous in Witchlight?'

'Well, rich at least.'

I glanced at Eva. This definitely wasn't her type of place.

'I've got to go to work now,' Ezra said, 'but you know you can ring me any time day or night if you need me.'

I hugged him across the console. 'I know – and back at you. Thank you for everything. Come on, Eva.'

I opened the back door of the truck and she immediately jumped out, but rather than her paws landing quietly on the ground the way they normally did, there was a loud clattering.

'You have to be joking,' I said, looking at the key chain that had fallen on the pavement in front of me. I bent down and picked it up. There were half a dozen keys, together with a couple of novelty items including a glittery letter N.

'Eva! You stole Nour's keys? Why did you do that? We *like* Nour!'

Eva's tail wagged happily as Ezra glanced out of the window. 'You weren't joking – you really do have a kleptomaniac for a dog.'

'She's only a kleptomaniac when it comes to keys. Could you drop these back for me? And maybe take Nour a bottle of wine to say thank you – and sorry about her keys? I was going to do it later, but I'm not sure when I'll get a chance and she'll need these back ASAP.'

Ezra rolled his eyes but it was only in jest. 'I'll give her a ring and see if she needs them now. If not, I'll take them over this evening along with a bottle of Malbec. She's a red wine woman.'

No wonder he'd grabbed me a glass of red automatically at Lorenz's opening night. 'Thanks, Ezra.'

A moment later, he was driving away. I looked down at Eva. 'That was deliberate, wasn't it? You wanted him to go back there.' I had to admire her audacity. Fingers crossed Nour would ask Ezra to open the wine and share a glass with her. I was certain there was still a spark between them that just needed fanning, and apparently Eva thought the same.

'I'm afraid this is going to be a lead situation.' I bent down and clipped her lead to her collar. 'And no stealing keys here, okay? I'm not sure the head vampire would see the funny side of it.'

I was about to open the door, when it opened and a familiar man stepped out: Lestat. 'Hi again,' I said, giving the deadly assassin a friendly smile.

'Good day.' He was about to walk around me but I reached out to touch him. He looked pointedly at my hand on his forearm and I snatched it back.

'Do you have a minute?' I asked. 'I'd like to ask you a few questions.'

'About?'

'Lorenz Matheson's murder.'

He arched an elegant eyebrow. 'You're not the police.'

'No. I'm a PI. Beatrix Stonehaven.'

'Stonehaven.' He looked at me with renewed interest. 'And why, Beatrix Stonehaven, are you looking into Lorenz Matheson's murder?'

'Sonny's hired me to do so.'

He nodded. 'The vampire with the extraordinary coffee.'

'That's the one.'

Lestat studied me with his black eyes. 'And what do you want with me?'

'You and Vlad were at the club.'

'And since we're assassins, you want to accuse us of killing Lorenz?' His voice was unemotional.

'No,' I said firmly. 'But I want to speak to you both. Vlad was talking about wanting to kill freely.'

A brief smile touched Lestat's lips. 'Vlad is our administrative assistant. To my knowledge he has never killed a living thing, nor does he drink from the source – he prefers blood bags. He is the least violent vampire I have ever met, though he enjoys the prestige that comes from being part of the Order of the Nightshades.'

That married up with my impression of the soft, doughy blond. 'And you?' I asked.

He smiled. 'Oh, I kill people all the time.'

I swallowed. 'Did you kill Lorenz?'

His laugh sounded genuine. 'I enjoy your boldness, little rock. No, I did not kill Lorenz Matheson. I gave Chief Inspector Greenridge my alibi, and Shady's CCTV footage confirmed that both Vlad and I returned to his venue prior to Mr Matheson's death. All the Nightshades were present and correct when Lorenz was killed. Whoever killed your leader, it wasn't us.' He tipped an imaginary hat to me, 'Good day, Miss Stonehaven.' This time I let him step around me.

If what he said was true, I suddenly didn't feel so good about Sonny's odds. If the killer wasn't part of the Nightshades – and I wasn't taking Lestat's word for that – then it had to be a local vamp, someone known to Julietta.

I opened the door to the estate agency. Although there was no jingling bell or annoying under-mat buzzer to announce me, a tall woman appeared in front of me almost immediately. She scanned me up and down and her nose crinkled slightly.

'Can I help you?' she asked. There was an implied 'What are you doing here?' as if she thought I was lost. Apparently no one who looked like me could be in the market for a luxury home. I looked down at my stained jeans; it was probably a fair assessment.

'I'm looking for Julietta,' I said.

'About?' she asked, tapping her toe. She was standing in the sunlight and her bare arms showing no hint of tattoos; from what I could see, she wasn't wearing any magical amulets either, so she wasn't a vampire. But she was definitely magical. Mermaid? Siren? I had no idea.

'It's private, actually,' I said.

'I'm afraid Julietta is very busy today,' she replied primly. 'If you leave your name and number, I'm sure she'll get back to you when she can.'

'I really need to speak to her,' I said. 'I'm happy to wait until she returns.'

'I'm afraid I don't know when that will be.' Her eyes fixed squarely on me, and I felt a strange tingling in the pit of my stomach.

From what I knew so far about my powers, they were definitely inclined to the more psychic side of things. Did that mean I could tell if someone was lying to me? Maybe if I touched her hand, I could find out more. I took a step forward, not entirely sure what I was planning to do, when a calm voice came from the back of the building. 'It's alright, Zara. Stonehaven and I have an appointment.'

Julietta was every bit as intimidating as I remembered from the previous night. Her perfect posture made me wonder if she'd been a ballerina. It would have made sense: turning into a cutthroat vampire leader should have been easy after the competition and pressure of the ballet world. You only needed to see the state of a dancer's feet to know that those women were tough as nails.

'Come into my office,' she said. 'I've been looking forward to talking to you.'

I couldn't help but feel that she was the spider and I was the fly. And I was stepping willingly into her web.

Chapter Thirty-One

Julietta Cortez had style, that was for sure. Just like the front of the building, the room I walked into didn't look anything like an office; it was more like a salon in a very expensive house. Sure, there was a large mahogany desk with a leather swivel chair, but there was also a comfy sofa. The walls were a deep green and several framed awards were displayed on one of them: *Realtor of the Year; Coastal Charm Real Estate Award; Property Pinnacle Award 2025.*

This was a woman who took her job seriously and I guessed she did the same when it came to running the vampire sect.

'A surprise visit by the selkie's mate,' she said. 'Tell me, Stonehaven, to what do I owe the pleasure?'

'Sorry?' I stammered, certain I'd misheard her.

'The leader of the water-shifter sect, Fraser Banks, the selkie – he gave you his coat, did he not? And by all the laws of magic, that makes you his mate.'

A surge of anger rushed through me. I hadn't imagined Fraser would choose to share *our* secret with the head vampire, especially not without mentioning it to me first. 'He told you that?' I demanded.

She laughed. 'No one *told* me.' She moved to a coffee machine and placed an espresso cup beneath it. 'You were rather loud last night when the leaders cleared out of Fraser's and I have this delightful vampire hearing.' She tapped her ears. 'It's useful to remember that. Secrets don't stay secret long in Witchlight Cove.'

My anger dispersed and a flood of embarrassment took its place. I'd waited until everyone was out of Fraser's house and the front door was closed before we'd started discussing matters, but Julietta could have been lurking around outside. Should I deny it? Was there any point? 'Well,' I began, 'it's... That situation, it's—'

'None of my business,' she interrupted smoothly. 'And I shouldn't have brought it up. I apologise. Unless, of course, you've come here to talk about a possible wedding venue?'

'No,' I said flatly. 'I'm not here to talk about wedding venues. I want to talk about Sonny. I don't think he killed Lorenz and I want to know if there are any other vampires who could have framed him. Does Sonny have enemies within your community?'

I thought for a second that she would refuse to answer my question but then she leaned back into her chair. 'Sonny's not your typical vampire, as I'm sure you're aware. There are many who frown upon his way of life.'

'Does that include you?' I asked.

One of her perfectly plucked eyebrows rose in an impressive arc. 'Surely you're not implying that I would wish to see one of my own kind behind a cell door?'

'No, of course not,' I said quickly. 'I'm just asking questions.'

'My job is to keep the peace. I've worked hard for many years to make sure that vampires are tolerant both of each other and the magical and non-magical creatures in Witchlight. This killing by a vampire goes against everything I have taught my people, so I find it difficult to believe one of them would be involved.'

'Do you think it's the Nightshades?' I asked. 'You think someone hired them to kill Lorenz?'

Her gaze was level. 'I certainly wouldn't accuse them of being involved.'

That didn't mean she didn't *think* they'd been involved. However, there was one gaping hole with the assassin theory: the Nightshades were reputed to be some of the best killers in the world who would complete a job without leaving a trace of their presence, so why would they need to frame Sonny? Why send that videotape? It seemed unnecessary, unless the murder was personal.

'Did Sonny have anything to do with the Nightshades?' I pressed. 'I know that Shady was hosting them for drinks.'

'Indeed,' Julietta replied. 'I see you've already eliminated the bar owner from your suspicions or you'd be questioning him more thoroughly.'

'I'm confident Shady wasn't behind it,' I said, even though I hadn't actually spoken to him other than that weird moment in the station after he'd seen his brother. But I'd gained the impression that he cared for Sonny deeply; he wouldn't have set him up like that.

I persisted. 'Back to my question. Do you know if Sonny had any connection to the Nightshades?' I pressed.

'You must ask him yourself, but I will say this – all the vampires here had very different lives before they came to Witchlight. Some were involved in dark, nefarious activities, others were struggling to make a living. I make it my business *not* to find out about their existence before they joined us, and I judge them solely on their behaviour in this village. I would hate to prejudice myself against them by knowing their past mistakes, and I would encourage you to do the same.'

'So you *could* have killers in your group? That's what you're telling me, isn't it?'

'We are vampires,' she said pointedly. 'We live by death. I expect that many of them have killed at some point but they know that to do so in Witchlight Cove would mean exile from the village, and I can't think of anyone who would take that prospect lightly.'

'Who do *you* think killed Lorenz?'

She shrugged. 'That is for Chief Inspector Greenridge to discover.'

'And if it *is* Sonny?'

'Then he will go to jail for a very long time.' Her voice was steely.

I stood up. 'Thank you for seeing me.' I paused. 'What was Lestat doing here?'

'The same as anyone who comes to an estate agent – he's thinking about buying a house.'

I blinked. 'Here?'

'Here.'

Huh. 'Thank you for your time, Julietta.'

She nodded and it was clear that I was dismissed.

I'd got as much as I could hope for, and the longer I stayed the greater the risk of Eva stealing something and deciding to make a chew toy out of it. I cleared my throat awkwardly. 'I also appreciate your discretion about what you overheard last night.'

She inclined her head. Weirdly, I trusted that she wouldn't go around blabbing the news about Fraser Bank's new mate. With a light tug on Eva's lead I prepared to leave, but then Julietta spoke again. 'Before you go, Miss Stonehaven,' she said, her voice softening slightly, 'I know it might be difficult for you to do, but if this were my investigation I would look at who has the most to gain from Lorenz's demise. Someone who wants to work their way up the ranks – and has already done so remarkably quickly.' Her gaze locked onto mine. 'Someone who was not born in Witchlight Cove becoming the leader of a sect within five years of moving here would raise my suspicions.'

I knew exactly what she was implying. 'Fraser was with me when Lorenz was murdered,' I said firmly.

'That doesn't mean he couldn't have hired someone.' Her eyebrow arched again. 'He's certainly rich enough. It's just something to think about. I'm sure you know what you're doing.'

Her smile widened; there was something about the twitch of her lips that made me think she didn't believe that at all.

Chapter Thirty-Two

Julietta was right: if I hadn't known Fraser and we hadn't been in this predicament, he would've been at the top of my suspect list. He had enough money and influence to hire the Nightshades to do his dirty work, plus he had a rock-solid alibi in that he'd been chatting with me and Maddie when Lorenz was killed.

But why would he frame Sonny? Fraser was one of the few people Sonny actually got along with, as much as he got along with anyone. Trying to think of Fraser as the killer felt like trying to fit a square peg in a round hole, but I needed to question him – and maybe talk to him some more about our bond. It had obviously connected us strongly enough for him to sense my pain and I needed to know how that worked.

It was still lunchtime so I didn't expect to find him at home. As I contemplated where the best place to look for him was, I realised I could use our bond to find him.

I already knew that if I thought about him strongly enough I'd get a vision of what he was doing as I had done the night after I was shot. Doing it now could save me from a lot of searching... Then I shoved the thought away; doing that would be an invasion of his privacy. Instead, I headed to the Smuggler's Rest.

Thankfully, the moment I opened the door I saw him standing beside the bar. When he turned, his eyes lit up with pleasure though I didn't miss the way he scanned me for signs of injury after the pain he'd felt from me earlier. 'Hey,' he said. 'Everything okay?' It was clear that he didn't know whether to greet me with a kiss or a hug; instead we settled on awkward smiles.

'I wondered if you wanted to come for a walk with me,' I said. 'There are a couple of questions I need to ask you – about the murder,' I added, so he didn't think they were about *us*.

He looked at me intently and for a moment I thought he'd refuse, but then he nodded. 'Let me tell the others and grab my coat.' He disappeared into the back of the restaurant then reappeared a few moments later with a coat and a cone of chips. 'Here.' He thrust the chips at me. 'You're hungry.'

I took them gratefully. 'I am.' The chips were salted to perfection and he'd even put a generous splodge of mayo on the side. 'How did you know I liked mayo rather than ketchup?'

'The same way I knew about the Oyster Bay – something told me and I listened.'

Once we were outside, he asked, 'What's going on? Is everything alright?'

I answered honestly. 'I had a problem with my magic but it's fine now. Let's focus on the case, okay?'

'Of course. I'm always here if you want to talk, though.' He cleared his throat. 'So, the case. Have you got any leads?'

'Not exactly.' I grimaced. 'None really. But it's possible that the Nightshades were involved, though they all claim to have been at Shady's when Lorenz died.'

'You don't believe them?'

'I find it hard to believe that a group with such a sterling reputation couldn't play with a timestamp to make it look like they were there when they weren't.'

Fraser nodded. 'I can see that.'

It was nice not to be automatically shot down the way Yanni would have done if I'd floated the theory by her. 'If they *were* involved, they were probably hired by someone who stood to gain from Lorenz's death.'

It took him less than a heartbeat to realise what I was saying. 'You mean me?' He looked amused.

'I have to ask—' I started.

'I understand. On the surface, it looks as if I profited from his death.'

'Not just on the surface, Fraser – you actually did. You're the leader now because Lorenz died.'

'I would have been the leader anyway. Lorenz was facing a lot of criticism after the mess with Gilbert Storcrest, and he and I had been in talks for months about me taking over from him. He wanted to step away and focus on his home life.'

I blinked. 'So you would have become the water-shifter leader anyway?'

'Yes. Lorenz was going to abdicate and support me taking over the position because there's no one else within our community with the same strengths and resources. I was a shoo-in, with or without his endorsement. If anything, his death has made the transition harder for me.' He eyed me. 'I'll prove it. Put your hand on my heart,' he instructed me.

'Sorry?' I stammered.

'Put your hand on my chest. You have visions when you touch me, don't you?'

'They're new,' I said, truthfully.

He nodded. 'If you use them with the bond, you should be able to tell if I'm lying or not.'

'Fraser—' I edged backwards.

'It doesn't mean you're accepting the bond,' he reassured me. 'It's just *there*. I'm sure you'll be able to feel whether I'm telling the truth or lying.'

My fingers tingled as if they were desperate to reach out and touch him, but it wasn't that simple. The last time I'd done this, I'd seen visions from his mind – and I'd also ended up flat on my back on his living-room floor. And that wasn't a bad experience compared to what had happened with Nour.

'I'm here,' he said gently, as though he were reading my thoughts. 'Nothing will go wrong. Focus on the question you want to ask me and you'll feel the truth.'

Was it cheating to use my magical powers to get an answer? I didn't see why: Yanni used her size to intimidate people, and no one called that cheating. Wolves used their speed to catch people, and that wasn't cheating either. This was just a skill I had; one I needed to learn to use. It was time to practise.

I took a deep breath, closed my eyes and prepared to place my hand on his chest.

'Sorry, I should take my jacket off first,' he muttered.

What? His jacket was unzipped so I could easily place my hand on his shirt – unless he meant I had to touch his bare skin.

'My pelt blocks magic,' he said, reading my confusion. 'The coat can do more than heal, it can stop a selkie from being bewitched or cursed. Amongst other things.'

'Such as?' I asked, both intrigued and keen to delay the whole touching-him-to-feel-his-innocence thing.

'If you're wearing it, a werewolf's bite won't affect you, and apparently it wards off a vampire's touch, though I've never seen that happen. I don't think it will interfere with what we're about to do, but I'll remove it to make sure. To be honest, now we're bonded you can do whatever you like to me and it wouldn't protect me.'

I knew he was talking about spells and magic, but my mind couldn't help wandering down a far earthier path. What would I want to do to Fraser Banks if I had the chance? There were so many, many things...

Realising that there was a real possibility he could read my thoughts – or at least my emotions – I cleared my throat. 'We should get started,' I said, trying to sound like I hadn't just been imagining him naked.

'Right.'

As he slipped off the pelt and slung it over his arm, a buzzing in my chest drew me closer to him. He held my eyes as he unfastened a couple of his shirt buttons.

I locked my eyes on his before drawing in a deep breath and placing my palm against his warm flesh.

Chapter Thirty-Three

The visions were similar to the ones I'd had previously in that they came in flashes, but unlike before I felt I was wielding control within them.

Did you kill Lorenz? I didn't need to speak the question aloud; I knew Fraser could hear me, or at least his subconscious could.

The reply came through loud and clear. *I swear on your life and mine that I didn't kill him.* There wasn't a flicker of uncertainty.

As I stayed there with my hand against his chest, another thought entered my mind.

I want to see the memory of the last time you were with Lorenz when he was alive.

This time, it wasn't a question: it was a demand. Straight away I felt his subconscious yielding; it didn't have a choice and it was going to show me what I wanted. In that moment, my power scared me.

A single flash took me to the bar with Lorenz in his dapper clothes greeting the guests at his opening event.

When he saw Fraser, his joviality faded a little. 'Banks.' His voice was stiff, formal. 'I appreciate you coming.'

'I wouldn't miss it.'

'My last hurrah before I hand you the reins,' Lorenz said tightly.

'We haven't worked out the details yet.'

'No, but it'll be soon. The pod is restless, dissatisfied with me. Don't think I don't know about Derek pressuring you to take over.'

'I'm not a man to bow to pressure,' Fraser growled back.

Lorenz laughed bitterly. 'No, but I am. I look forward to my life becoming easier.'

'Leadership can be a burden.'

'Damn right, and few people appreciate how hard it is juggling everyone's needs. Frankly, I'm ready to speed things up.'

'Noted. We can discuss it tomorrow.' Fraser looked around. 'You've done a good job here.'

'Coming from a property developer, that's a real compliment.' Someone across the room grabbed Lorenz's attention. 'I'm needed – I'd better go. Speak tomorrow.'

'Tomorrow,' Fraser agreed.

That was it: that was the last time Fraser had seen Lorenz. I no longer needed to rely on Fraser's word to believe him because I had seen it for myself.

I wanted the visions to end and they did; I'd cut the bond between us. A moment later I opened my eyes to find I was looking straight into Fraser's. I cleared my throat. 'Thank you. I believe you.'

He was too close and he was looking at me with a mixture of attraction and wonder that made my breathing hitch. I wanted to remove my hand from his chest but it felt like it was superglued there and removing it would hurt us both. The longer the moment went on, the more his eyes darkened. Wonder fell away from his gaze, leaving only stark, raw attraction.

Instead of pulling away from him, I ached to press my lips to his.

Moving slowly, giving me plenty of time to object, his hand slid under the back of my T-shirt and his fingers brushed the skin at the small of my back. He drew me gently towards him and lowered his lips to mine. I surged upwards to meet them.

Thankfully there were no visions; all I felt was him. I gave a low moan when his tongue touched my lips. The heady scent of him surrounded me and suddenly the smell of the ocean seemed heavy in the air, too. My other hand slipped up around his neck, pulling him against me.

Finally we drew apart and his gaze was instantly contrite. 'I'm sorry, I didn't mean that to happen. I didn't want to pressure you.'

I released him and put my hands on my hips. 'Don't tell me you regret that kiss!' I said indignantly.

He smiled slowly. ' I loved it – and I'd love to repeat it – but I was planning to go slowly. Slower than slow. Glacial, really.'

'Glacial is for ice, Fraser. I am not ice.'

'Not you're not,' he agreed. 'You're hot.'

My cheeks warmed. 'Thank you,' I responded awkwardly. I wasn't used to being called hot. 'Right, anyway. That was nice,' I mumbled.

'Nice?' He looked mildly affronted. 'If it was only *nice,* I didn't do it right.'

My blush intensified. 'It was better than nice.' It had sent a rush of blood to all the good places, but he didn't need to know that. I cleared my throat. 'You should get back to work.'

'Yes, I should, but I was wondering if you'd like to come round tonight? Not to be less glacial,' he added hastily, 'but to talk about the Eternal Flame. I found a couple of places where there might be one – you might want to check them out.'

A surge of excitement ran through me. He'd found something and that was *huge*. And spending a little more time with Fraser wouldn't be the worst thing in the world. 'I can come round for six? There's another lead I want to follow up this afternoon.'

'Six is fine,' Fraser replied. 'Can I ask what the lead is, or is it top secret?'

I laughed. 'Actually, it's not so much a lead as a hunch. I'm going to speak to the Nightshades.'

He looked alarmed. 'You've got to be joking, Beatrix!'

I narrowed my eyes. 'Do you have any right to tell me what I can and can't do?'

He heard the warning in my voice and winced. 'No, of course not. I'm not telling you what to do – but I'd worry about *anyone* going to see the Nightshades. They're assassins – *paid* killers!'

'I'm not paying them to kill *me*,' I said drily. 'But I need to find out if someone hired them, because right now they're the only suspects apart from Sonny. Julietta's convinced none of her vampires would've killed Lorenz.'

'Of course, though I'm pretty sure Lorenz said none of his shifters could be murderers either,' Fraser said, referring to Gilbert.

It was a good point but I chose to ignore it. 'I'm not going to do anything to aggravate them,' I assured him.

His expression didn't soften. 'Let me come with you,' he said after a moment. 'At least let me wait outside.'

'I'll be fine,' I insisted. 'I'll have Eva. And I've been a PI for a long time.'

'In the non-magical world,' he pointed out, his concern evident.

'Where I dealt with demons and crazed elves and all sorts that you wouldn't believe. Look, I don't tell you how to run your businesses, and I'd appreciate it if you did me the same courtesy.'

I could see straight away that those words had stung and I felt a little bad. It was clear that Fraser respected me – he'd already shown that – but I needed him to back off. Thankfully my words finally did the job.

'I'm just worried, that's all. Can you call me after you've met them so I know you're alright?'

'You'll know I'm alright because I'm coming to your house, remember?'

'That's in five hours and I'll be in knots by then. Please, Bea. Do this for me?'

He was genuinely distressed at the idea of me going alone to see the Nightshades, so I nodded. 'Fine.'

'Do you know where they're staying?'

'Up at the Watchtower Hotel. One of them came into the station to let Yanni know they'd arrived in town so I'm assuming they're still there.'

'I think they are. Just ... be safe, okay? I care about you, Beatrix Stonehaven.'

The last vestiges of my anger fell away. He cared about me. I smiled. 'Don't worry about me,' I said firmly. 'I'll be fine, I'll text you afterwards and I'll see you this evening.'

Before I could think about it, I reached up on my tiptoes and kissed him on the cheek. I loved the feeling of his stubble against my lips, and it was hard not to go back for more. 'I'll see you later,' I called as I hurried away with Eva at my side.

Chapter Thirty-Four

The Watchtower Hotel was a misleading name because it wasn't a single tower but four; it looked like an ancient fort or castle. It had been built for the first vampire who'd lived in Witchlight Cove so it made sense that the Nightshades would choose to stay there, though I couldn't remember the last time one of the undead had actually owned it.

It had been a hotel for as long as I could remember and I'd been there as a child for school fayres and dances, not to mention the annual Witches' Conference where every witch from every coven in Witchlight came together. As I approached it, the thought of those times made me uneasy. We'd needed the space back then because there were so many witches; if the Nightshades had booked the whole place ... exactly how many of them were there?

Whatever: I only needed to speak to the most senior among them and that would be Vlad's Candy – or Candice, as the more diplomatic called her.

Given that my car was still in London and Eva needed a decent walk, we trekked the three miles around the outskirts of the village. The closer we got to the hotel, the slower Eva's pace became and I didn't think it was because she was getting tired. She knew what was inside that building and wasn't keen on spending her afternoon in a building with a load of trained killers. I could relate.

When we arrived at the door she sat down and refused to move no matter how hard I tugged at her lead. 'Come on, girl,' I said. 'The quicker we get in, the quicker we can get out.'

Eva whined softly. 'It's alright,' I said. 'It's still daylight. Worst-case scenario, we run outside if things get scary.'

Assuming they don't have daylight wards tattooed on them, I thought grimly, though I didn't voice my concerns to Eva.

She still didn't move so finally I unclipped her lead and let her stay outside. Lucky pooch.

Taking a deep breath, I pushed open the heavy front door.

So much of Witchlight Cove felt like stepping back in time but nowhere more so than the Watchtower Hotel with its dark wood, plush velvet chairs and tapestries on the walls. Who hung tapestries these days? Really old people, that's who – and vampires.

Summoning as much confidence as I could, I pulled back my shoulders and marched over to the reception desk. A tall man with silvery wings – a fae – was standing behind it. That seemed odd because, as far as I knew, there was no love lost between vampires and the fae folk, but I guessed that when it came to business, money was money.

'Hello.' I flashed a polite smile. 'I'm here to speak to a member of the Order. Her name is Candice. Could you call her?'

The fae's lips parted, though it took a moment for him to speak. 'Um, I'm not sure I can do that,' he said.

'If you don't know her,' I continued, reciting Maddie's description, 'she's tall and has incredible hair. And only wears designer clothes.'

'I know Candice.' He leaned forward as if sharing a secret. 'She's head of the Nightshades.'

'Great,' I said. 'Now, are you going to fetch her for me, or should I wait out here so she can see how you treat her guests?' That was nothing more than a bluff; I was on seriously thin ice, but there was no point doing things by halves.

He grimaced. 'She's in a meeting.'

I feigned confusion. 'Really? That's odd, because this is the time she told me to meet her.'

'Maybe it's best if you contact her to sort out a better time. I don't think I should go and get her. They're ... busy today.' His lips pursed. He wasn't being unpleasant , but it wasn't the warmest welcome; something about his demeanour definitely felt off.

Deciding it was worth the risk, I lowered my emotional barriers slightly to let his feelings wash over me. The heat of his fear hit me immediately; he was terrified of the Order, and summoning one of the deadliest creatures who'd ever visited Witchlight Cove was not something he was eager to do.

'What if I wait in the bar?' I offered. 'You said Candice is in a meeting in there?' I gestured to the conference hall entrance. 'When she comes out, you can let her know I'm waiting. Would that work?'

Relief flashed across his face. 'Yes, that sounds much better.'

'Let's do that,' I said confidently, trying not to worry about what might have imbued such fear in him.

As I headed to the bar, I checked the time; it was already 3pm and I only had an hour left on Fraser's ticking clock. I texted him to let him know I was at the hotel and waiting for someone so I might be delayed.

I didn't know where the day had gone but, on the plus side, it was definitely late enough for a cold glass of Oyster Bay while I waited.

Since it was a hotel, the wine prices were astronomical; it was an absurd amount for a glass and only a slightly less absurd price for a bottle, so I figured I might as well buy the bottle. I could take anything I didn't finish to Fraser's. It was the smart thing to do – at least, that was how I justified it to myself.

I sat at the bar. Just beyond the window, Eva was sitting and staring at me. That was surprisingly reassuring even though there was a thick pane of glass between us. I could also see the doors to the conference room, so I would see Candice emerge.

As I waited, my mind drifted back to my parents and my magic. I was no closer to accepting that they had stripped me of my powers, particularly as I could never speak to them about it.

An imperious voice interrupted my thoughts. 'So you're the idiot foolish enough to demand an audience with me?'

Shit. Candice had moved so silently that I hadn't noticed her approach – in fact, I hadn't even noticed the conference doors opening. I recovered quickly. 'Candice, it's lovely to meet you.'

Maddie hadn't been joking about her being intimidating; she made Julietta look like a puppy who might roll over and show her belly. Candice's posture was so straight that it almost defied nature, and her dark eyes had a reddish hue. They seemed to pierce straight through me.

During the walk to the hotel, I'd gone over the situation a dozen times in my head. I couldn't ask outright if the Nightshades had been involved in Lorenz's murder but perhaps I could use my powers to divine an answer as I'd done with Fraser. All I needed to do was to touch her hand and search for anything connected to Lorenz's name. I'd felt fairly confident it would work – until I saw her up close.

This would be a one-shot situation; there would be no second chances.

I stood up. 'Thank you so much for speaking to me,' I said. Keeping my breathing steady because she'd certainly notice any hesitation, I reached out to shake her hand and prepared myself to dive into her memories of Lorenz.

The minute our skin touched – *wham!* It was as though I'd been slammed against a brick wall both mentally and physically.

As I staggered back against the bar, I heard Eva barking outside. I tried to signal to her that I was fine, but it was difficult when I was struggling to stand upright. When I'd nearly fainted after touching Fraser that had been *my* doing, but this was *hers.*

Candice looked amused. 'Well, that was a silly thing to do, wasn't it?' Her smile was predatory. 'I should kill you right now for trying a stunt like that,' she snarled.

Eva was growling protectively as she ran away from the window, most likely to find a way inside the hotel, but I knew that wouldn't help. I needed to defuse the situation fast before Candice sunk her fangs into my neck.

'I'm so sorry! I'm … I'm new to my powers,' I stammered. 'I only started experiencing them two days ago and half the time nothing happens when I touch someone. I really am sorry.'

Common wisdom had it that vampires could tell if you were lying, so hopefully she could see that I was telling the truth – technically – and she'd believe that trying to invade her mind had been an accident. Even though it hadn't been.

As her silence swelled around us, I decided that it was probably best if I carried on talking. 'I came to ask about Lorenz, the water-shifter leader in our town, who was killed by a vampire a couple of days ago.'

She looked down at me with such cold disdain that I knew she didn't believe me. 'Our order has already spoken to the police,' she said curtly. 'I assured your Chief Inspector that we had nothing to do with that murder.'

'I'm not working for the police,' I said quickly. 'I'm working for the vampire who's been accused of the crime.'

'Be careful.' Her voice was suddenly dangerously soft. 'You're making a grave mistake if you think you can treat us the same way you treat your locals. They've gone soft – even the well-respected vampires here are a disgrace to their name.'

I swallowed hard. She clearly wasn't a fan of anyone in Witchlight Cove.

'I can't help you. And even if I could, I'm not inclined to.' I could tell from her tone that the conversation was over.

Just as I was about to call it a day, Vlad ambled up to Candice holding a clipboard. 'Hey, Vlad,' I greeted him.

He blinked. 'Do I know you?'

'We were chatting at the bar during the opening events at the night club – though I guess you were quite drunk.'

A slow flush worked its way up his face and he tugged at his collar. 'Right.'

Since I was getting nowhere with Candice, I decided to fire another shot before I was chucked out of the hotel. 'Do you know who killed Lorenz Matheson?'

The rotund vampire frowned and looked down at his clipboard. As he flicked through a few of the pages, Candice sighed audibly though she made no move to stop him. Vlad's lips moved as he mouthed Lorenz's name. 'Nope,' he said finally. 'Matheson wasn't on this year's hit list. Was he someone we killed last year?' he asked Candice.

She tapped her long fingernails impatiently on the bar. 'Matheson wasn't someone we killed *any* year. He was the shifter that died in the bar where you got heinously drunk.'

Vlad's blush deepened and I felt quite sorry for him. 'He wasn't *that* drunk,' I defended him.

'He was calling himself Vlad the Impaler.' Lestat joined us, his amusement clear. 'Miss Stonehaven,' he greeted me.

'Stonehaven?' Candice's eyes narrowed in a fierce glare. 'I thought you said you were just discovering your magic and now I find out you're a Guardian?'

'By all accounts she *is* magically inferior,' Lestat drawled.

Ouch. Direct hit.

'She can't be,' Candice snarled. 'She's related to bloody Bleakman!'

The world narrowed. 'You know my grandmother?' I whispered.

She grimaced. 'Not well, thankfully.'

I licked my suddenly parched lips. 'When did you last see her?'

'Why do you want to know?'

'Was it within the last decade?' I needed to know if my grandmother was still alive, because if she was that changed *everything*.

'Six years ago, wasn't it?' Lestat said. 'Or was it seven?'

Candice sent him a look of such fury that, if it had been me, I'd have had my fists up instantly. Instead I looked around for something to use as a weapon. There was a butter knife on a plate next to the remains of an afternoon tea; I could grab it, but could I use it before she ripped out my throat?

No one is going to be ripping throats. Lestat's voice in my head was amused. *She wants to see the Flame.*

'I tell you what,' Candice suddenly purred, her demeanour so changed it gave me whiplash. 'You let me see the Flame and I'll tell you everything about Dahlia Bleakman, including what she was doing, where she was doing it and who she was doing it with.'

God damn it: I needed to know all of those things, but I had no Flame to show her. I slid off the stool. 'Sorry, I can't do that.' Needing to distract her, I asked, 'Can I ask you one question?'

She tilted her head slightly as she studied me. 'You can ask, but I'll decide whether to answer,' she said finally.

'I was just wondering what an assassins' AGM is like. What do you talk about? It's not like you have village fêtes to organise.'

I thought I saw the tiniest twitch of amusement at the corner of Candice's lips and Lestat made no effort to hide his broad grin.

'We are a large organisation, Stonehaven. Organisations require administration: finances, delegation, management, assessments, appraisals, recruitment…' Candice intoned.

That was depressingly mundane. 'Right,' I said. 'Sure.'

'Now, about the Flame…'

'Sorry. That's still a no.'

She smiled; it was a terrifying sight. 'For now,' she said drily. 'That will change.' She reached into the breast pocket of her suit and pulled out a black business card. There was no name, just a number embossed in grey. 'Call me when you change your mind.'

'Yes, absolutely,' I said quickly. I remembered my wine. 'I've only had half a glass from that bottle,' I said. 'You should have the rest. It's really nice – Oyster Bay.'

Everyone knows what a vampire's drink is and it's definitely not white wine, so I thought she was going to refuse and sneer at me for offering. Instead, she echoed my words,

'Oyster Bay?'

'Yes – and it's cold.'

With a smooth, sweeping movement, she grabbed the neck of the bottle and whipped it out of the ice bucket. 'Don't take this to mean you're forgiven. I just like Oyster Bay,' she said, before disappearing back into the hotel.

I turned back to Vlad and Lestat. 'I guess she's not sharing.'

'She doesn't play well with others,' Lestat noted, making Vlad snicker. 'Not enough hugs as a child.'

'Right. Well, thanks for chatting.'

Lestat swept me a low bow. 'I have no doubt we'll see each other again, Beatrix Stonehaven.'

Not if I saw him first. He'd spoken into my head deliberately and I had no idea how he'd done it. Did he have magic psychic skills? Did all vampires have them or just him? My textbooks suddenly seemed entirely too brief on the subject of vampires.

I could feel their gaze on my back as they watched me leave. I wouldn't tangle with the Nightshades again in a hurry but, like Julietta, I believed Candice that the Nightshades weren't involved. That meant either Julietta was wrong or an outsider had come in.

I suddenly thought about Kaz and her barrier monitoring equipment. Maybe she'd recorded someone unusual coming to Witchlight. I rang her but she didn't pick up, so I left a voicemail. 'I really need to speak to you. Give me a call when you get this. It's about Lorenz.'

If Kaz had recorded some footage, we might finally take a step forward. That would be a relief because so far this case had been worse than a game of snakes and ladders.

Chapter Thirty-Five

Eva had somehow made her way into the foyer and the receptionist was looking less than pleased. 'We have a strict no-dogs policy,' he sniffed. 'I don't even know how she got in! She must have opened the door.'

'Sorry. I'm taking her now.' I clipped on her lead and we scurried out of the hotel.

When we were out of the grounds, I let her off her lead. I'd been a couple of hours since I'd seen Fraser, and I hoped the selkie was still calm. I waited until I was a decent distance away before I rang him; I wasn't making the same mistake that I'd made with Julietta and letting the vampires overhear everything I'd said.

'It was fine,' I said quickly when he answered.

'Thank the Mother,' he muttered. 'Did you find out anything useful?'

'Well, the head of the vampires likes Oyster Bay,' I said, trying to sound upbeat. 'And she doesn't appreciate having her mind poked into.'

'*Beatrix!*' he said, aghast.

I laughed; winding up Fraser was kind of fun. 'It's fine – *I'm* fine. There's no need to worry.' I decided to save the little titbit about her tangling with my grandmother until we were together.

He made a sceptical sound; he obviously didn't believe me.

'I'll see you later,' I added. 'Six o'clock.'

'I'm looking forward to it, Beatrix.'

'Me too.' I hung up.

I'd have to buy another bottle of white wine, but given that the first one had hopefully stopped me from making an enemy of a powerful vampire organisation, it was money well spent.

Back at the house, I was surprised to find Maddie sitting in the kitchen with several of my mother's cauldrons laid out in front of her. 'What's going on?' I asked curiously.

She flashed me a grin. 'I had another meeting with Ernie today,' she said. 'He mentioned that potions are the closest magical skill to alchemy. He said there's a chance that if I'd grown up without the Eternal Flame, I might've ended up as a potions witch.'

'Can that happen?' I asked. 'I thought whatever type of witch you are is ... just whatever you are?'

She shrugged. 'Lots of people have more than one type of skill, it all depends on where you focus on in your studies. He seems to think that if I work on my potions skills, I might develop some of the same techniques I've been using for alchemy.'

'That sounds amazing. Could you do your tattoos again?'

Her grin widened. 'Yes!'

My mother had been an earth witch, my dad had called himself a knowledge witch, a term he'd made up though it was fitting considering how much time he'd spent buried in his books. My parents had occasionally harnessed the power of the Eternal Flame, which made sense given that they had continual access to it. What *didn't* make sense was why they'd encouraged Maddie to use it and done everything they could to strengthen her magic while putting a bind on mine. Had they wanted Maddie to be the Guardian?

I studied my best friend with too-wide eyes.

'What?' asked Maddie. 'You're looking at me weirdly.'

I was, but I wasn't ready to share my thoughts with her yet so I decided to relay what Nour had told me. 'Something happened today,' I started. 'A few things, actually.' I told her about my discussion with Candice.

Maddie paled. 'Bleakman is alive?'

'If Lestat is to be believed, she was six or seven years ago.'

'And did you believe him?' she asked.

I considered before nodding slowly. 'Yes, I did.'

She shuddered. 'What should we do about the wards? I can maybe—'

'Maddie, relax. The wards are still up. We're still safe.'

'You weren't safe that night when your parents died,' she whispered.

'My grandmother caught me outside the house's wards and lured Dad outside of them to rescue me. The wards themselves are secure – anyone meaning harm to us or the Eternal Flame *can't* get in. So just, take a deep breath.' I realised Maddie was shaking. 'I'm sorry,' I murmured. 'I didn't mean to upset you.'

'No, it's fine – but that was the worst night of my life.'

I nodded. 'Mine too. But even if my grandmother *is* alive, she hasn't come back since then.'

'No, she hasn't,' Maddie agreed. 'But you haven't been here.'

And now I was. I went cold. 'We can speak to Ernie about putting on some more wards as a precautionary measure.'

Maddie sagged against me. 'That's a great idea.' She smiled weakly. 'Now can we talk about something that doesn't petrify me?'

'Sure. For starters, why didn't you tell me Nour is so lovely?'

The tension eased from Maddie's frame as she thought about Ezra's ex. 'She's sweet, isn't she? They made a great couple. I was furious when they ended things.'

'I really like her.' I paused. 'We even talked about forming a coven – with you.'

Her eyes widened. 'Are you serious?'

'We were half-joking – but only half. It might be worth looking into.'

Maddie nodded, then her expression became serious again. 'Until you leave again, you mean.'

I licked my lips. 'I'm not so certain that I *will* leave. Being back here has just—'

Maddie beamed, leapt up from the cauldrons and pulled me into a hug. 'Oh my gosh! Really?'

'My feelings might change,' I cautioned her. I knew that could happen, particularly if things took a bad turn with Fraser, but at that moment I wanted to stay. Badly.

'This is the best day ever – apart from the stuff about your grandmother. But if you're staying, we definitely need to get Ernie to help with the wards.'

I cleared my throat. 'I've got more news. You know I said my powers were acting strangely? Well, I was right. Something has happened to them.'

'What do you mean?'

I took a deep breath. 'It seems a bind was placed on me when I was very young. When Fraser's magic saved me it also broke the bind. Now it's slowly unravelling, which means that I might actually get the powers I was supposed to have.'

From the way Maddie was frowning, I knew she'd realised *who* had bound my magic. 'Yes, it was my parents,' I admitted.

'That's ... hard. Are you okay?'

'I'm not *not* okay – does that count? Can we focus on the positive part?'

Maddie nodded, then she sent me a radiant smile which transformed her serious expression. 'New powers! This is amazing! Do you know what powers you're getting – oh my God, are you a fire witch? That would be awesome!'

I laughed. 'I don't think so. Everything so far seems to be to do with people's minds. I heard Yanni's thoughts once, and Lestat's – and I've seen a couple of people's memories by accident.'

'You're a psychic witch!'

'It looks that way. I wondered if you could help me?' I wanted to try the exercise that Ezra had made me do earlier. I'd failed with him, but I'd managed with Fraser – and I felt like I *could* have succeeded with Candice, had she not had wards the size of the Eiffel Tower. My parents had told me that confidence was one of the keys to making magic work and I could feel mine growing: I was *sure* I could do this.

'I want you to think about what you had for lunch,' I asked. A beat later I sent her a flat look. 'Unless it was a tuna sandwich, because you always have tuna sandwiches.'

She grinned. 'I didn't today! I branched out.'

'In that case, think about it and give me your hand.'

'Oh my God.' She leaned forward.

I took her hand. *Lunch,* I thought. *I want to see Maddie's lunch from today.*

For a moment I felt woozy and thought I might faint as I had at Fraser's, but somehow I steadied myself. I was in Maddie's place now, sitting at a desk with a bowl in front of me. No ... not a bowl, a mug. A massive mug with cream on top. I inhaled. 'You had a frappé for lunch?' I asked incredulously. 'Do you know how unhealthy that is?'

'You did it! This is incredible! How do you feel?'

As I released our hands, my elation ebbed. 'It's good,' I admitted, 'but I still don't understand why my parents put a fucking bind on me.'

'I'm sorry, Bumble Bea. But it makes sense, doesn't it? I'd be willing to bet that your parents put the bind on you to protect you from your grandmother.'

I knew she was right, but that didn't stop the sting.

'We need to celebrate you coming into your powers,' Maddie went on. 'Shady's is open tonight. Cocktails? What do you say?'

I tried to keep my expression neutral. 'That would have been lovely, but I can't. I've got plans.'

'Plans?' Her gaze narrowed. 'You're going to dinner with Fraser!'

'It's work-related – Eternal Flame-related,' I said firmly.

'Uh-huh.' She grinned. 'Is it Eternal Flame related with wine?'

'Wine helps me think,' I said solemnly.

She smirked. 'Well, if it's *just* work, then I guess you won't want to look through my wardrobe for something to wear, will you?'

Damn. She had me there.

Chapter Thirty-Six

Being the owner of a big dog with light-coloured fur makes it difficult to dress up for a night out, especially if she's coming with me. If I wear black it shows the fur that's moulted onto me; if I wear white I can guarantee Eva will trail in some mud and deposit it on my clothes.

Thankfully, Maddie's wardrobe was impressive and I ended up choosing an emerald-green jumpsuit, a denim jacket and flat trainers – I didn't want to look as if I'd tried too hard.

'You look hot as hell,' Maddie said as I came downstairs. 'Way too hot for a "work" meeting,' she teased.

'I just wanted a chance to dress up a bit,' I said without quite meeting her eyes.

'Well, have a good night,' she said. 'And don't do anything I wouldn't do. Not that that leaves much out. And don't forget that I'll need updates.'

I picked up my bag and threw her a mock glare. 'I'm not texting you from Fraser's.'

'Oh, come on!' she whined. 'I have to live vicariously because I have no love life of my own. Maybe you can send me psychic messages instead? That would be so awesome.'

'Sadly, that is far beyond me. Have a nice night, Maddie. Good luck with the potions.' I opened the front door and blew her a kiss. 'Love you!'

'Love you, too.'

It made my heart warm to see how easy those words flowed between us now. Our old friendship had been well and truly dusted off and I would never leave it untended again.

I walked down to the waterfront with Eva trotting in front of me. She kept a slight distance away from me, as if she knew I didn't want dirt on my clothes. She really is the best dog in the world.

When I reached Fraser's house, the gate was wide open. I walked up the drive and knocked on the door; a moment later, he opened it. I immediately felt pleased I'd made an effort with my outfit because he looked beyond handsome. I had no idea how the hell a man could look so good in a crisp blue shirt and barefoot in jeans – but he did. And he smelled divine, a musky scent of saltwater and vanilla.

'Hey.' He leaned in to kiss my cheek, then hesitated. 'Is it alright to touch you like that?'

'Yes,' I said, a little breathlessly. 'It's only been a day, but I seem to be getting a little control over my powers.'

'That's great,' he said, and kissed me gently on the cheek.

I was wrong: I wasn't ready for it at all. A bolt shot through me, not a memory or a vision, just pure desire. My pulse shot up in a way it hadn't done for years. Fraser's lips against my cheek and his scent in the air were enough for me to want to forget about bonds and the missing Eternal Flame and all that shit, and just drag him upstairs.

I pulled myself together. No sleeping with Fraser until we knew what the hell was between us. Glacial was what we needed here. 'The food smells lovely.' I blurted out the first words that came to mind – before I realised I couldn't actually smell any food.

He grinned as he took my denim jacket and hung it up. 'I haven't started cooking yet. And I'm afraid I cheated a little. I ended up staying late at the restaurant, so I asked the chef to whip us up something.'

'No need to apologise if I'm getting dinner cooked by your chef! I brought wine.' I held out the second bottle of Oyster Bay I'd bought that afternoon.

'I'll put this in the fridge – I've already got a bottle chilling.' He shot me a wry look, 'Apparently, I can't go shopping now without picking up a bottle of your favourite.'

'I guess I'll have to keep coming round to help you drink them,' I said lightly, then immediately wished I could take back the words. Did I sound too pushy?

'I'd like that,' he smiled.

I followed him into the kitchen. After he'd poured us each a glass of wine, he passed mine over and our fingers touched. I wished like hell that the attraction between us was less magnetic.

'Cheers,' we said simultaneously.

'So do you want to see what I've got?' he asked suddenly.

'You want to show me what you've got?' I repeated huskily.

'Information about the Eternal Flame,' he clarified.

'Oh yes, of course,' I said, praying I hadn't gone as red as I felt. 'The Eternal Flame.'

'I'm more than happy to show you what else I've got.'

'What happened to glacial?'

He grimaced. 'Around you, my plans go to shit.'

'You say the nicest things,' I laughed. I took another sip of my wine, grateful that I was the one with psychic powers and not him. 'Come on,' I said, taking hold of his hand in a way I'd never done before. 'Why don't you show me what you've got – Eternal-Flame wise?' I added hastily.

His laughter was the best sound I'd ever heard.

I don't know what I'd expected – a couple of bits of paper, some open books, maybe a few notes jotted in the margins – but I should have known not to underestimate Fraser Banks. His dining table was covered in books with Post-it notes sticking out from their pages. In the centre of his table, multiple tabs were open on his laptop screen.

'You've done all this research on the Flame?' I said, impressed.

He nodded. 'I looked at some of it before,' he reminded me. 'When I thought there might be a chance it could heal my mother.'

A pang of sympathy struck me. His father had beaten his mother so badly that Fraser had considered kidnapping her and bringing her to Witchlight Cove to see if the Eternal Flame could save her. Unfortunately, she'd passed away before he could try. 'I'm so sorry, Fraser.'

'It's okay. Obviously, that's how I discovered the Cove, but there were other places where I thought there might also be Eternal Flames – one in Scotland, another in the Mediterranean and one in the Caribbean.'

'I wouldn't say no to a trip to the Caribbean,' I said with a grin.

'Under the guise of research, obviously?'

'Obviously.'

'I haven't pinned down the exact locations yet, just landmarks. I've narrowed the one in Scotland down to eight possible locations, and the one in the Caribbean to twelve islands. I hadn't looked into the Mediterranean one yet.'

Much as I loved the idea of going to the Caribbean, the difference between eight and twelve was significant. Not to mention it would be quicker and easier to travel around Scotland than go tropical island-hopping – even if I could have done with some sun.

'I'll put the food in the oven to warm up,' Fraser said, 'then we can see if we can narrow this down a bit more. Check if we can identify any of the landmarks? I'm hoping something will call to you, maybe jog a memory.'

'Sounds good,' I said.

As Fraser headed into the kitchen, I stared at the pages spread across the table. We needed to find another Eternal Flame, and perhaps if its Guardian was obliging they'd explain why my Flame had vanished. I tried to ignore the dark thought that it had vanished because *I* had, and after a decade it had given up waiting for me.

I sat down and picked up the nearest book, but I'd only read the first line of the passage that Fraser had highlighted when my phone buzzed.

Jesus, Maddie, I thought, certain she was calling to check up on me. I was taken aback to see a different name on the screen. 'Ezra,' I said. 'Is everything alright?'

His voice was frantic. 'Trixie, thank God you answered. I need you to come to the hospital.'

'What? Why? What's happened?'

'It's Pepper. Someone hit her with their car. Please, I need you to come now!'

Chapter Thirty-Seven

'Apparently it was a hit and run,' I said to Fraser as he drove me to the hospital. 'That's all I know.'

'Do you want me to wait for you?' he offered. 'I don't mind sitting in the car.'

I shook my head and forced a smile. 'No, it's fine. I'll call you if I need you, if that's alright.'

'Always.' The sincerity in his tone made my heart do a backflip, but I didn't have time to think about that now because Ezra was already running out of the hospital towards me.

'What happened?' I asked as I jumped out of the car.

'They said she was hit outside her house. She'd only just come back to the village after her concert. Paul was inside and he didn't see it happen.'

I guessed that was both a blessing and a curse: less trauma for Paul, but fewer witnesses.

Ezra looked wrecked; there was apprehension and tension in every inch of his body. 'What do you need?' I asked.

'I don't know, Trixie.' He ran a hand through his hair. 'I just thought maybe you could help.'

'Help how?' I asked. 'I certainly don't mind trying to find her attacker, but hit and runs are difficult...'

'Not that. Can I explain inside?'

I nodded. 'Sure.'

Fraser was already driving away as we walked quickly toward the hospital entrance with Eva close behind us. 'If anyone asks,' I said to her, 'you're a pet therapy dog and we forgot your vest, okay?' She barked.

Ezra shook his head. 'She's not normal. You know that, don't you?'

The waiting area was crowded with at least a dozen of Ezra's family members. Nour was standing a little to the side of them. When she saw me, she hurried over and hugged me tightly before releasing me to take hold of Ezra's hand.

'Have you spoken to Yanni?' I asked him.

'She's gone to the scene of the accident to check for any traces of the car, but it's a long shot. Nour had an idea, though, and we think maybe you could help.'

'Me? How?'

He lowered his voice. 'Hit-and-run suspects are almost impossible to catch – they ditch the cars, change the plates, respray them. But maybe you could use your new powers.'

I froze. 'You want me to *what*?'

'Pepper's in a coma but her mind might still be intact,' Nour said gently. 'If you could look into her thoughts, you might see the moment it happened – see the car and the driver.'

That wasn't like reading Maddie's thoughts to learn what she'd had for lunch; they wanted me to find the person responsible for an attempted murder. 'I don't know if I can,' I said honestly. 'There has to be another witch who's better equipped.'

'Even though I only saw fragments of your aura,' Nour said firmly, 'I can tell that you're the strongest psychic witch I've met, bind or no.' She grimaced. 'And you're the only witch I know who would even consider helping a werewolf.'

I shook my head. 'I don't think it's safe. What if I hurt her? I'd never forgive myself.'

'I understand your concern but I trust you,' Ezra said. 'And Nour trusts you. Besides, we can't wait. Pepper was hit at least twenty minutes ago, and for all we know the driver might already be going through the barrier. Please try, Trixie. If it doesn't work, we'll find another way.'

'I don't—'

He cut me off. 'I've never asked anything of you, not once in twenty years, and I've done everything you've asked of me. I stayed out of your life when I desperately wanted to come and find you. But now I'm begging you. Do this for me.'

He was right; he'd never asked anything of me before. And as far as friends went, Ezra was as loyal as they came. He didn't just want me to do this. He *needed* me to.

'If something goes wrong—'

'No one will blame you,' he said firmly. 'I promise.'

'I can anchor you,' Nour offered. 'Keep you from using too much power on her.'

I nodded slowly. 'All right, then. Take me to her.'

As Ezra excused himself to go and speak to Pepper's family, Fraser appeared in the hospital corridor. 'I thought you went home!' I exclaimed, startled. Instinctively, I stepped into his arms and he instantly drew me closer and pressed a kiss onto my hair.

'I was on my way,' he explained as he drew back, 'but then I thought that I should be here for you. It wasn't a bond thing,' he added hastily, 'more of a moral thing, I guess.'

'It's okay,' I said, surprised at how intense my feeling of gratitude was at seeing him. 'I'm glad you're here.'

'What's going on? Can I help?'

I met his gaze as I tried to steady myself. 'Pepper's in a coma. There's no way of knowing who ran her down before they hide the evidence, so I'm going to try to enter her mind and get a vision of the car that hit her.'

'You're going to use your powers on her?' Fraser's voice was calm but reserved.

'I am,' I said firmly, preparing to argue with him about why I should do it.

'Okay.'

His simple answer disarmed me. 'You think it's a bad idea, don't you?' I asked.

'Absolutely not. I think you can do anything you put your mind to, Beatrix Stonehaven.' There was no hesitation in his tone, and I felt energy radiating from him into me, a steady current of belief in me that somehow felt miraculous.

'Go on,' he said. 'I'll stay out here and comfort the Bentleys, if I can. If you need me, I'll be right here.'

I nodded before I leaned up and kissed him lightly on the lips. His smile was like the sun. 'Could you take care of Eva for me?' I asked.

'Of course, I can.' Eva went to him happily, tail wagging.

As I left Fraser's side, I made sure my emotional barriers were firmly in place. I knew I'd be hit by a wave of emotions when I entered Pepper's room but I couldn't let it sway me.

Still holding Nour's hand, Ezra led me to Pepper's bedside. Two older women – her mothers – were sitting on one side of her, and on the other was a pale-skinned, dark-haired, man, presumably her vampire husband, Paul.

'Aunt Kath, Aunt Wyn,' Ezra said softly. 'You know Beatrix?'

The women looked up briefly, their faces etched with pain. There was only a faint flicker of recognition.

'Paul, this is my friend Beatrix. Beatrix, this is Pepper's husband, Paul Polter.'

'Nice to meet you,' I murmured, wincing internally at the banality of my words.

'Beatrix is a witch with strong psychic powers,' Ezra explained. 'She might be able to explore Pepper's mind and find out who did this so we can catch them before they get away.'

The women's demeanour shifted immediately. Kath's eyes filled with desperate hope, while Wyn's hardened with anger. 'Whoever did this deserves to rot in hell,' she said sharply.

'Absolutely,' I replied.

'Do you think you can really find out who it was?' Paul asked.

‘I don’t honestly know,’ I admitted. ‘But I’ll try my hardest.’

‘Could it harm Pepper?’ Kath asked.

‘No,’ Nour said firmly. ‘The accident happened so recently that the memory will be at the forefront of Pepper’s mind so Beatrix won’t need to do any digging. It’ll be absolutely fine. And to make extra sure, I’ll anchor Beatrix’s magic to make sure she doesn’t use too much.’

The three family members exchanged glances. ‘Okay, do it,’ Paul said, his voice trembling. Kath nodded her agreement and laced her fingers through Wyn’s.

I hesitated then took a step forward. ‘I might need a little space,’ I said.

‘Of course.’ Kath stood up, Wyn followed reluctantly and then Paul a moment later.

‘Whatever you need me to do, Trixie,’ Ezra said, his eyes steady.

‘You go.’ I wanted privacy; the last thing I needed was to feel self-conscious. I didn’t know what the fuck I was doing, so I certainly didn’t need witnesses – besides Nour that is.

When we were alone, I sat beside Pepper’s bed, and Nour took hold of my left hand. She murmured some words to Hecate that I tuned out. Placing my hand on

Pepper's head felt too intrusive, so I mimicked Nour's move, and picked up Pepper's hand instead.

'Ready?' I asked Nour.

She nodded, eyes closed in concentration. 'I've got you.'

I focused on Pepper and lowered my barriers. 'Who did this to you?' I whispered to her. 'Show me. Show me what you need me to see.'

I was pulled forward by the force of her subconscious – it was like being caught in a current. My body stayed seated but my mind was winding through the tributaries of her thoughts. 'Show me the car,' I urged.

Flickers of memory started to form, but something else tugged at me, pulling me toward another scene. 'I need to know about the car,' I said more firmly.

But Pepper's mind took me elsewhere and I flashed into another scene, another memory. Pepper was standing outside somewhere that I'd been before ... Lorenz's bar.

I realised with a chill that I was seeing the night that Lorenz was murdered. Pepper was pushing her way out against the tide of the queue, and someone else was pushing their way in: a vampire with a black hood hiding their face. All I could see were painted red lips and fangs, but I *felt* Pepper's flare of recognition.

My God! Pepper knew which vampire had come into the bar just before Lorenz was murdered. That was why she'd been targeted; she'd been hit by the car deliberately.

Having shown me what she wanted to, Pepper's mind pushed me back to the scene of the accident. The current turned into a riptide as bursts of yellow light flashed through the darkness and grew brighter and brighter.

Headlights. Massive headlights from a black SUV. Pepper had been staring directly at them moments before the impact.

Then I was thrown from her mind. I fell backwards and went flying, dragging Nour with me.

Hearing the noise, Ezra rushed in. 'Nour!' He rushed to her, helping her up first before turning to me. 'Did you see it? Did you see who did this?' he demanded as he helped me up too.

'Pepper knows who killed Lorenz,' I told him tightly. 'This wasn't an accident – she was targeted.'

'Tell me you know who this psycho is!'

I shook my head. 'I didn't see their face clearly, the glare of the headlights blinded Pepper from seeing the driver, but I saw the car. A black SUV.'

Ezra pulled me into a tight hug. 'Thank you,' he said, his voice breaking. 'Thank you for this.'

As I pulled away, my mind was racing. There might have been a dozen black SUVs in Witchlight, but surely there couldn't be many owned by a vampire? We finally had a way to identify the culprit.

Chapter Thirty-Eight

The moment I stepped into the hospital foyer, Fraser engulfed me in his arms. I wanted to stay there forever, to let his warmth block out what I'd just seen. I might not have been hit by the car, but I'd experienced everything Pepper had felt. The fear, the pain – and then the nothingness.

He moved back so he could look at me more clearly. 'What do you need? Do you need to sit down? A drink?'

'In a minute,' I said. 'I need to talk to Yanni first.'

Nour and Ezra were beside me too. At any other time I would probably have been embarrassed to be seen clinging to Fraser like a limpet to a rock, but at that moment I didn't care. 'Is Yanni here?' I asked him.

'She's just arrived. I saw the police car outside.'

Releasing myself from him, I darted to the door. Yanni was walking towards me with Dove at her side; Eva was already bounding up to them.

'Bea,' Yanni said when she reached me. 'What's going on?'

'I know what sort of car hit Pepper,' I said. 'I saw it.'

'You *saw* it?' she asked. 'You were there?'

'No, it's ... it's magic-related. I'll explain later, but right now you need to put out an alert for a black SUV.'

Yanni frowned. 'There are a lot of black SUVs in Witchlight Cove. And what kind of magic are we talking about?'

'The magic part is complicated, but the car isn't. Pepper was hit only twenty-five minutes ago so there's still time to find it. And you need to cross-reference it with vampire owners because whoever hit her killed Lorenz, too. And call Maddie, ask her to monitor the barriers so you don't lose the vehicle before it's too late.'

As I spoke the words, a chilling thought hit me: Pepper had been hit just after she'd returned to Witchlight Cove, as if someone had known she'd just come through the barrier. And the easiest way to know that was to *monitor* it.

Oh my God. I knew who'd done it. I knew who'd murdered Lorenz and run down Pepper.

I turned and glanced at the hospital windows. Dozens of pairs of eyes were staring in at us expectantly, waiting to see if Yanni had any news, but I was only looking for one person.

'Nour,' I called and waved her over.

'What is it?' she asked.

'Can any of your relatives do a spell to locate a vampire? It's for the person who hit Pepper with their car – and who murdered Lorenz.' I licked my lips. 'It's Kaz.'

Her jaw dropped. '*Kaz*? Kaz who works at Sonny's? Are you sure?'

'All the signs point to her. We need to find her before she puts anyone else in danger.' Guilt surged through me; I'd left Kaz a message asking her to speak to me about Lorenz... Had she thought I'd already identified her and attacked Pepper because of my message?

I felt sick.

Yanni frowned. 'Beatrix, this is a grave accusation. To accuse someone of murder without physical evidence—'

I interrupted. 'Believe me, she's behind this.' The affection in Kaz's voice when she'd spoken of Sonny ... she loved him, I was sure of it. I'd assumed it was platonic love but maybe I'd assumed wrongly. She *loved* Sonny and he loved someone else. Had she believed that Sonny would seek comfort from her if Lorenz was dead?

Pepper had seen Kaz sneaking into the club so she had to be eliminated as soon as she returned to Witchlight from her concert. Kaz had the feed from the barrier on her laptop, ostensibly to monitor when there would be a rush of customers – but the café had been *closed* and she'd been using it to monitor Pepper's return.

'One of my cousins can do a locator spell.' Nour turned to her phone. 'Though I don't know how easy it will be to do without an item of Kaz's.'

Yanni was looking at me apprehensively. 'Are you going to tell me how you know Kaz is behind this? And what kind of magic was involved? Because if Maddie is using—'

'No, no, she's not,' I said hastily. 'Maddie's not touching dark magic, I promise. It was me.'

'Beatrix Stonehaven.' Her face turned thunderous. 'After everything that happened to Maddie, you're telling me you're messing around with evil magic?'

'No!' I protested, realising how the confusion had arisen. 'No, it's not *dark* magic, it's *my* magic. I've been getting stronger. I can't go into it now.'

She studied me for a moment. 'We're going to have a long talk later, but for now I suppose I have to trust you.' I could have kissed her.

Nour came closer to me, phone clutched in her hand. 'Can your cousin help?' I asked hopefully.

'We don't need her to,' Nour said, shaking her head. 'My aunt has spotted Kaz.

Apparently, she's walking towards the Watchtower Hotel.'

'Where the Nightshades are,' I murmured.

'Exactly. My aunt tried to ask her how things were at the cafe, but she said Kaz seemed strange. She was brusque and walked away very quickly.'

'Maybe she's hoping the Nightshades will take her in,' Dove suggested. 'Protect her.'

Candice had been disdainful about the local vampires because she thought they were weak; would Kaz change her mind? I was fairly certain Candice would have no compunction about taking in a murderer – in fact, it was part of the job description. And once Kaz was a Nightshade, she'd be outside the law.

A memory hit me from my meeting with Candice. 'One of the Nightshades I spoke to mentioned that recruitment is one of their topics at the AGM,' I said. 'Maybe Dove's right and Kaz really is hoping to join them. Killing Lorenz might have been a test to prove herself.'

'Then why frame Sonny?' Yanni frowned. 'Nightshades are normally discreet.'

I didn't mention my theory about Kaz's love for Sonny; I had zero evidence of that, and Yanni was all about the hard evidence.

'Was Kaz in her car?' I asked Nour.

'No, she was walking. My aunt offered her a lift,' Nour replied.

'She's probably hidden the car so we can't see the damage,' I said grimly. 'We need to move fast.' I turned to Yanni. 'Can you change the barrier to make sure no vampires can get in or out?'

Yanni grimaced. 'The Nightshades won't like that, but it's possible. It'll drain a lot of power, though. I'll make the call and head straight to the hotel.' The edge to her voice was a pointed reminder that the barrier was tied to Eternal Flame and draining it further would push it closer to a breaking point.

'I'm coming with you,' I said.

'You've done enough. You get to take a step back now, Bea.'

Before I could object, Fraser stepped forward. 'We'll follow in my car.'

Yanni raised an eyebrow but nodded. 'Fine. Just don't get in the way of police work.'

'I promise,' I said, already fully aware this was a promise I wouldn't – couldn't – keep.

Chapter Thirty-Nine

Yanni had the sirens blaring and I could tell that her foot was pressed hard on the accelerator, but even so her car wasn't particularly fast. Living in Witchlight Cove, she'd never needed to do much in the way of car chases so she'd not seen the point in investing in a faster vehicle. After this, I would convince her that it was a must.

I groaned. 'We need to speed up ,' I complained. 'I don't know how far Kaz was from the Watchtower Hotel when she was spotted, but if she gets to the Nightshades and they take her in, she'll have diplomatic immunity and we'll be fucked.'

'Don't worry, we'll get there,' Fraser said confidently. He pulled out his phone. 'But just in case, I'll call Alistair,' he said.

'Alistair?'

'He's the head of the fae sect – he owns the hotel.' A beat later, his tone lost all trace of friendliness. 'Alistair,' he said brusquely. 'I've got a situation. There's someone heading your way – Kaz, who works at Sonny's. Don't let her in. She's a vampire but she's not part of the Nightshades.'

There was a pause, while he listened then he continued, 'She killed Lorenz, and I need your co-operation.' He was glaring; I guessed he and Alistair weren't all that close. 'On behalf of the sect council, I request that you put up a ward to prevent her entry to your hotel.'

Alistair obviously said something rude because Fraser's face tightened. 'I'm calling it a request in order to be polite, but we can call it what it is if that makes you happy. It's a demand, Alistair. Do it.' He hung up.

I stared at Fraser. 'You're not a fan of Alistair's?'

'He's a horrible bastard,' Fraser growled.

'He seemed pretty scared when I met him.'

'The fae manning the front desk? That's Orion. He's scared of Alistair, too, and with good reason. He's not a man to mess with.'

'And yet you're locking horns with him? Thank you,' I murmured with feeling.

'No worries, it's the right thing to do. The issue we've got is that the fae can only hold a ward over ground that they're physically touching, and with a quick ward like this one, they can't be inside the ward either. Which is problematic because fae defence is mostly about misdirection and illusions; they're not strong fighters. The fae can ward the hotel, but those doing the warding will be vulnerable to attack from Kaz. Fae are scared of vampires at the best of times.'

'Huh.' I frowned. 'Given that the fae are so scared of vamps, it seems crazy that they let them stay at the hotel.'

'No doubt Alistair is off site, damned coward that he is. I expect he was given a hefty payment. And there's always the possibility that the Nightshades made a booking under a false name.' Fraser reached across the car and took my hand. 'What you did back there with Pepper was incredible.'

'It was pretty terrifying,' I admitted. 'But it got a result. Having the power to see into someone's thoughts is incredibly invasive, though – I hate the thought of someone doing it to me.'

'Then the world is lucky that you're the one with the power because you won't abuse it,' he said with absolute certainty.

'Thank you,' I said, my cheeks warming.

We turned off the main road and onto the narrow, pothole-ridden lane that led to the hotel. 'We never did get around to having our dinner,' I said after a moment. 'Maybe after tonight, we can fix another date.'

'Of course,' he said easily. 'I've still got all that Witchlight information to go through when you're ready.'

'Yes, that too.' I hesitated for a second. 'But actually I was thinking maybe we could have dinner without talking business.'

His eyebrows lifted. 'You mean ... like a proper date?' he asked.

'Yeah,' I admitted. 'Just like that.'

'Let's get this done first,' he said. 'And then I'm all yours.'

Promises, promises.

'Look over there! That's her, isn't it?' I said excitedly, pointing ahead. Fraser's eyes flicked in the direction I'd indicated. 'Just there. Turn left,' I urged.

'There's no road to the left.'

'You've got a 4x4. Quickly!'

He yanked the steering wheel hard to the left.

Without a doubt it was Kaz, and even from a distance I could see her fury. She was hammering her fists against the air – or rather, the boundary ward the fae had put in place to keep her out.

I spotted a female fae about fifty metres away from her on the wrong side of the ward. If Kaz noticed her, the fae would be dead and Kaz would have a way through to the hotel and the Nightshades. I wasn't going to let that happen. She needed a distraction and I was going to give her one.

I unclipped my seat belt. 'Don't slow down. She needs to be distracted by both of us. Keep going for her, alright?'

'I don't like this,' Fraser said tightly.

'You don't have to like it, you just have to trust me.' I turned and glanced at Eva. 'Wait until the car stops, then join me. Okay, girl?' She barked and pricked her ears.

'Beatrix, don't—' Fraser started as he braked hard.

I didn't wait to hear the rest, nor did I wait for the car to stop completely, before I threw open the door and launched myself out. A lifetime of martial arts had taught me how to hit the ground and roll – though even so, the ground was hard and unforgiving. Luckily, adrenaline was surging through me, protecting me from pain.

I pushed myself to my feet. 'Move!' I snarled to Fraser, and the car barrelled towards the vampire.

'Kaz! It's over!' I yelled. 'I know what you did!'

Fraser came to a stop in front of the fae, obscuring her from Kaz's vision.

Meanwhile Yanni, seeing that we'd disappeared from her rearview mirror, had turned back and was rattling towards us as she navigated the bumpy field in her battered car.

Kaz finally stopped her relentless pounding on the invisible boundary and turned to me, her face a mask of fury. Her fists dropped to her sides as her sharp eyes zeroed in on me. 'Beatrix,' she said, her tone all sweetness. She began walking toward me. 'I was hoping to see you. I wanted to thank you for your help with that graffiti.'

'It's not going to work, Kaz,' I said flatly as I closed the distance between us.

Her smile didn't falter, but her eyes flickered with something dark. 'I don't know what you're talking about,' she said breezily. 'I was just going for a walk. I thought I'd head up to the Watchtower's bar – it has such a wonderful view.'

I continued moving towards her. Eva was keeping pace beside me, and Yanni and Fraser had left their cars so they were pinning her between themselves and me. There was no escape for Kaz except through us – and that made her all the more dangerous.

'We both know you're running to the Nightshades for diplomatic immunity, Kaz, and the only reason you'd do that is because you killed Lorenz. I'm still not sure why – though I could make a good guess – but I know you did it. When you got my voicemail, you panicked and you mowed down Pepper as she came back to Witchlight Cove. She'd seen you sneaking into Lorenz's bar, hadn't she? She probably thought you were trying to queue jump, but that wasn't the reason, was it?'

'Really, Beatrix, I have no idea what you're talking about.'

Yanni stepped forward and pulled out a pair of yellow cuffs that were radiating magic. Getting them around the superfast vampire's wrists wouldn't be easy. 'Kaz,' she said calmly, 'we need you to come to the station. This will all be cleared up easily if you cooperate.'

Kaz's eyes flicked to the cuffs and her lips pressed into a thin line. 'This is a massive misunderstanding,' she said tightly. 'Whatever you think you have on me, you don't. I was at home when Lorenz was killed. As for the car – I bumped into a deer a couple of days ago. It left a nasty dent, but that's all – there's not a drop of blood on it.'

Of course not, I thought bitterly. She'd probably licked it clean.

'Why did you kill Lorenz?' I asked. 'And why frame Sonny? You told me that he took you in, looked after you. He *cared* for you, Kaz.'

Her smile returned, sharper now as if she were mocking me. 'I really don't know what you're talking about,' she persevered. She wasn't going to crack. My visions wouldn't count as evidence, and she wasn't going to admit anything. Unless...

'I know the truth,' I said, stepping closer to her. 'So we can do this the easy way or the hard way.'

She looked unnervingly smug. 'Sonny did it,' she spat. 'Hard as it is for me to admit it, he murdered Lorenz.'

'I guess you're choosing the hard way, ' I murmured.

Before she could react, I grabbed her firmly by the shoulders and pushed into her mind.

Chapter Forty

I was fully aware that, as a vampire, Kaz could have had barriers up like Candice had done but this time I wasn't going to be taken unawares. I was going to be faster and stronger.

I flung my mind at hers with all my strength, pushing so forcefully that I practically tumbled into it. The barriers weren't there; instead, I found myself in the same vision I'd seen back at the hospital – only now I was in the driving seat of the car and heading straight for Pepper.

Bingo! Since I was there, it made sense to clear Sonny's name. I needed proof that Kaz had killed Lorenz. *Show me more,* I said firmly. *Show me why you killed Lorenz.*

Her mind fought back, fragments of resistance splintering like static but she couldn't fight me off. For the first time in my life, my magic was strong. *Show me, or I will find the visions myself,* I told her.

As soon as I'd thought the words, I knew that was what I was going to do.

I pulled the images to me and they blurred in a storm of time and space over which I had only a modicum of control. Kaz was fighting me, refusing to lessen her grip, but I was stronger. I just had to hold on until she gave in.

I landed in a memory and the swirling stopped.

Kaz was lying in a hospital bed and Sonny was standing over her. I could feel the awe that filled her. 'You came for me?' she asked him and her voice trembled.

'I couldn't leave you to die,' he said gruffly. 'A promise is a promise.'

Gratitude radiated from her.

How could she have done this to him when she felt that way? How could she have set him up when she owed him everything? The scene skipped forward.

She was standing with a group of vampires and I recognised one of them: Shady. 'You're not doing yourself any favours hanging around with Sonny,' he warned.

'Sonny's a good man,' she shot back.

'You've been here long enough to know the ropes. You need to think about your future. I love Sonny too, but you need to wake up. He's an outsider, and if you hang off his apron strings, you will be too. If you want to make anything of yourself, you need to reconsider what you're doing.'

'I know exactly what I'm doing with Sonny beside me,' she said, her voice filled with longing.

The vision shifted again, the kaleidoscope of memories hurtling me forward.

She and Sonny sitting in the coffee shop laughing together, though the image disappeared almost as soon as it formed. The next one showed them on the sofa together, watching a film, pure contentment rolling from Kaz.

Suddenly the scene shifted again. The décor in the café wasn't the same as it was now; this had happened a couple of years ago at least.

Kaz leaned towards Sonny, lips trembling, trying to kiss him.

'I'm sorry,' he said, pulling away gently.

'I don't understand,' she said, her voice so much smaller than the Kaz I knew.

'It's not about you,' Sunny said firmly. 'It wouldn't be right. Not for me, and not for you.'

'Because you're my sire?' she said.

He sighed. 'You're amazing, Kaz, but I can't do relationships. I need you to move on. There are good people out there who deserve your love and they'll be lucky to have you. But it won't be me. I will always be on my own. That's just how it will be.'

I felt her heart shatter as if it were my own.

'We can still be friends? Pretend this never happened?' she asked.

His smile was warm and filled with relief. 'I would like that very much.' The embrace that followed told me that they had ended the conversation on good terms. So what had happened?

The answer came before I was ready, and it wasn't from a vision. It just made sense: Kaz had found out about Sonny and Lorenz.

Instantly I was immersed in another of her memories and the image hit me like a gut punch. *She'd seen them together, gazing into each other's eyes, their love so palpable that even as an observer I felt its warmth – and the anguish it caused Kaz.*

That was the moment she'd changed.

'You said you would always be alone! But it was me *you didn't want!'*

I assumed she was shouting at Sonny but she wasn't: it was a photo of him and her together down at the waterfront.

'The Nightshades were never involved at all, were they?' I asked her.

Her resolve was weakening and for the first time since she'd screamed at me, she directed her thoughts into a response. *'No. I planned to ask for sanctuary.'*

'They're cold, hard killers – you're a girl who had her heart broken and made a bad decision. Tell me about setting Sonny up. You got the CCTV footage of them?'

'I just wanted to talk to Lorenz,' she said. *'Tell him to back off – but then I heard them fighting. I thought that maybe Sonny had seen sense, so I watched them…'*

A flash took me to the moment.

Kaz was in a small broom-cupboard sized room where the CCTV was set up, watching Sonny and Lorenz fight. I could feel the adrenaline rush as she hoped this would be it; the moment they ended their ill-fated relationship and she swept in and took her place beside Sonny. But all of that changed because a moment later they kissed. Fury took hold of her, so deep and vehement it was as if her entire soul had turned black. If she couldn't have Sonny, no one could.

All the thoughts that had rolled through her head in the hours after seeing the kiss bombarded me, her determination to make them pay. I saw her back in the broom cupboard, loading the video clip onto a USB stick then clearing the computer. I saw her standing outside the bar, watching from a distance as the first people were let into the club.

'Show me how you killed Lorenz,' I demanded.

Kaz wasn't fighting me now or pushing against me. A bright flash shifted me again to the night at the bar.

She stormed into the bar, almost knocking into Pepper as she went. Pepper glared and in that moment sealed her own fate: she would have to die, too. But not yet; Kaz wasn't there for Pepper.

Once inside the bar, she waited by Lorenz's office for the moment when he would slip away for five minutes' peace. She would give him a lifetime of it.

'Hey, can I talk to you?' Kaz asked in that same sweet voice she'd tried to use on me. 'It's about Sonny. I'm worried about him.'

Anxiety shaded Lorenz's expression. 'Is he okay?'

'Can we talk in private?'

The second Lorenz opened the door to his office, she sank her fangs into his neck and her paralysing venom sank into his blood stream. She'd never used it before and it was kind of fun watching him freeze.

She had no interest in draining him dry; she didn't want any part of him in her. Instead she retracted her fangs and watched him topple over. She'd bit into his carotid artery and every beat of his heart sent another spurt of his blood onto his lovely new office floor. His eyes met hers and she held his gaze smugly as he died.

I had seen more than enough. *You need to tell Yanni,* I commanded. *Admit what you've done. If you own up, the councils might be lenient with you.* I braced for her to fight back but there was nothing, no response. Just silence. *Do you hear me? You have to tell her.*

Was she agreeing to confess? The only way I would know was if I got out of her mind.

Gasping for air, I opened my eyes and found myself in the present. The only thoughts in my head were my own.

I released Kaz's shoulders and stepped back. I raised my fists, prepared for her to come at me but she didn't – she couldn't.

Because the moment I let go of her, Kaz crumpled to the ground.

Chapter Forty-One

'Beatrix, what happened?' Yanni's voice cut through my spiralling thoughts as she ran over and dropped to the floor beside Kaz. 'She's still got a pulse!'

I hadn't known that vampires still had pulses; obviously they weren't as undead as common lore suggested. My brain felt sluggish as if my thoughts were crawling through molasses to reach me.

Yanni pulled out her phone and dialled. 'We need an ambulance.' She rattled off our location then secured Kaz with the cuffs. Finally she turned back to me. 'Bea, tell me what happened?'

'I don't know. I don't know!' I stammered. My breathing was uneven and shallow. 'I thought I was doing the right thing. I thought she was going to tell you…' The words barely came out. I couldn't breathe. What had I *done*?

I knew the answer, of course: I had gone into her mind, taken control and now she was catatonic.

‘Will she be okay?’ I whispered fearfully.

‘I don’t know.’ Yanni’s voice was clipped with fear. ‘Beatrix, you need to go.’ She directed a comment over her shoulder. ‘She’s in shock – get some sugary hot chocolate into her.’

‘Fraser gave me his pelt,’ I said to Yanni, my mind still not working. I hadn’t told her yet and that had been weighing on me. ‘And now we’re bound together forever.’

Yanni’s eyes filled with sympathy. ‘I know, love. Go on now, everything will be okay.’

I felt gentle hands on my shoulders, pulling me away from Kaz. ‘Come on, Beatrix,’ Fraser murmured. ‘I’ve got you.’ His voice was steady though I could hear the tension beneath it.

‘I didn’t... I didn’t mean to...’

‘I know you didn’t. It’s okay.’

Even as Fraser half-dragged me toward the car, my eyes stayed fixed on Kaz’s crumpled form on the ground. *What had I done?*

He wrapped his pelt around me and bundled me into the passenger seat of his car then slid in the driver’s side while Eva bounded into the back. ‘Whatever happened, this isn’t your fault,’ he said firmly. ‘*She’s* the killer.’

'Yes,' I breathed. 'She killed Lorenz and she hit Pepper with her car – but that doesn't make what I did to her right,' I replied shakily.

Fraser clipped the seatbelt around me. 'You did the right thing. A murderer is off the streets and none of the fae were harmed.'

'But Kaz was.'

'She killed Lorenz.' Now his voice was harsh. 'He and I didn't always agree on what was best for the water shifters, but he was a good, honest man. And she could have killed Pepper, too. Don't you dare feel bad about bringing her killing spree to a stop. You have to stop some people by force, Bea.'

I knew that he was thinking about his father. 'Maybe,' I whispered. 'But if Kaz isn't capable of confessing, Yanni needs solid evidence.' I sat straighter. 'Kaz had a USB drive with CCTV footage on it.'

'Beatrix—'

'Take me to her apartment,' I interrupted. 'I'm not finished until we have the evidence to free Sonny.'

'Beatrix, you've just had a huge shock. You should go home and rest.'

'I need to go to her apartment,' I repeated, more loudly. 'If you won't take me, I'll go by myself. I only need ten minutes – you can come with me if you want, or not, but I'm going.'

He sighed and nodded. 'Ten minutes. We find the memory stick, then we call Yanni. Do you know where Kaz lives?'

I did: I'd seen her home in the flashes in my mind. 'A little cottage by the railway on Hope Street.'

He turned the car around and we drove off.

When we arrived, he turned to me. 'You said I could come with you,' he reminded me. 'And I have to – you've been through so much and I am *not* leaving you right now.'

I wanted him by my side as much as he wanted to be there because his presence felt steadying. I'd grown used to handling situations alone, but it had been a lonely existence. In that moment, I knew I wouldn't leave Witchlight Cove, not now, not ever. Regardless of what happened with Fraser, this was my *home*.

'Wait here for a second,' I negotiated. 'You're head of a sect now – you don't want to have to lie about seeing your possible mate breaking and entering.'

There was a palpable flicker of emotion from him when I said 'possible mate', but I didn't have time to linger on it. I needed to focus.

Leaving him in the car, I went to the front door and pulled out two of my many hairpins before crouching in front of the lock. Straightening them out, I used one as the wrench and the other as the rake. It was nowhere near as easy as doing it with a proper lockpick set, but I'd left mine at home; it hadn't seemed necessary for a date with Fraser.

After a long few minutes of fiddling, the door clicked open. I headed back to the car. 'You can come now. The door was open,' I lied.

His wry smile said he didn't believe me for a second, but he wasn't going to call me out. We left Eva snoozing in the car; we didn't need golden hair everywhere to show we'd been inside Kaz's home.

I stepped inside and flicked on the lights. Fraser followed close behind, his presence solid at my back. 'I think this'll count as evidence,' he said dryly. 'I don't think we'll need the USB drive.'

I followed his eyes and my stomach lurched. 'Yeah,' I said, feeling relieved. 'I think you might be right.'

Chapter Forty-Two

'Can you call Dove?' I asked. 'She needs to take some pictures of this.'

The cottage walls were plastered with photos, hundreds of them: Sonny and Kaz smiling in the coffee shop with her in her work uniform; the two of them getting matching tattoos, probably done by Maddie; them splashing in the water under the moonlight. But it was what had been done to each photo that made my stomach churn.

Sonny's image had been defaced in every single one. Some had black marker crosses through his eyes, others were gouged with compass points. Over more than one photo, Kaz had scrawled: *Mine, or no one's!*

There was a photo of Lorenz, Kaz and Sonny together; across Lorenz's face there was a single word written in thick black ink: *Die.*

The hatred, the fury, were suddenly too much; they seemed to be embedded in the very fabric of the cottage. The atmosphere was heavy and oppressive and it was sinking into me like London pollution used to sink into my pores.

'I can't be in here,' I blurted to Fraser and bolted outside. Leaning against the cottage wall, I gulped in calming breaths as the second-hand rage slowly left me.

'All right?' Fraser asked softly.

'There's so much fury in there,' I explained. 'The need to kill was overwhelming and it affected me – it was like black tar sliding down my windpipe, choking me with its vileness.' Involuntarily, I was clenching and unclenching my fingers.

Fraser looked down my hands. 'You're hurt,' he said, frowning.

Only then did I realise he was right. My hands were covered with scrapes, and no doubt there would be dark bruises on my body. There was a difference between doing my rolling-out-of-a-car stunt and hitting the floor repeatedly in the dojo on a pile of crash mats.

I shrugged. 'They're nothing,'

He held out his jacket. 'Put it on.'

'I don't need—'

'Put it on,' he repeated. 'I *hate* to see a woman in pain, especially you. Please.'

It was the please that did it. I settled the pelt over my shoulders and instantly it sent a soft tingle through me as it healed me. It made me think of Fraser's mum. 'When your dad hurt your mum, couldn't she put her pelt back on to heal?'

He closed his eyes for a moment. 'My dad took it from her and hid it. I never found it.'

'God, that's horrible! I'm sorry.'

'Even worse, she couldn't shift without her coat, couldn't commune with The Mother.'

'The Mother?' I asked.

'The ocean. She's at the heart of our powers. I am strong in her call,' he admitted. 'Even from here, I could send someone to her depths. Permanently.'

I blinked. In this part of the village, we were more than a mile from the coast.

I started to take off his coat but he stilled my hands. 'It wants to be with you a while longer.'

Suddenly tears stung my eyes. He really *did* trust me. His father had hidden his mother's pelt, forcing her to stay with him in a wretched existence, and yet Fraser trusted me with his. 'I would never keep this from you,' I promised.

He smiled. 'I know. You may be a siren, but you would never entrap me.'

I snorted. 'I'm no siren.'

'And yet you call to every inch of me,' he admitted. '*My* siren.'

At that moment, Dove's car juddered up the street and she climbed out. 'Okay, Beatrix? Yanni filled me in. None of what happened is going in the official report.'

I blanched; they were covering up for me and that didn't feel good.

'What have we got in there?' She tilted her head towards the cottage.

'Evidence,' Fraser said. 'The door was open when we arrived. Kaz must have been careless.'

'Uh-huh.' Dove's tone made it clear she didn't believe us, but she was willing to roll with it.

'We called you instantly and stepped back out,' Fraser went on. 'We haven't touched anything.'

'Kaz had a USB,' I said. 'She put the footage of the argument between Sonny and Lorenz, and of Lorenz's death on it before she wiped it from the security system. Find the memory stick and you'll have what you need to lock her away.'

'All right. I've got this now, Beatrix. You two go home.'

We left Dove to her business and returned to Eva in the car. All I could think about was Kaz's mind yielding to me; I had thought I was using my magic in the right way and instead I had been destroying her. The guilt ate at me. What I had done was *wrong*.

'Dove's got this now,' Fraser said. He studied me and sighed. 'We're not going home yet, are we?'

'No. I want to go to the hospital to see how Kaz is.'

'Beatrix,' he said carefully, 'you don't need to do this. Kaz is a murderer who framed somebody else, attempted to run down an innocent woman and tried to seek sanctuary with a bunch of assassins. She doesn't deserve your guilt.'

All true, but it was the things he wasn't saying that mattered. 'She was also a young girl, who was saved by Sonny and fell in love.' I looked at him pleadingly. 'Please. Take me to see her.'

He held my gaze for a moment. 'Okay. But I'm not leaving your side – you've had a shock, and you're not on an even keel yet.'

I nodded, relieved. 'I'm happy for the support.'

Sensing my distress, Eva scrabbled over the centre console to land on my lap. She was heavy and furry and I couldn't have cared less. My heart eased as she licked my face. 'Thanks,' I murmured. 'I love you, too.'

When we went into the hospital, the crowd gathered in the foyer erupted into cheers. Even more surprisingly, Ezra engulfed me in a massive bear hug. 'Ez!' I gasped. 'What is it?'

'Pepper woke up about fifteen minutes after you left!' His voice was breaking with emotion. 'The doctors think whatever you did helped bring her round. You saved her, Trixie.' He hugged me again. 'She's with us again because of you.'

'I'm so glad, Ez, really I am. But what about Kaz? Was she brought in here? Have you seen her?'

He frowned. 'Fucking Kaz, I can't believe it! I *liked* her.' His top lip curled in a snarl. 'They brought her in on a trolley ten minutes ago. She didn't look good – the nurse said she might die.' He actually seemed a little pleased about that. Werewolf justice was rough and ready.

Tears welled in my eyes. 'It's okay,' Fraser squeezed my hand. 'It's alright.'

Ezra suddenly stilled. 'Trixie? What is it?'

My throat was tight with guilt. 'I just need to go and see her,' I managed, my voice barely above a whisper.

If I'd killed her, I needed to know.

Kaz was surrounded by doctors. When one of them approached me, I summoned the courage to ask the question that was consuming me. 'Will she be okay?'

'Are you next of kin?' the doctor asked.

'Not exactly,' I hedged.

The doctor frowned at Eva. 'Dogs aren't allowed in here.'

'She's a therapy dog,' Fraser lied smoothly.

'She needs her vest on.'

'We'll get it,' Fraser agreed. 'But tell us about Kaz first, please.'

The doctor grimaced. 'She's gone too deeply into her mind. At the moment I can't tell if she can't come out of this state or if she simply doesn't *want* to.'

'But she will come out of it at some point?' I pressed.

'I'm afraid I can't answer that,' the doctor replied. 'She might stay like this forever.'

Fuck. Forever was a very long time for a vamp.

'Magic did this,' I said as I thought it through. 'So surely magic can fix it.' I could hear the desperation in my voice, and judging by the doctor's expression so could she.

'I'll need to research old spells, remedies.' She eyed me and clearly connected the dots. 'You're the witch that did this, yes? Am I correct in believing that you are a Stonehaven?'

'Yes.'

'Then your magic is linked to the Eternal Flame. Perhaps you could use its power to develop a remedy.'

'The Eternal Flame,' I murmured.

'Yes. It might be worth exploring.'

I nodded dumbly. So the missing Flame might be the key to saving Kaz.

There was nothing more to ask, and nothing more the doctor could tell me.

We had enough evidence to ensure that Kaz would be held accountable for her crimes. Sonny would go free, and his relationship with his brother would probably be better than ever But none of that erased what I had done to Kaz; nothing could erase it but saving her. And my best chance of doing that, apparently, was the Eternal Flame. And it was missing.

I was doomed and so was Kaz.

Silently, I walked out of the hospital with Fraser and Eva close behind me. As we walked into the cold night air, we saw Ezra and Nour. They were standing close and they jumped apart, though Ezra kept hold of Nour's hand.

From the sympathy in the smile Nour offered me, I knew that Ezra had told her what had happened. Soon everyone would know. I was a Stonehaven, and perhaps I was more like my grandmother than I'd ever thought possible. Death and destruction followed in my wake, too.

We went to Fraser's car, but before I could get in he pulled me to him for another much-needed hug. I dropped my head onto his chest, wishing his magic could take away just a tiny part of what I was feeling.

This wasn't like before, when my grandmother had attacked and killed people to get to me. Back then, I'd felt guilty about *her* actions; this time the guilt was my own.

I lifted my tear-streaked face. 'I bet you wished you'd given your pelt to someone else now,' I said, my voice breaking.

'Not even for a heartbeat, mo chridhe,' he replied. 'I am drawn to you like a selkie to the sea. But we don't need to talk about that now, not for years, if you don't want to. Not ever, if that's what you decide. I'm still here for you, come what may.'

I brushed a hand across my face. 'Well, you know that first date I mentioned? I was wondering if we could change it slightly?'

'Of course,' he said gently. 'There's no rush. I promise.'

'No, I didn't mean postponing it…' If the last few hours had shown me anything, it was that Fraser was everything I could want and more, and that I one hundred percent didn't deserve him. But that was something I couldn't think about now because whether I was deserving of him or not, I needed him.

'What I meant was that instead of going for dinner or drinks or something, maybe we could go on a road trip?'

His brows lifted slightly. ‘A road trip?’

‘I’ve heard Scotland is nice this time of year… ’

It was time to get the Eternal Flame back, even if I had to beg another Guardian to help me. We had eight potential locations to check. How hard could it be?

Other Works by Heather

The *Witchlight Magical Mysteries Series* with Ella Stone

Secrets of the Frostbound Cottage – Book 0.5 (a prequel story),

Secrets of the Forgotten Heir – Book 1,

Secrets of the Deadly Nightshades – Book 2; and

Secrets of the Eternal Flame – Book 3.

The *Portlock Paranormal Detective* Series with Jilleen Dolbeare

The Vampire and the Case of her Dastardly Death - Book 0.5 (a prequel story),

The Vampire and the Case of the Wayward Werewolf – Book 1,

The Vampire and the Case of the Secretive Siren – Book 2,

The Vampire and the Case of the Baleful Banshee – Book 3,

The Vampire and the Case of the Cursed Canine – Book 4,

The Vampire and the Case of the Perilous Poltergeist – Book 5,

The Vampire and the Case of the Cozy Christmas – Book 5.5,

The Vampire and the Case of the Hellacious Hag – Book 6; and

The Vampire and the Case of the Malevolent Mermaid – Book 7.

The Other Realm Universe:

The *Other Realm* series

Glimmer of Dragons- Book 0.5 (a prequel story),

Glimmer of The Other- Book 1,

Glimmer of Hope- Book 2,

Glimmer of Christmas – Book 2.5 (a Christmas tale),
Glimmer of Death – Book 3,
Glimmer of Deception – Book 4,

It is recommended that you read *The Other Wolf books 1 to 3* before continuing with:

Challenge of the Court– Book 5,
Betrayal of the Court– Book 6; and
Revival of the Court– Book 7.

The *Other Wolf* Series

Defender of The Pack– Book 0.5 (a prequel story),
Protection of the Pack– Book 1,
Guardians of the Pack– Book 2,
Saviour of The Pack– Book 3,
Awakening of the Pack – Book 4,
Resurgence of the Pack – Book 5; and
Ascension of the Pack – Book 6.

The *Other Witch* Series

Rune of the Witch – Book 0.5 (a prequel story),
Hex of the Witch– Book 1,
Coven of the Witch;– Book 2,
Familiar of the Witch– Book 3; and

Destiny of the Witch – Book 4.

The *Other Detective* Series

Frustrated Justice – Book 0.5 (a prequel story),

Veiled Justice – Book 1,

Mystic Justice – Book 2,

Arcane Justice – Book 3; and

Savage Justice – Book 4

About The Author – Heather

About Heather

Heather is an urban fantasy writer and mum. She was born and raised near Windsor, which gave her the misguided impression that she was close to royalty in some way. She is not, though she once got a letter from Queen Elizabeth II's lady-in-waiting.

Heather went to university in Liverpool, where she took up skydiving and met her future husband. When she's not running around after her children, she's plotting her next book and daydreaming about vampires, dragons and kick-ass heroines.

Heather is a book lover who grew up reading Brian Jacques and Anne McCaffrey. She loves to travel and once spent a month in Thailand. She vows to return.

Want to learn more about Heather? Subscribe to her newsletter for behind-the-scenes scoops, free bonus material and a cheeky peek into her world. Her subscribers will always get the heads up about the best deals on her books.

Subscribe to her Newsletter at her website www.heathergharris.com/subscribe.

Too impatient to wait for Heather's next book? Join her (ever growing!) army of supportive patrons at Patreon.

Heather's Patreon

Heather has started her very own Patreon page. What is Patreon? It's a subscription service that allows you to support Heather AND read her books way before anyone else! For a small monthly fee you could be reading Heather's next book, on a weekly chapter-by-chapter basis (in its roughest draft form!) in the next week or two. If you hit "Join the community" you can follow Heather along for FREE, though you won't get access to all the good stuff, like early release books, polls, live Q&A's, character art and more! You can even have a video call with Heather or have a character named after you! Heather's current patrons are getting to read a novella called House Bound which isn't available anywhere else, not even to her newsletter subscribers!

If you're too impatient to wait until Heather's next release, then Patreon is made for you!

Heather's Shop and YouTube Channel

Heather now has her very own online shop! There you can buy oodles of glorious merchandise and audiobooks directly from her. Heather's audiobooks will still be on sale elsewhere, of course, but Heather pays her audiobook narrator *and* her cover designer - she makes the entire product - and then Audible pays her 25%. OUCH. Where possible, Heather would love it if you would buy her audiobooks directly from her, and then she can keep an amazing 90% of the money instead. Which she can reinvest in more books, in every form! But Audiobooks aren't all there is in the shop. You can get hoodies, t-shirts, mugs and more! Go and check her store out at: https://shop.heathergharris.com/

And if you don't have spare money to pay for audiobooks, Heather would still love you to experience Alyse Gibb's expert rendition of the books. You can listen to Heather's audiobooks for free on her YouTube Channel: https://www.youtube.com/@HeatherGHarrisAuthor

Stay in Touch

Heather has been working hard on a bunch of cool things, including a new and shiny website which you'll love. Check it out at www.heathergharris.com.

If you want to hear about all Heather's latest releases – subscribe to her newsletter for news, fun and freebies. Subscribe at Heather's website www.heathergharris.com/subscribe.

Contact Info: www.heathergharris.com

Email: HeatherGHarrisAuthor@gmail.com

Social Media

Heather can also be found on a host of social medias including her Facebook Page, her Facebook Reader Group, Goodreads, Bookbub and Instagram.

If you get a chance, please do follow Heather on Amazon!

Reviews

Reviews feed Heather's soul. She'd really appreciate it if you could take a few moments to review her books on Amazon, Bookbub, or Goodreads and say hello.

Other Works by Ella Stone

The *Witchlight Magical Mysteries* Series with Heather G. Harris

Secrets of the Frostbound Cottage – Book 0.5 (a prequel story),

Secrets of the Forgotten Heir – Book 1,

Secrets of the Deadly Nightshades – Book 2,

Secrets of the Eternal Flame – Book 3.

The *Dark Creatures Saga*:

Dark Creatures - Book 1,

Dark Destiny – Book 2,

Dark Deception - Book 3,

Dark Redemption – Book 4, and

Dark Reckoning - Book 5.

The *Bloodsucker's Blog Trilogy*:

Life Sucks – Book 1,

Love Bites - Book 2, and

Lost Souls - Book 3.

About the Author - Ella Stone

About Ella

Ella Stone has always been enchanted by the magic of stories. From sneaking late-night reads of The Magic Faraway Tree and The Borrowers to getting completely lost on the staircase with Harry Potter, books have been her doorway to other worlds.

Now, as a writer of urban fantasy and magical mysteries, Ella weaves her own worlds filled with intrigue, humour, and a touch of romance. When she's not crafting stories, you can usually find her hiding in a quiet corner of her tiny house surrounded by her cats, trying to squeeze in "just one more chapter."

Stay in Touch

Ella has a great website, which also offers you some free books if you join up for her newsletter, so have a rummage around at: https://www.ellastoneauthor.com/

Social Media

If you're a social soul, then track Ella down at her Facebook page, Ella Stone Writes!

Printed in Dunstable, United Kingdom

67958602R00221